FOGLAND PO

"Elegant prose, a veritable Chinese box of puzzles, and authentic, well-rounded characters make this a standout."

—*Publishers Weekly* (starred review)

"*Fogland Point* is first-class fiction, a multilayered and original mystery underscored by fine writing, fully developed characters, and a wonderful sense of place. Doug Burgess writes with humor and poignancy while creating an eerie, atmospheric tale that is sure to please."

—Michael Koryta, *New York Times* bestselling author

"Drop everything and read this book. A terrific story in a terrifically honest voice—it's intelligent and original, hilarious and heartbreaking, evocative and charming. A beautifully written tale of murder, dementia, family, love—and surprises! Standing ovation."

—Hank Phillippi Ryan, award-winning nationally bestselling author

"If only we all had friends like the Laughing Sarahs: fiercely loyal, mordantly funny and murderously clever. Doug Burgess' *Fogland Point* brings a wildly original amateur detective to the table of the most secretive small town in New England. I can't wait to go back."

—Francine Mathews, author of the Merry Folger Nantucket Mysteries and several spy thrillers

"Readers...will find Burgess' debut strongly evocative of a distinctive place, presented in a compelling first-person voice that manages to be beyond illusions but never cynical."

—*Kirkus Reviews*

Fogland Point

Books by Doug Burgess

Seize the Trident
The Pirates' Pact
The World for Ransom
The Politics of Piracy
Engines of Empire
Fogland Point

Fogland Point

Doug Burgess

Poisoned Pen Press

First Edition 2018

10 9 8 7 6 5 4 3 2 1

Library of Congress Control Number: 2018930802

ISBN: 9781464210228 Hardcover
ISBN: 9781464210242 Trade Paperback
ISBN: 9781464210259 Ebook

Poisoned Pen Press
4014 N. Goldwater Blvd., #201
Scottsdale, AZ 85251
www.poisonedpenpress.com
info@poisonedpenpress.com

Printed in the United States of America

For Elise and Don, Irene and Tom

"Observe constantly that all things take place by change,
and accustom thyself to consider that
the nature of the universe loves nothing so much as
to change the things which are,
and make new things like them."

—*Marcus Aurelius*

Chapter One

Little Compton sits on a tiny spit of land on the wrong side of Narragansett Bay. Everything else—Providence, Newport, URI, and civilization—is west. Little Compton is east. It used to be part of Massachusetts, but they didn't want it and it got handed over to Rhode Island in some obscure Colonial boondoggle back in 1741. The town patriarch was one Colonel Benjamin Church, who led the Colonists' war against the Wampanoag and slaughtered two hundred of them at the Great Swamp Fight in 1676. A plaque in the square celebrates this historic achievement.

You don't come here by accident, or pass through on the way to someplace else. There is nowhere else. The town is a peninsula. The main road narrows, runs along the coast, passes a few scrubby beaches and the tatterdemalion fleet at Dowsy's Pier, hunkers down into the swamplands of Briggs Marsh, and finally reaches a desolate spot where the only thing around you is gray, sullen ocean. Fog envelops the car. You're not in Rhode Island anymore, not anywhere, really. Little Compton is a void where the North Atlantic should be.

Our town square is a graveyard. I know how that sounds, but it's literally true. Look it up on Google Earth and see for yourself. The United Congregational keeps watch on the graves from the top of Commons Street, a view it shares with the post office, elementary school, and community center. You can't get anywhere in town without passing the cemetery first. It forms the backbone of all local directions.

Here, marked by a Celtic cross with a fouled anchor at its heart, lies my Great-Great Grandpa Ezekiel Hazard, a captain on the Fall River Line ferry to New York. He spent fifty years at sea and drowned in his bathtub after slipping on a bar of Yardley soap. Just to his left is a little granite wedge for Millicent Hazard, 1909-1918, dead of influenza but "*Resting in the Arms of the Lord.*" An imposing obelisk marks the remains of Howland Prosper Hazard, who served one term in the Continental Congress and spent the rest of his life telling the story of how he loaned a half-crown to George Washington for passage on a stagecoach back to Yorktown, where Washington triumphed over the Redcoats. Howland's epitaph declares him the "*Financier of the Revolution.*"

And, a few paces away, under a blighted beech tree, rests my mother.

The only Hazards left now are me and Grandma. My father, not technically dead, read himself out of the family at Thanksgiving a few years ago, which is also where I received the sickle-shaped purple scar on my left shoulder. I didn't like how it looked so I covered it with a tattooed rose. Then I didn't like how it made the other shoulder seem bare, so I covered that with a bloody skull. Don't ask what they mean. I got them out of a book. Dad's somewhere in Massachusetts; I don't care to know where.

Grandma's house is one right and two lefts from the cemetery, on Fillmore Road. In her kitchen is the last pink rotary phone in the world. It even works, though we had to pay the electrician to install an adapter. Now when she turns the wheel it connects to a motherboard inside that translates her analog commands into digital language. It's like she's calling from 1974.

Next to the phone is a list of numbers with "Emergency" written on top. I never thought about it until now, but that list is basically her whole life. The first are the pediatrician and vet, both dead, fire department and police. After that comes a different hand, my grandfather's. It gives the name and number of the electrician, plumber, and a direct line to St. Miriam's. This was when he found out he had lung cancer.

The other names are in her handwriting, shaky but recognizable. There are the Laughing Sarahs—more about them later. My number is there, and my father's. These were numbers she used to remember, but not anymore. The last entry is the saddest. It is her name and phone number. Now the emergency is her.

The avenues of my grandmother's mind are closing down, one at a time. Dr. Renzi described it like that: a great city becomes just a town, then a village, then a hamlet, then a single street with a vacant house and broken windows staring blankly. Right now we're somewhere between the town and the village. But the village still has a telephone, and Grandma's phone has become the only link to an increasingly shrinking world. Her calls are incessant and strange. Once she interrupted a meeting between me and the department chair to ask why Ronald Reagan stopped making movies.

"Because he's dead," I answered abruptly.

There was a long, shocked pause. "My God, has anyone told Nancy?"

Another time she dialed AT&T because a zeppelin was

trying to dock to her satellite antenna. Then came an endless stream of phantom burglars, mashers, and would-be rapists. The last afternoon Pastor Paige came for coffee, she snuck into the front parlor and called Billy Dyer down at the police station. "He wants to do those sex things again," she whispered, horrified.

At the end of the month the bill would come in, full of bizarre notations. Grandma apparently spent three hours on a Thursday afternoon talking with the Office of the Governor General of Canada. Cost: forty-five dollars and eight cents. Calls to a florist in Poughkeepsie, to a charter boat company in Nantucket, to dozens of private numbers whose identities I can only imagine; calls going out in all directions, all day long—distress signals from a foundering liner demanding rescue from anyone near enough to help.

Mine comes on an afternoon in early October. I let it go straight to voicemail. Lately Grandma has taken to calling me every time she mislays something—reading glasses, television remote, keys. I've become her Lar, god of the household, even though I haven't set foot in the place for months. Our dialogue follows a familiar track:

"Did you look on top the television?"

"Of course I did. What d'you take me for…? Oh."

But today I'm not in the mood. Back in my little cubbyhole at Faculty Housing, staring at a room that has just ceased to be mine. There is still a tub of peppermint ice cream in the fridge and half a bottle of vodka left over from a welcome-back party weeks ago. It turns out they go well together. So it's not until evening that I finally pick up the phone and listen to her message.

"*…gotta come over here and help me, there's blood everywhere, on the sink and countertop and all over the floor, I don't know what to do I just found him and I'm sure he's dead and the lobsters and it looks like his head is—*"

She cuts off abruptly. There is a rustle and a thump, like she's dropped the receiver. The next three minutes are static.

Dr. Renzi warned me that her delusions would become more fantastic as the dementia eats away at her sanity. She could become violent or terrified or amorous all in the space of ten minutes, shifting like a one-act tragedian from one scene to the next. "Sooner or later," he said, "you're going to have to bring in professional care. The question is not if, but when." It looks like that moment has come. I call Renzi's office and leave a message with the triage nurse, requesting an appointment for Maggie Hazard as soon as possible.

Then I call Grandma.

The phone rings and rings. I imagine it jangling through the house, buzzing the extension in the back parlor, irritating the solemn black Bakelite with its long cloth cord in Grandpa's old office. But there is no answer. Panicking a little, I ring up Irene, Constance, and Emma—Grandma's closest friends. No one picks up. I leave a string of increasingly hysterical messages on their answering machines and end up staring at the quad outside my windows, a bare patch of scrubby grass.

I could call Dad. But I don't. Not yet. Don't open that box. Instead, I take out the overnight kit from my desk drawer—kept ready for just such an occasion—and toss it into a rucksack with a spare shirt and a dog-eared copy of Borodin. Five minutes later I'm on Route 95, heading south past the outlets at Wrentham, the monitory spire of the Fleet Bank building, the floodlit capitol with its naked *Independent Man* glowering down on the shoppers at Providence Place Mall. Over the Mount Hope Bridge, and into the clinging country dark of Tiverton. I didn't bother leaving a note. After all, it's not like anyone will miss me. I've just been fired, but that's a story for another time.

•••••

It is past ten and the house is dark as I approach. Even the porch light is off. Grandma's place is the biggest on the block, shaped like a foreshortened T. From the road it looks oddly backward, showing its shingled tail to passersby while its white clapboard face stares out to sea. But there is a reason. The house was built on a sloping hill by Captain Ezekiel Barrow in 1704. Its tall windows look out to Narragansett Bay, where Captain Barrow could watch the ships sail in and out of Newport. He even added an extra storey and a widow's walk with lead-glass windows that opened on a hinge. Old Barrow was a wrecker, and from his lofty perch he watched for ships in distress like a vulture circling carrion. Inside is a patchwork of flotsam from his prizes: a carved Spanish staircase in mission oak with pineapple finials, tall French doors with silver handles, Delft tiles that frame the front room fireplace. Captain Barrow came to a bad end in 1713 when his sloop overturned in a squall as he attempted to claim a prize; his corpse washed up on Breakwater Point.

Gravel and crushed seashells crunch under the tires. The sound usually wakes up anyone within, but not this time. Part of me already imagines the scene I'll find behind the polished oak door: Grandma sprawled out at the foot of her stairs, neck broken; or slumped over the kitchen table; or tucked into bed like a child with one cold hand resting on the pillow. I've seen these visions often enough. When I was young I used to watch her labored breathing as she napped, counting each breath and waiting, terrified, for the rattle and cease. Now it would be a comfort, and I'm angry and ashamed at myself for thinking such thoughts. Nevertheless, even as I move round the house, trying the doors and peering through curtained windows, a cold, clinical part of me is already making lists: call the hospital, the undertaker, her lawyer Mr. Perkins; get out her best black dress with the piecrust collar and seed-pearl piping. Empty the refrigerator. Call the Sarahs.

"David? Is that you?"

The sound of her voice makes me jump. Grandma is standing on the back porch, cigarette in hand, wrapped in a green tartan bathrobe that used to be Grandpa's. The smoke forms a wreath around her head. She looks at me quizzically, but without surprise. "You all right there, kiddo?"

"Grandma! Are you okay?"

"Why shouldn't I be?"

"You called me. You sounded really upset. You said…" Here comes the awkward bit. "You said there was a body."

She raises an eyebrow. "A body? Whose body? What are you talking about, boy?"

Honestly, I wish I knew. But the bloody corpse has already flitted back into the Lethe of my grandmother's imagination. And I've just driven all the way from Boston for nothing. "What are you doing outside this time of night?" I ask instead. "It's freezing."

She shrugs. "I like to watch the waves." Her cigarette semaphores towards the sea, making a fiery arc. "Want to join me? The *Dixieland* oughta be passing by pretty soon." This is a private joke. The *Dixieland* ferry—ludicrously named, filled with day-trippers from New York—passed by our house every day at noon. Sometimes Grandma and I would stand on the bluff, wait until it approached, and then drop skirts and trousers and let our asses hang in the breeze. She chuckles at the memory.

"Grandma," I say again, bringing her back to the present, "you called me. You said something was wrong. Do you remember?" Even as the words leave, I regret them. Her face darkens. She hates to be reminded of "Fuzzy Acres," as she calls it.

"Of course I remember," she snaps, and we both know she doesn't. "But I'm fine now. You can go along back up to that college. I don't want you failing 'cuz of me." Sometimes she knows I'm an assistant professor now, sometimes not.

"It's okay. Let's go inside."

She shrugs again but doesn't resist as I take her arm. The house is utterly dark. I wonder how long she's been standing on the porch. "Did Emma bring dinner yet?"

"I think so."

But the kitchen is cold and untouched. Aunt Emma always rinses the dishes and puts them on the counter—the counter is bare. "Let me fix you something," I say.

"Whose house is this? You sit down. I'll fix you something."

Before I can protest Grandma puts on the coffee, plugs in the toaster, and pulls out a loaf of bread from the cupboard. While the toast heats she makes scrambled eggs, a perfect yellow disc at the bottom of the pan. This she cuts in two and sprinkles with a dust of salt and castor sugar. At that exact moment the toast pops up. I've watched her do this all my life and it still amazes me that she can time it so well. Even the coffee is brewed. Grandma sits across from me and helps herself to eggs. In a moment they're gone, and most of the toast, too. She eats ravenously, licking her fingers, all delicacy forgotten. I'm beginning to wonder when she ate last.

"Did Emma give you your pills tonight?" I can see the little orange bottles still atop the fridge. "Here, I'll do it."

"Emma does it," Grandma corrects, mulishly. "You let her do her job."

Emma is Grandma's next door neighbor and best friend, but lately Grandma has taken it into her head that she's some kind of paid housekeeper. I can't blame her, really. For months now Emma's come by every night to give Grandma her dinner, pick up the clothes she left strewn on the floor, straighten the furniture, and sort the mail. I've learned not to offer her money. Truth is, Emma was always Grandma's guardian, even before Fuzzy Acres. When Grandpa died it was Emma who chose Grandma's funeral outfit, dressed her, and fixed her hair while Grandma stared blankly at the mirror, numb with grief. When Grandma started forgetting things—little things, appointments and birthdays and children's names—it was Emma that kept track. On my birthday I received a Hallmark card with a twenty-dollar bill inside. The card was signed in Grandma's handwriting but it was addressed in Emma's. In her own quiet way she gives Grandma the greatest gift any friend ever could, by allowing her to remain herself. But when I tried to express my gratitude, Emma was curt. "Never you mind. You don't know what she did for me." Then she changed the subject.

Now I peer out the kitchen windows, over to Emma's house. Her ancient Buick is parked out front and there is a light on in the kitchen. It's Thursday night, which means Emma will be watching her shows. Cop dramas mostly, the gorier the better. It's always been a strange side of her otherwise buttoned-up personality. "Give Em a semi-decomposed corpse in a lonely field," Aunt Constance likes to say, "and she's a happy woman." A flickering blue light reflects on the grass outside her parlor windows. But why hasn't she come by?

"I'm gonna go check on Emma," I say.

Grandma doesn't look up from her toast. "Tell her those eggs she brought last week were bad. Feathers and blood. Had to throw half away."

Outside the air has a definite chill, and there's a hint of frost on the lawn. I shiver in my shirtsleeves. Emma's house is smaller than Grandma's, a gray saltbox Colonial whose austerity and uncompromising squareness always reminded me of Emma herself. A pot of nasturtiums greets callers at the door. I knock, ring the bell.

"*My God, what is that? Is that a body?*"

The television blasts away in the front room. Emma has grown rather deaf lately. I try the door and, sure enough, it's unlocked. It opens right into the parlor, where a rocking chair is pulled up close to the television set. Dr. Ross and Detective Stone peer down at a mangled corpse on the screen. But the chair is empty.

"Emma?"

"*Dead some days I expect. There is hypostasis on the lower back and forearms, suggesting…*"

The inside of the house is small and plain, with only a few stickback chairs in the living room, and a kitchen with a built-in table just behind. A kitchen light with a wicker shade dangles overhead. The light is on, gleaming off a pile of copper pans strewn on the floor. The shelf above the stove is skewed at a cockeyed angle, one plank dangling loosely from a single bent nail.

"Emma, you there?"

The kitchen island is one of those old-fashioned stainless-steel models with ceramic sides and a grooved draining board to catch the juices. On the floor behind the island a pair of bare, bluish legs stick out at an odd angle. Fuzzy pink carpet slippers point upward toward the ceiling. Emma's fingers curl loosely around the handle of a stockpot. The saucepan and braiser lie at her feet. The skillet, polished steel with a weighted iron base, rests gently against her gray curls. A dark smudge on its rim corresponds exactly to the deep wound across her forehead.

"Yes," says a voice behind me, "that's just how she was when I found her."

Grandma is standing in the doorway holding an unlit cigarette and studying the corpse of her best friend with a dispassionate eye.

"How *you* found her?"

"Sure. Came by a couple hours ago to ask if she had any strawberries, and there she was. Head bashed in something awful."

"But…" My brain is working sluggishly. "But you said it was a man!"

"A man? What man?"

"I don't know! You said it was a man, that there was blood everywhere, something about lobsters…"

We both stare as if the other had gone completely insane.

"My God." I take hold of the kitchen island to steady myself. "Why you didn't call the police?"

"I *did.* I called them, and Connie and Irene. I called everybody. I called you, David."

Of course. And Irene, Constance, and Billy down at the police station had all reacted just as I had. Which is to say, not at all. "I kept calling and calling," Grandma goes on, sounding a little peeved, "but nobody answered, so finally I just gave up. What else was I supposed to do?"

"But why didn't you tell me when I got here…? Oh…"

That look comes back into her eyes, half combative and half terrified. The Revenge of Fuzzy Acres. "I'm sorry, Grandma."

She shrugs. "Had to happen someday. And this was quick, at least. She prob'ly never felt a thing." Still, Grandma shudders.

"It's okay," I tell her. "I'll call the police."

"Maybe you'll have better luck."

Grandma decides this is a good exit line and makes her way back to the house. I'm about to follow when something brushes against my shoe. Something large, dark, and prehistoric is scuttling along the floor, making its laborious bid for freedom.

A lobster.

•••••

Within the hour the police are called, an ambulance ordered, and Grandma is back in her kitchen with a shawl wrapped round her shoulders, a mug of tea in her hand. Aunt Constance remains at Emma's house, manfully directing the ambulance crew and policemen. Everyone says she is splendid in an emergency. Aunt Irene comes by to keep Grandma company.

Irene is not a small woman, and tonight she has thrown an alpaca shawl over her knitted wool coat and plush pink nightgown. Fabric billows out in all directions. "Ouf!" she cries, collapsing into the chair next to Grandma. "What a night! You all right there, Mags?"

"Irene," Grandma answers, looking at her coolly over a raised cup, "what the hell is wrong with you? It's almost ten. What are you doing here?" She casts a knowing glance. "Has Phil got 'company' over again?"

Irene, already flushed, gets redder still. "Phil's dead," she answers, more brutally than usual. Then she turns to me. "Hey, sweetheart. Sorry you had to deal with all this."

"Where's Emma?" I ask.

"Down at Newport General. They'll keep her till we make other arrangements. I already called Mr. Fuller. He's up in Tiverton but does all the services at the United Congregational down the road. Very tasteful."

"Was she a Congregationalist?"

"Who knows? It don't matter, anyhow. There's only but one big church in town, so they tend to do all the marriages and funerals. Except for the Jews. But there's only a couple of them, and they go 'cross the bridge to Touro." She sips her coffee. "I spoke with your dad."

"And?"

Her lips form a thin line, which is as close as Irene ever comes to showing displeasure. "He knows you're here. I guess he'll see you at the funeral. Probably not before."

"Bastard," I mutter. Grandma doesn't hear, and Irene pretends not to. I gather up the plates and rinse them in the sink. Irene joins me, and under the sound of the gurgling she leans in. "Sorry! I thought I'd make it here earlier. Was she extra weird?"

"No. Almost normal, actually. Seems to be taking it pretty well. Too well, really, for someone who just lost her best friend. She forgot that she found the body, but then when she saw it again it was like—I dunno, like finding a stain on the carpet or something."

Irene nods sagely. "It's like that with a lot of things now. Doesn't want to admit she can't remember, so she fakes it. Poor thing doesn't even know what emotions she's supposed to feel. Ah, well, there's one comfort, I suppose. In a couple hours she won't remember Emma's gone. Poor Emma. What a way to go."

"I'm so sorry, Aunt Irene." And I am. Of all the Aunts, Emma was the most like actual family to me. Neither as smart as Aunt Constance nor as kindly as Aunt Irene, she was somehow more real than either, more solid. She tutored me on geography and physics when Dad was away and Grandma too busy. She let me build a tree house in her yard. "What can I do?" I ask, knowing the answer already.

"Well, Constance is handling all the funeral arrangements, and I need to be at the shop…"

I take a deep breath, let it out slowly. Once the words come they cannot be taken back. "Shall I stay with Grandma for a while?"

"Oh *would* you?" Irene gushes, seemingly surprised by the offer. She spoils the effect by adding, "We'll make up your room just like it was. It won't have to be very long. And we never see enough of you, David. Connie was saying just the other day she can't remember the last time you were down."

I remember the last time I was down. I suspect Irene does, too. It was when Grandma decided I was a burglar and then, even more disturbingly, that I was Grandpa. We had five minutes of extremely awkward conversation before Aunt Irene intervened and drowned Grandma with *The Late Show*.

"So tell me," Aunt Irene leans closer, "can you square it with the college, being gone? Can you take sick leave?"

I realize there's no point in hiding it from her. The whole story is going to come out anyway. "No," I answer, as calmly as I can, "they fired me when they found out."

"*What?*" Irene drops her plate into the sink with a clatter. "They can't do that!"

"Sure they can," Grandma calls from the table. "They do it all the time."

"Who?" Irene asks her, curious.

"*American Bandstand*," Grandma answers darkly. "Can't believe a single damned word."

Irene turns back to me and lowers her voice. "How did they find out?"

It's my turn to shrug. "I had to turn in a prescription form to Benefits. It had my old name on it, and medical history. Somebody asked a question. Supposed to be confidential. Guess it's not."

"Just like that." She shakes her head. "Frigging Catholics. If only you'd gotten that job in Buffalo..."

"Well, now I can go back and ask for it," I say with a smile. But we both know what's really coming. Months of unemployment followed by adjunct Hell in some godawful community college. Living from week to week. And no medical, of course, which is going to be damned inconvenient. The shots alone run about a hundred-fifty dollars a pop. But my problems are still a ways off; Grandma's are right at hand. "What happens...after?" I ask, nodding towards her.

Irene's hands clench slightly. "It'll have to be the Methodist Home," she answers in a whisper. "Connie already called them. There's a waitlist, but poor Mrs. Everard has stage-four liver cancer so it can't be long now. A couple months, at most."

"I can stay here till then, if you'd like."

"Oh, that's lovely. We'll help, of course. I'll bring over the groceries every Friday night, and Connie's been handling the household finances..."

"What are you two whispering about?" Grandma demands.

Irene paints a sympathetic smile on her face and turns around. "We were just talking about how we will handle things, now that poor Emma is gone. You'll miss her, won't you Maggie, dear?"

"Miss Emma? Miss Emma?" Grandma's eyes shift out of focus. She goes on, dreamily, "That's her problem, of course. Always a miss, never a missus. If only Teddy Johnson had married her..."

"Poor Teddy!" Irene responds, recognizing an old cue.

"That would have been different. I always said Emma would be a splendid mother. She has all the right instincts. Too late now, I guess." This seems a lucid comment, and Irene nods enthusiastically. But then Grandma continues, "She needs to get out more. Can't stay cooped up in that house all day. If she hung 'round the Boy and Lobster like the other girls do, she'd find someone right enough. Nothing wrong with her looks. And a pretty little sum in the bank, too. A man could go farther and fare worse. How old you suppose she is?"

Irene is making frantic semaphores at me, but stupidly I answer, "She was eighty-one."

Grandma scoffs. "Don't tease. In fact, you seem a likely enough young cub. Got a girlfriend?"

"I…no."

"Well we've got this friend, see. She lives next door. Kinda shy, but you can work past that…"

"Maggie," Irene interjects with forced cheerfulness, can't you see that's David? Your grandson?" She says this as if Grandma's spectacles aren't strong enough.

"Grandson?" Grandma repeats. "No. That's not right. I never had a grandson." She looks at me blankly. "You do look familiar, though. But your hair's too short. And there's something wrong with your…"

"It's time for bed." Irene announces chirpily.

Grandma accepts this and stands up. Irene massages her shoulders. "Need any help getting up the stairs?"

"Never have, Irene." She turns looks me up and down. "Let me know if you'd like an introduction. There's a dance at Pawtuxet next Friday. Everybody'll be there."

"Okay, Grandma," I answer sadly.

"Won't that be nice?" Irene tweets. She had apparently decided to indulge this fantasy. Perhaps she, too, remembers the Pawtuxet dance. "I'll wear my Alice Blue chiffon. And you've got that sexy black number, Mags, as I recall. What do you suppose Emma will wear?"

"Emma?" Grandma looks scandalized. "What's the matter with you, Irene? Emma's dead. She just got walloped with her own pots."

And so to bed.

Chapter Two

The day of the funeral is neither hot nor cold, sunny nor rainy, but everything at once, a New England allsorts of bluster and wet sunshine. The air is a separate element, so thick with mist that it turns the lamps in the sanctuary into halos of yellow light.

Fog seeps in under the doors, through the cracks in the windows, into my grandmother's mind. The others are worried. I see them watching her, wondering if she can make it through the service. But this is one of her good days. She shows up on time, wearing her pearl choker and a black dress that buried her mother, father, two uncles, and husband. Her makeup is sparse but correct, a thin line of pale lipstick and even fainter eyeliner. She never opens the hymnal; she knows them all by heart.

"*Eternal father, strong to save…*"

It's a pretty good turnout, all things considered. Aunt Irene and Aunt Constance sit across from us, Irene in a voluminous mantilla that could have been borrowed off an extra from *Carmen*; Constance looking nunlike in a crisp black dress and piecrust collar instead of her usual blue jeans and sweatshirt. Neither of them is crying. The rest of the congregation are the kind of people who would always turn up at a funeral: distant relatives, local acquaintances, and gawkers. Wally the Postman is here, with his blowzy wife. She's sixty if she's a day but has somehow managed to squeeze herself into a black leather halter top. Her nails are lacquered vermilion; her hair is fire-engine red. Wally sits hunched over, face like a rotten grapefruit, John Deere cap pulled low over his eyes. He's the only self-proclaimed Trumpkin in Little Compton. His wife has a pair of plastic chickens on her mailbox that she dresses up for the holidays. Right now they are Mr. and Mrs. Dracula.

Our local GP, Dr. Renzi, has put on a tie and smoothed back his silver hair, and looks very distinguished next to batty Mrs. Thurman, who has dressed for the occasion by pulling a black trench coat over her bathrobe. The Karabandis sit with their seven children and look around them hopefully. They are here on approval. It was not well taken when they decided to purchase Dykstra's Dry Goods after Jim Dykstra had his last heart attack. Not because they were Bangladeshi—Little Compton has voted Democrat every year since 1908—but because they were from Flushing, Queens. They brought with them a typical urbanite's notion of what a "quaint" country general store should look like, filling Dykstra's with plush toys, jams, homemade soaps, and scented candles. Mrs. Karibandi dispenses penny candy from glass jars. Now locals have to drive all the way to Middletown if they want spaghetti sauce.

In the far corner of the nave, lit with watery sunlight from the window above, is a couple I've never seen before. The wife is in her late thirties, with an aureole of perfectly coiffed blond hair and a body that speaks of personal trainers, long jogs, and yoga. She is dressed with insolent simplicity in a charcoal skirt, white blouse, and six-inch black heels that even from across the aisle I recognize as Jimmy Choos.

Her husband looks like he is running for something: dark pinstripe double-breasted suit, midnight blue tie, autumn tan-and-black hair turning genteelly gray at the temples. Set against Little Compton's caravansary of grotesques, this couple seems fantastically *de trop*, like extras from a cruise line brochure. I can't wait to ask Irene about them.

And at the back, leaning up against one of the pillars, is Billy Dyer. *Chief* Dyer now, though he still has freckles on his nose and a wedge of strawberry-blond hair that sticks up all over his head like he's been electrocuted. The blue uniform hangs lumpily on his thin frame. I heard he got married a couple months ago. Debbie Antonelli, with her squashed-pug face and chunky jewelry. Aunt Irene tells me there's a little stranger on the way in the spring. "Well, *almost* spring," she amends, significantly. Billy catches me staring at him, and stares back. We both look away at the same time.

It is not a long walk to the grave. Constance, her two sons, Mr. Fuller, the undertaker, and I all serve as pallbearers. The coffin is polished pine with a garland of summer jonquils. It feels too light, and as we make our way down the steps one of the sons, Petie, loses his footing and we all hear the unmistakable thump of the body shifting inside. Constance grimaces. We reach the burial mound where Pastor Paige is waiting, a prayerbook open in his hands.

A few tourists wander past and snap photos. I don't blame them; it's picturesque in an Edward Gorey sort of way. Wraiths of gray cloud swirling around black figures, with a title like *The Anstruthers Await the Inevitable*. But the cameras affect Maggie. Her eyes narrow. "That's just not right," she mutters.

"It's okay, Grandma," I whisper back. "They'll be gone soon."

"Dammit," she says, "just because he's the President, that doesn't make it right."

Pastor Paige has donned his whitest cassock for the occasion. He's a nice old boy, but the fact that he was born on the wrong side of Ireland has forever doomed him to be denied his most cherished ambition, which is the priesthood. He still wears his dog collar out and about, even though no one expects it from a Congregationalist.

"In the midst of life, we are in death," Paige intones, and drops a trowel of dirt over the grave. We bow our heads. Constance steps forward and reads the Twenty-Third Psalm in a clear, crisp voice. One of the Karibandi boys fidgets and draws a smiley face in the dirt with his toe, until his mother reprimands him.

Grandma catches sight of a mockingbird escaping its nest in the willow tree above and laughs. "Go on, you old hen!" she calls after it, while the rest of us stare at our shoes. "Go on south! Winter's coming, and it'll be cold as a witch's left tit from here to Bangor. If I was an old hen, I'd fly south too!"

The choir takes this as a cue, and breaks into a decent a cappella "Blackbird": "*All your life, you were only waiting for this moment to arise...*"

The well-groomed couple stands too near the grave. The husband could be a professional mourner, so deeply felt appears his grief. But his wife takes surreptitious glances at her watch. I can feel the attention they are attracting, not all of it welcome. Aunt Constance clears her throat meaningfully. The husband notices. He whispers something and they retreat tactfully back into the crowd.

"*Blackbird singing in the dead of night,*

Take these sunken eyes and learn to see,

All your life, you were only waiting for this moment to be free."

Suddenly I find my throat closing up and the unmistakable prick of tears. They are not for Aunt Emma. They are for me, for the body I left behind and this new one that I barely recognize or understand. For Grandma, caught like a ghost between a past that suddenly seems very real and a present that is slipping away. For my mother, whose funeral I never saw because Dad thought it would be too upsetting. She just left to get groceries and never came back. After the funeral Dad went back to his ship and I moved in with Grandma and Grandpa. But for weeks Grandma was prostrate with grief and Grandpa was out on his boat, so it was Emma that came every day and made my breakfast, packed my school lunch, made sure my hair was combed and my shoes laced up. And it was she who finally told me that my mother had gone and would not be coming back, and held my small, furious body as I fought against that truth. So maybe these tears are for Emma too, a bit.

• • ● • •

We hold the wake at Grandma's house, since Emma's is too small. Every proper New England home has a ghost, and Grandma's is so big it has two. Captain Barrow lurks around the parlor, not far from where his portrait hangs above the fireplace. Everyone in the family has seen him at some point, including me. He sits in a large wingback chair and stares into space, a grim, lantern-jawed man in a blue coat whose brass buttons twinkle in nonexistent firelight. I caught him there at Thanksgiving one year, and came back to the dining room asking Grandma why the nice man had to eat his meal out in the front room. "Why don't you invite him to join us?" Grandma answered. But when I tried to relay this invitation, he was gone.

The second is less forbidding, but antic. Grandma calls it the Hired Help because it likes to fling pots and pans around, and occasionally turns a hand to light housekeeping: switching on the vacuum cleaner at two in the morning, throwing open the kitchen windows in January to let in the fresh air, turning up the gas burners with empty pots atop them. I once asked Grandma if the Hired Help might actually be Captain Barrow himself, but she was appalled at the idea.

"A fine, dignified gentleman like the captain would *never* mess about in the kitchen," she scoffed. Her own theory was that it was a kitchen maid who had served when Great-Grandpa William was a small boy, and threw herself in Briggs Marsh after the family discovered she was pregnant.

Today, as guests file in from the funeral, the house looks just the same as it always has. This used to be comforting, but now it's sad, as though nobody told the house the bad news. All my grandmother's things are waiting for her to come back: the oversized wooden spoon above the range, Norman Rockwell plates, a winsome ceramic owl on the banister. Why owls? I used to wonder. What was this mid-century fascination with decorative owls? I remember as a kid every house had them. If someone didn't, you almost wanted to ask what happened to it. Now I see them in the junk shops on Wickenden Street, knitted owls and porcelain owls and macramé owls with button eyes.

Somebody had the foresight to turn on the furnace, so the old radiators hiss and gurgle. The house is stiflingly hot. Aunt Constance and Aunt Irene hand out sandwiches, and Grandma sits in her rocking chair. Emma's family came down from Fall River. Two elderly cousins and several flat-faced middle-aged second cousins. The men are heavyset and jowly; the women have that hard, lacquered look that is incomplete without a cigarette dangling from the lips. Emma didn't bother much with blood kin, it appears. Aunt Irene plies them with gin and tries to engage them in conversation, without success. The elderly look uncomfortable, but their children find a quiet corner and begin to talk to Mr. Perkins about the will.

"Vultures," says Aunt Constance, passing by with a tray. "Tuna or liverwurst?"

Constance Heckman, Irene Belcourt, and Maggie Hazard are now the three surviving members of the Laughing Sarahs. Aunt Emma was a member, too. The Sarahs meet in the back parlor of my grandmother's house, the one next to the kitchen that's really a pantry, every Saturday. The name is a Protestant joke. The Lord came to Abraham and told him his wife, Sarah, an old woman, would soon be with child. Sarah burst out laughing. Puzzled and a little annoyed, God turned to Abraham and asked, "Why did Sarah laugh? Does she think I can't make her pregnant, or something?"

"I didn't laugh," said Sarah.

"Oh, yes, you did," said God.

This story might be mangled in the telling, but it makes a great deal of sense. Sarah was like an old Yankee, no nonsense about her. She took the news much the same way my grandmother would have, or any of her friends.

The Laughing Sarahs began as a social club composed of married ladies for whom God's little miracle would be a similar surprise. Grandma, Constance, and Irene even own a company, New England Wrecking and Salvage. Aunt Constance founded it with Uncle Phil, Irene's husband, and Grandpa Mike, but they're both dead. The widows took it over with Constance at the helm. Not much changed. They still operate out of the same converted boathouse down at

Dowsy's Pier, with a sign over the door that never quite conceals the ghost of "Salty Brine's Best Littleneck Clams" in washed-out gray beneath. The front office is the "shop," where Grandma, Irene, and Constance have their desks. The boathouse fans out behind, and has a sexy history: it was built during the war to house submarines, one of a dozen or so secret bases along the New England coast. It's a long, narrow tin structure with a flat roof and corrugated sides. The interior still has the old gantries and concrete slabs, even the original klaxon horn to announce when a sub was coming in. I played secret agent there for years.

Aunt Irene is the scout. She drives her ancient Dodge C-Series up and down the coast as far as Fall River, looking for scrap. It has so many dents and bruises that it's become shapeless, a faded blue dumpster with wheels. Aunt Constance is the skipper of the *Eula May*, a wrecker that was once a Navy minesweeper during the war. Her two boys, Blue and Petie, act as crew. They scour the coast for abandoned fishing trawlers, pleasure craft, and the like. Hurricane season is a godsend.

Grandma is bookkeeper, or was, until the crisis. These are actual books, green leather ledgers with red penciled lines, along which she carefully notes every pound of scrap metal coming in, every bill going out. As a child they fascinated me. The books are kept in a tall case behind her desk and go back as far as 1954. I could turn to any page and find her clear, precise handwriting. If one turns to November 22, 1963, the news of the day is not the Kennedy assassination but "4.91 tons best steel from scrapping *Northern Endeavor*. Paid Jim Cobb." On August 17, 2007, the day my grandfather died, Grandma stopped by the office on the way home from the hospital and reported that the electric bill had been paid, $76.05. But next to this she drew a small cross in black ink.

This was nowhere near as depressing, however, as what came later. The last ledger is dated this year. Entries are still rendered in a clear, crisp hand, but they make no sense. Who is "J.R.D" and why was he paid $450? What was the "Overlook Prize Commission," and what did they do to deserve nearly five thousand dollars? Too late, we found out. The scammers had gotten her number. Earnest young ladies got her on the phone and promised instant prize winnings, millions of dollars, trips to Aruba, and free automobiles. All she had to do was pay the taxes. So she did, again and again, entering the sums in the company ledger with calm certainty of a promise to be fulfilled. By the time Aunt Constance intervened, Grandma had given away nearly five hundred thousand dollars and New England Wrecking and Salvage was broke.

They are not my aunts, of course. It was Grandma who encouraged the idea. "Say hello to your aunties!" she would say, and gradually they and I got used to it. My father was unperturbed. Little Compton is so small and isolated that everybody is related in some way, so it's just a question of degree.

The party, if one could call it that, is winding down. People who came for the food have already eaten it and left. Others who came out of a sense of duty have seen that duty fulfilled, and they are next to go. Emma's family members are staying to hear the will read. I breathe a little bit easier and begin to wonder if Irene used up all the gin. Like a bottle imp, she appears at my elbow.

"Did you see our local celebrities?" she asks, nodding toward the well-dressed couple from the funeral. They stand off by themselves in one corner. The husband pretends to be interested in the books on the shelf beside him; the wife looks bored.

"Is he running for Senate or something?"

Irene chuckles. "Looks like it, don't it? No, they're just rich. Name of Rhinegold. Marcus and Alicia."

"Where are they from?"

She shrugs. "People like that don't really come from anywhere. They just move from place to place. Came in on a big yacht called the *Calliope* last summer and liked it so much they stayed. Well, most people would get a beach house near the pier. But Mr. Rhinegold decided he'd rather have the old Armstrong mansion up on Fogland Point."

I know the place. There's a pier and a little beach at the base of the hill where children play among the rocks. "I didn't know that was for sale."

"It wasn't. That conservancy owned it for years, but nobody's lived there since the Cavendishes left. You remember them. I guess Rhinegold made the conservancy an offer they couldn't refuse. And, as if that weren't enough, he bought all the land around it—basically all of Fogland Point. Now it's just one long driveway. But that's not what got everybody so worked up. They're going to pull down the house."

"No!"

"Fact. Rhinegold got some county inspector to declare the place unsound. The crew's coming in a week from Wednesday."

The Armstrong mansion is a local institution, a big, gaudy High Victorian with crenellated rooftops and a wrap-around porch. It's ugly, but of the kind that fascinates rather than repels. When I was a kid it was the most popular trick-or-treat house in town. "Everybody must have been wild."

Irene nods. "The Historical Association had a few words to say, that's for sure. They even tried to get the place declared a national landmark, but since nothing's ever happened in

Little Compton that didn't get very far. Then they tried picketing the shop, but Connie came out and gave them a stiff talking-to, and they went home."

"*Aunt Constance?*"

"Well, sure. Who'd you think is gonna do the wrecking? We'll be up there for a whole week."

So Rhinegold is not a complete fool after all. He had infuriated the town, yet salvaged some of his reputation by hiring the most local of local firms to do the actual dirty work. In fact, I rather admire his nerve. "But what is he doing *here*?" I ask.

Irene makes a face. "Trying to look like a native, I expect," she sniffs. "Did you see how close they were standing to the grave? Closer than the family, even! They've got a lot to learn."

I agree, but think to myself that they probably will learn, sooner or later. The rules of a New England town are not hard. Once Mr. Rhinegold gets himself some old dungarees and topsiders, and his wife trades in her Jimmy Choos for a nice comfortable pair of hospital flats, they'll be just fine. The secret to village life is concealment.

Mr. Perkins puts on his glasses and clears his throat, which means it's time to read the will. He sits behind the big partner's desk in the study. Me, the Laughing Sarahs, and Emma's potato-faced family all gather round. The Rhinegolds melt into the other room; I never see them leave. "The terms," says Mr. Perkins in his dry voice, like crackling paper, "are perfectly clear. But the execution is rather less so, as you will appreciate. Ahem." He clears his throat ostentatiously. " 'I, Emma Lynn Godfrey, of 434 Fillmore Road, Little Compton, Rhode Island and Providence Plantations, do hereby in this year of two thousand and eight, by my hand and in front of these witnesses…"

"You can skip all that," one of the male relatives growls. "Just get to the fun part."

Mr. Perkins is scandalized. His practice is mostly confined to the shore communities here. Newport is Far Away; Providence is a foreign country. These Riversiders might as well be Ashanti tribesmen. He clears his throat again. "Yes, well, I suppose we can dispense with the preliminary material. 'I hereby leave my home and all its contents to my cousin, Minerva Jardyce, nee Godfrey..."

"That's more like it!" the male cousin growls approvingly, rubbing his hands together. The elderly cousin—Minerva, presumably—sighs and shakes her head.

"And all other goods, chattel, and income to my daughter, Arabella Johnson, in the hopes that she might remember her mother fondly."

There is a long silence. "Arabella Johnson?" someone repeats. "Who the hell is that?"

"Her daughter, obviously," says Aunt Constance with a wicked smirk.

"But *where* is she? She's not here." The cousins look around, as if Arabella will suddenly pop up behind the aspidistra.

"Efforts are currently being made to locate Miss Johnson," Mr. Perkins informs them. "Miss Godfrey set aside a portion of the remaining estate to hire private detectives. She was explicit, however, that no efforts were to be made until her decease."

Something about the way Perkins annunciated that phrase "a portion" hints at great things. "Just how much are we talking about?" the male cousin asks warily.

Now it's Mr. Perkins' turn to smile, rather timidly. "After the settlement of all just debts, the liquidated estate is valued at approximately three million, four hundred-seventy-five thousand dollars." He folds his hands on the desk.

The uproar is immediate. The cousins rise up en masse, crying aloud and shaking their fists. Aunt Irene tut-tuts. Aunt Constance still smiles grimly.

Finally Mr. Perkins bangs the palm of his hand on the table for attention. "Please! Please! Ladies and gentlemen, I beg of you! A little decorum, if you don't mind. Now, as I said, efforts are being made to find this Miss Johnson. That is her birth name, so she might be married under a different name now—"

"But how could Emma never tell us?" one elderly cousin objects plaintively. He turns to Aunt Constance. "Did you know about this?" Slowly Constance shakes her head.

"Emma...Miss Godfrey, I should say, was adamant that no one should know," Perkins explains. "The money came from the sale of some properties owned by her father, Ephraim Godfrey."

"She never said a word," Irene marvels, shaking her head. "Not one word."

"Paid all her bills on time, though," Aunt Constance puts in.

All this rank sentiment at a funeral has the cousins incensed. "That's all very well," one of them says nastily, "but what exactly happens if the detectives *don't* find this lucky Miss Johnson?"

"Then, after a due process of inquiry, the estate will be awarded to the other legatee, Mrs. Jarndyce."

"See that, Ma? You may be a rich woman yet," the cousin says happily.

"Unless," Mr. Perkins raises a finger, "Miss Johnson is located or, in the case of her decease, any surviving heirs."

"Bad scran on the lot of them," one of the female cousins snarls.

Minerva Jarndyce finally speaks. "Emma was a bitch. Five years ago my boy Stevie was up for assault. No evidence.

But she wouldn't hire a lawyer, wouldn't even put up parole. He got six years upstate."

"Where," Aunt Constance interjects smoothly, "he has so far beat up two inmates, a guard, and the prison chaplain. Emma was no fool, Mrs. Jarndyce."

"Who the hell are you, and what business is it of yours?"

"No one, and none, Mrs. Jarndyce."

"I think," says Mr. Perkins, rising, "that we have covered all the main points. I will, of course, be in communication with you as the search for Miss Johnson progresses. After one year's time without success, by the conditions of the testator, the remainder of the estate will devolve to the legatee. I trust that's clear enough?" His only answer is a collective growl. "Very good. Then, in that case, I bid you all a good evening. I'll show myself out."

Chapter Three

By nine o'clock the cantankerous cousins have all left, and the temperature in the living room drops at least ten degrees. It continues to fall. The house is like a freshly dead corpse, halfway between life and corruption. Grandma is still in her rocking chair, sleeping. Each breath releases a tiny puff of condensation into the damp air. It's easier when she is asleep to pretend that when she wakes up everything will be as it was. This used to be true. She would fall into a doze, the batteries of her mind replenished themselves, and she awoke with a fresh charge. That lasted until April.

Now the two surviving Laughing Sarahs are back, with cake. "I was going to bring this out as a surprise," says Aunt Constance, "but then I saw that family of hers and thought, nah." She puts the cake on the coffee table with a possessive thud. Sugar sponge studded with almonds and icing hearts. It looks delicious, but decidedly out of place.

"You made it?" I ask.

Aunt Irene laughs. "No, honey, Emma did."

Is there something ghoulish about eating a dead woman's last cake? What if Aunt Emma had been reaching for the cake tin, when the cake tin came to her? But Aunt Irene has already handed me a slice. I dip in a fork, thinking I will just have one bite, and realize, *This is really good.* The frosting is buttercream, the cake thick and moist with the tiniest hint of anise, like a wry smile. Emma was always the best baker.

The cake, it turns out, is not the only act of larceny being contemplated. Aunt Constance takes a sip of coffee and says quietly, "The appraisers are coming in the morning. Figure on that bunch to not even wait for the body to cool. It's going to be a long night."

I understand everything except the last part. "Why?" I ask.

Aunt Irene smiles and pats my knee. She is often given the unlovable task of softening Constance's decrees. "Emma was our family," she says gently. "She was your grandma's best friend. Her house is full of memories, and we don't want them to just disappear into the back of a truck."

"So you're going to…take them?" I'm thinking of the Chippendale chairs, the Morris hutch, the glassware brought back on a tea clipper by Great-Uncle Elias, whose picture still hangs in Emma's parlor.

"Not all of it—" Irene avers.

Constance cuts her off. "You bet, all of it," she interjects. "All the good stuff, anyway. Want anything?" There has always been a hint of pirate rascality about Aunt Constance.

Grandma wakes up with a snort. "Where's Emma?" she asks at once.

The two ladies look at each other. "She made you this cake, dear," says Aunt Irene.

"Why are you eating it, then?"

We all laugh, and Irene hands her a piece. Grandma's table manners haven't left her. She unfolds a napkin and places it in her lap. The cake is consumed in six remarkably dainty bites. A few minutes later her head nods, and Aunt Constance takes the plate from her lap.

Irene leans over to me. "I've been dying to tell you," she begins conspiratorially, "about the latest with Wally and that floozy wife of his. You know she left him for some nightclub bouncer in Cranston. Well *that* ended, but only because he took her purse with all her cards, and now she's back, but neither of them—"

This interesting narrative is interrupted by a sharp knock on the back door. There stands Billy Dyer, resplendent in his light blue uniform with polished silver badge identifying him as police chief of Little Compton. He still looks about fifteen years old.

"Hiya, Billy."

"Hey Ro…er, David."

Oh, so it's going to be like that. Okay, then. "Heard you got married to Debbie Spaghetti," I say brutally. "Congratulations."

He shifts from one foot to the other. "Can I come in?"

"Better than standing outside."

The Aunts look up as I bring him into the parlor. There is something wary in Constance's expression. "Evening, Chief," she says. "If you've come for the obsequies, you're too late."

"Not exactly. Can I sit down?" His voice sounds oddly strained. Constance waves toward a chair, and Aunt Irene automatically cuts him a slice of cake. Just as automatically he begins to eat it. "Hey," he says finally, looking up from an empty plate, "that was good."

"There's coffee in the kitchen," Irene tells him.

"No, no, that's okay." He looks at me and swallows rather painfully. I can actually see his Adam's apple bob up and down. "So, David, how you been keeping?"

"Not bad, considering. You?"

"Oh, you know, about the same."

"That's good."

"Would you lovebirds like some privacy?" Aunt Constance cuts in. Billy blushes to the roots of his hair.

"I haven't seen you since you left for grad school," he goes on, still awkwardly polite. "You look..."

"Different," Constance supplies.

"So handsome!" Irene adds.

"Bigger."

That can't be the word he was hoping for. "I mean," he chokes, "you know, *fuller*."

Silently Aunt Irene hands him another slice of cake. He shovels in a mouthful, as if to prevent any more words from escaping.

"Yeah," I say, taking pity on him. "That happens sometimes. You look good, though. Married life agrees with you. And I hear a little stranger is on the way."

I meant it kindly, but Billy's face falls even more. Clearly the subject is delicate. "It's good to see you, Billy. But did you just come here for cake and a social call?"

"Not exactly. Fact is...well..."

"Is this an official police matter?" Constance inquires with a raised eyebrow, rolling off the syllables unctuously.

Billy answers by saying nothing. Suddenly there is something else in the room, a different kind of tension. Cold, as if Death brushed us with its wings.

"My God," Irene whispers, "what is it? What's happened?"

"Is it true Emma Godfrey was worth millions, and they're looking for the heir?"

Even in the age of Internet and text, nothing is faster than the Little Compton bush telegraph. "That's about the size of it," Constance confirms.

"Damn. That's bad."

"Not so bad for the heir, or heirs."

"No, it's just...well, I got the coroner's report back about an hour ago. It's not good."

Chief Billy has been reduced to monosyllables and Constance seems frozen in her chair, but Irene looks puzzled. "Not good? But Emma was sound as a bell!" she protests. "If it weren't for the accident, she might have gone on for years."

"Yeah," Billy sighs, "that's kinda the problem. I know she was your friend, and there's no easy way to say this, but it looks like we might have a homicide case on our hands."

The two ladies stare at him. I realize I'm still hovering like a ghost in the doorway, and sink down onto the divan next to Irene. "Homicide?" she repeats blankly. "Who was killed?"

"Emma, you twit," snaps Constance.

"No. Oh, no. That's not...no." Irene shakes her head. "That's nonsense, Billy. She was reaching for a pot when the shelf collapsed."

Billy nods. "That's how somebody wanted it to look. But I examined that skillet myself. There's a dent on the base. If it just fell from a shelf it might have cracked Miss Emma's skull, but there's no way it could have gone that deep. Someone swung it overhead and brought it down on her. Then they pulled all the pots down to make it look like an accident."

Irene still looks incredulous, but Constance hums appreciatively. "Clever," she muses.

"But Connie," Irene turns to look at her, "you don't believe this, do you? For God's sake, it's Emma! Who on Earth would ever want to hurt Emma?"

It is Billy who answers her. "You heard yourself. She had three million dollars in the bank, and some very greedy relations. Not to mention this mysterious Arabella Johnson, wherever she is."

Constance scoffs. "I've got a pretty healthy savings account and a whole gaggle of worthless relatives. None of them have taken a swing at me yet."

"You wouldn't let them near enough," Irene mutters under her breath.

Billy pretends not to hear. "You're right, Miss Constance, but the fact is somebody probably did."

Since there is no answer to this, we sit in silence. I'm thinking of the hook-braid rug in Emma's front parlor, the watercolor of Block Island on the wall, how relentlessly normal it all looks. And yet on the floor, a body. A house where murder was done. It all seems unreal, unnatural. "Why did you come to tell us this?" I ask. "Isn't it normal to keep investigations under wraps?" The lingo comes right from one of Emma's cop shows, and I wonder if I sound ridiculous.

"Oh, David," sighs Constance, "isn't it obvious? He's here to question us."

Irene gasps, but Billy shakes his head. "Not you, Miss Constance. But Miss Margaret was the one that discovered the body. And she was probably the last one to see Emma Godfrey alive. I need to talk to her."

"Good luck," Constance mutters, glancing over at Grandma's recumbent form still snoring in her chair. She turns back to Billy. "I take it," she says slowly, "that you have considered the impracticality of an eighty-year-old woman with arthritis and Alzheimer's braining her next-door neighbor and then having the presence of mind to conceal the crime in this colorful manner."

"My God, of course! But she may be an important witness. In fact she may be the *only* witness."

"Poor Mags," murmurs Irene. "She's all alone now."

"We'll wake her presently," Constance tells him, "but you might as well know she won't remember a thing. Never does anymore. And if she thinks you're looking for a story, she'll quite happily concoct one. Most of what she says these days is one part old memories and nine parts delusion."

"I know, I know."

"Billy," Aunt Irene interjects, studying his face deeply, "are you *sure* about this? I mean, I'm not a pathologist or anything, but isn't it possible it was just an accident, after all? Couldn't the pan have just dropped a certain way?"

Billy shrugs. "Sure, I guess. That's what the Providence police think, too. Dr. Renzi did the autopsy, and even he couldn't be certain. Plus Providence is up to their knees in tax records from Plundergate. They're not gonna waste much time on a little old lady in the boonies."

The sudden and dramatic collapse of Ocean State Building and Loan, coupled with charges of embezzlement, graft, and extortion, has kept three police divisions and the FBI happily occupied for months. Last week the state speaker of the House was hauled off to jail; they say the mayor is next. But Aunt Constance cocks a quizzical eyebrow at Billy. "You've already got a suspect."

"Pardon?"

"Oh, come off it. Providence and the coroner tell you it's just an accident, but you think it's murder. Well, the four people who knew Emma best are all in this room right now and you haven't asked us a single question about alibis or anything. For all you know, any of us might have whacked her. God knows I've been tempted a few times."

"*Constance!*" Irene cries, scandalized.

"Well, it's true, ain't it? He knows who killed her. Don't you?"

Faced with a frontal assault, Billy surrenders. "I don't *know* anything yet, Miss Constance. But there is this fellow, I've got the name here somewhere..." He begins to fumble with his notebook.

Constance answers wearily, "I suppose you mean Marcus Rhinegold."

"How on Earth did you know that?" I ask, amazed.

Constance shrugs. "It's Little Compton. Nobody comes here, nobody leaves. Nothing ever happens. Then two months ago a big fancy yacht pulls up in the harbor and now there's a murder. Not exactly rocket science."

"Right," Billy concurs. "He's an outsider. Nobody knows a thing about him. He came to the funeral, though. And I understand you do some work for him."

"We were hired to take down the Armstrong place. But I'm not privy to his secret demons, and I gather Irene isn't either."

"Certainly not," Aunt Irene concurs, shivering a little.

Some obscure instinct for academic impartiality leads me to come to the unknown Rhinegold's defense. "But Billy," I protest, "that's not fair. Just because this guy's not from around here doesn't make him a murderer, for Christ's sake."

"It's not just that. We've got a report that his car, a big black Mercedes, was in the area that afternoon. It's a dead end street, so either he got lost and was turning around, or he was here to visit someone. The car passed by right about four o'clock, according to my witness."

"Gladys Furman," Constance says knowingly. "That woman don't miss a thing. But she's crazy as a loon, Billy, and I'm not sure she'd know a Mercedes from a Pinto with those big specs of hers."

Billy coughs into his hand noncommittally. "Yeah, well, anyway, I'll be along to see this Rhinegold as a matter of course, but I doubt he'd have much to say to me. But maybe if you talk to him…"

"*Us?*" Irene bleats.

"You're up at the Armstrong house all the time. And you're the only people in town who actually know him."

"We don't know him. Not like that. For God's sake, Connie?" Irene turns to Aunt Constance and spreads her hands in mute appeal.

"This seems a little…unorthodox," Constance says slowly.

"Of course it is. But Providence won't back me up—it's my case, for what that's worth. And I figured with you all being so close to Emma, you might want to help."

That's it, of course. The vision of her lying cold and alone in one of those grisly filing cabinets down at Newport General is in all our minds. Constance puts it into words. "So what you're really saying is that if we don't help you, Emma's killer might never be found?"

Billy takes a breath, lets it out. "Well, I'm still not saying Rhinegold is the killer but…yeah."

Aunt Constance crosses her arms and is silent for a moment. "We'll do what we can," she answers, surprisingly. "But he isn't likely to say much to us. Not part of his world, if you know what I mean. Might have better luck with David here."

"Me?"I stare back in disbelief. "I've never said a word to him."

"Exactly." Aunt Constance is sibylline. "You're an outsider, too, more so than the rest of us, anyway. And you're closer in age. We're just a couple of old broads."

"Oh, Connie, I don't know," Irene says worriedly. "Should David get mixed up in all this?"

I have to agree. But Billy runs a hand through his hair, which means he's thinking deeply. He looks at me as if seeing me for the first time. "Not a bad idea, that."

"Is it normal procedure for the police to deputize random history professors to interrogate suspects?" I protest.

"Oh, please," scoffs Constance, "calling Billy 'the police' is like calling Fred Barnes down at Narragansett Savings the Secretary of the Treasury."

I can see Billy isn't exactly flattered by this, but he plows ahead, "You're smart, David. Smartest person I ever met. And it's not very much, just a friendly conversation."

"What if he doesn't want to talk to me?" I object, rather feebly.

"He will," Aunt Constance affirms. "I'll just ring him up and tell him you want one last look at the old Armstrong place before we take it down. You're a historian writing a book on ugly old Victorian homes. Couldn't be simpler."

Billy squirms a bit. "Just be careful," he says awkwardly.

"The thought had occurred to me. But what am I supposed to get out of him? It's not like I can go, 'Hey that's a nice moulding. By the way, did you kill any old ladies this week?'"

"Get him to talk about himself," Constance suggests, as if it had all been her idea. "Ask if he has any relations in town. You could start by asking why he went to the funeral of a woman he supposedly never met."

"You don't have to do it, David," Irene adds. "You can say no. After all, Emma was our friend."

"She was mine, too," I say quietly, and for the first time realize it's true.

"It probably won't come to anything," admits Billy. "But Rhinegold's all I've got. And I was really sorry about Miss Emma. She was always good to me. Gave me a loan for the police academy. Even said she'd pay for the wedding if we ever…"

"Coffee, anyone?" Irene interrupts.

Now Grandma is awake. She stares unblinkingly for a moment at Billy, then turns slowly to me. "You can't have the wedding now," she announces, "It's too damn cold. Wait till May at least."

"I guess I'll be going." Billy is on his feet. He stares down at his notebook.

Irene protests, "But didn't you want to talk to…?"

"Later. There's no hurry. Thanks for the cake, ladies. David, I'll be seeing ya. Let me know how it goes." The door slams behind him.

"Well," says Grandma, absorbing his exit, "that was weird. What did he want?"

"To deputize David."

"Don't be disgusting, Constance. That isn't even legal in some states. Anyway, in my day, we called it plucking the rose."

Chapter Four

"Be patient and let time pass," Queen Elizabeth once advised. What was good for the Virgin Queen seems to be the order in Little Compton as well. Days pass without word from Chief Billy—not that I expected any. Aunt Constance and Aunt Irene dutifully tried to engage Marcus Rhinegold in a friendly conversation about his antecedents, relatives in town, future plans—and were politely and firmly rebuffed. They tried again with his wife, Alicia, and got the same—more firm, less polite. "Well, so much for that," Aunt Constance reports at dinner.

"Did you mention me?" I ask, hoping my voice betrays no anxiety.

"Sure. He seemed a little more receptive there. Wanted to know if you were at the funeral, and made me describe you in some detail. I had to fudge a bit about what your doctorate is actually for, but I don't think he cares. I'm not sure I know, anyway. You may hear from him, you may not."

On this unsatisfactory note Emma's would-be murder investigation rests. I check the papers every morning, just in case Billy decides to go public, but there is nothing in the *Journal*, save various sweating councilmen being paraded past klieg lights into the courthouse. Plundergate rolls on.

True to their word, the Aunts left few scraps for the appraisers to pick over. An elegant sideboard appears suddenly and mysteriously in Grandma's dining room, and there is a watercolor of Block Island hanging over my bed. "Oh, stop fussing," Constance says, waving aside my protests. "Emma would've wanted you to have it." Even Aunt Irene now sports a Fair Isle jumper in green tartan which seems snug on her large frame.

The Aunts come by most nights to keep Grandma company, and give me a chance to rest. They play bridge around the baize-topped table in the study. Emma's hand is a dummy, but her green eyeshade still rests next to it. I've never offered to take the empty chair, and they've never asked. Sometimes Aunt Irene will read interesting bits from the paper, most of which I read on my iPhone hours before. But it passes the time.

On an otherwise unremarkable Wednesday the post arrives with a letter from Xavier College, formally terminating my employment as an assistant professor "for reasons which are well known to all concerned." Irene and Constance must have sensed something in the air, for that night they are more solicitous than usual. Irene brings a gigantic Victoria sponge cake lined with homemade raspberry jam, and even Aunt Constance unbends enough to ask my opinion on the refugee crisis in Syria. Grandma eats her cake and focuses on her hand. Somehow, with most of the wires in her head lying in a tangled heap, she can still play bridge. But her conversation is desultory.

The fourth hand ends in a spectacular grand slam for Aunt Constance, and by common instinct all three women look to the television. "It's nearly ten," Irene says, wolfishly.

"Who's got the remote?" Constance demands.

"Right here." Grandma fumbles with the slippery plastic, points and shoots.

"I really don't know what you see in him," I offer. "He's not even that good-looking."

"Shut up," all three chime in unison.

"*Blue Bloods will not be shown tonight so that we can bring you a special report from our correspondent at the capital, where we have the latest on the Plundergate scandal that has already implicated...*"

"For God's sake, turn it off," growls Constance, disgusted.

"Another week without Tom," Irene sighs. "If this Plundergate lasts much longer, I may lose my will to live."

Such is the rigid order of our lives that the postponement of a single program has thrown the entire Wednesday askew. We stare at each other. "Well," Grandma asks of the room, "what now?"

"Oh!" cries Irene suddenly. "I have an idea!" She jumps up from the table and disappears. A moment later she is back, holding something black and plastic with a cord dangling down behind. "Meant to give this to you days ago," she tells me.

It is a tape recorder as big as a shoebox. "Thanks?" I tell her, puzzled.

"It's for you to record us," Irene says mystifyingly. "You know, like those Israelis did with the Holocaust—like that!"

I am not even one half-step ahead of her. "You want me to make you talk about the Holocaust?"

"No, silly. Oral history. We tell stories, talk about our lives, whatever we remember. And you record it all. Because, let's face it, in a few years we'll be gone, and this whole place will just be one giant condo project."

"And because some of us may forget things soon," Aunt Constance puts in.

"You mean me," says Grandma.

"I mean you."

I'm beginning to understand. The Laughing Sarahs have been conferencing. The subject is me. I've lost my job and I'm back living in a town I told to fuck itself about six years ago. In my grandmother's house, no less. Where my own father won't visit. So, they asked themselves, what can we do to keep David from getting bored, restless—even… suicidal? Yeah, they remember that, too. A quick trip to Newport General when I was sixteen, complete with twist-tie restraints pinning down my arms. Dad was in Guam. Fun times.

But I have to say, their solution has a manic kind of brilliance. Give him a project! Us! "This could be fun," I admit. "What do you want to talk about?"

"Well, you're the one with the PhD in history, Smartypants," Constance answers snappily. "What do you want us to talk about?"

The giant tape recorder sitting on the table seems to ask the same question. Where to begin? Whose story do you want to hear? Should we talk about rationing during the war? Or Aunt Constance's second husband Edgar, who took acid in the '60's and now believes he's the Shah of Iran?

"Tell me something about Emma."

There is a collective intake of breath, felt rather than heard.

"What do you want to know?" Constance demands. "She lived over in that little house for fifty years. Then she died. You know as much as we do."

"Not everything. You went through Emma's things. Did you find the letters?"

"Letters?" Constance repeats, all innocence. "What letters?"

"The letters that kept coming for fifty years," I say doggedly. "Teddy Johnson's letters. The ones you said you'd never tell me about as long as she was alive."

"Oh *those* letters. No, we didn't find them. Just bills and circulars." She stares into the fire as if trying to read a message in the coals.

"I'm going to take Maggie up," Irene announces. She takes Grandma firmly by the hand. "Say goodnight to the folks, Gracie."

"Goodnight to the folks, Gracie!" Grandma mimics, grinning. Half the time she doesn't know who I am, but she can remember a Burns and Allen skit from 1935. They disappear up the stairs together.

"I don't believe you," I tell Aunt Constance quietly.

"Can't help that. Anyway, what are you bothering about those letters for? It's all over and done with."

"Are you sure? What if she was killed because of something in her past?"

"Oh, please. This is Rhode Island, not the Moulin Rouge. Emma didn't have a past. She got old, and died."

"She didn't die, Constance. She was murdered."

A voice from above our heads calls gently, "I think David is right, Connie. He deserves to know." Irene comes down the stairs, leaning heavily on the banister.

Constance grimaces at this new betrayal. "We were there, Irene. It was all just a stupid love affair that fizzled out."

"Not before producing a kid, apparently," I put in.

"I didn't know about the daughter," Constance answers. "Emma went abroad for a while. She must have had the baby then. But she didn't come back with it. So if she didn't tell us, chances are she never told Teddy."

"Pretty rough on him."

"He was pretty rough on her. Never came back, did he? Never claimed his bastard."

"Connie…" Irene is distressed.

"No, I mean it. I'm telling you the truth, David. We

didn't find the letters. I don't know what they said, and I don't care."

"You still haven't told me about them," I remind her gently.

Aunt Constance looks at me for a moment, shrugs, and walks over to the bookshelf. For one mad moment I think she is actually going to produce the letters themselves. Instead she comes back with a box of scrapbooks. "We took these out of her house that night," she says. "Here." She chooses one, flips it open and shows it to me.

Three girls in bathing suits pose alluringly on the hood of a Pontiac convertible. My grandmother's hair is long and straight, pulled into a braid. Aunt Irene is already slightly plump, with a cheeky grin. The third figure is Aunt Emma, draped over the radiator grill. She is by far the most beautiful: heart-shaped face, almond eyes, and a long willowy figure like Katharine Hepburn. Her hair is wet and serpentine around her shoulders. The date on the picture is 1950.

"That's Teddy behind the wheel," Aunt Irene tells me.

It must be summer, because Teddy is shirtless. His muscled bicep is folded casually on the doorframe, hand resting on the wheel. Thick, blond hair is pulled back from a razor-straight scalp. He has dark eyes with long, almost feminine lashes, and very white teeth.

"Wow," I say.

"Yeah, that was Teddy," Aunt Constance sighs. Her lips form a thin line.

"He was so handsome," Irene sighs, "Movie star handsome, like Cesar Romero, but not Italian."

"Cuban," Aunt Constance corrects.

"Teddy most certainly was not Cuban!" Irene snaps back.

Constance opens her mouth, closes it again. "Well, anyway, you get the idea."

"But how did it all start?" I press. "And why did they never marry? What happened to him, anyway?"

"What makes you so sure this has anything to do with her death?"

"What makes you sure it doesn't?" I retort.

Aunt Constance considers this for a moment. "Fuck it," she says finally. "I'm headed home. Irene, you can do the honors." She makes it as far as the door before turning round. "But remember this," she says, pointing an accusing finger at both of us, "Emma was a damn good woman, and the only thing she ever asked for was privacy. If she had secrets, they were hers and hers alone." With that, she turns and marches out the door.

Irene, admonished but unrepentant, cuts herself another slice of Victoria sponge. "Connie's always so forceful. I always said she'd make a splendid Baptist preacher, the hard-shell kind. But her people were Episcopalians."

"About the letters…?" I prod.

"Oh, it's such a beautiful story! But Connie is right, love, it can't have anything to do with Emma's death."

"You said…"

"I said I think you should know. But not because of… all this. It's not like that. I don't think Emma would've minded you knowing, not now anyway. And after all, it's just another old New England fairy tale."

I chuckle. Most New England fairy tales end with a pirate ship preying for souls or a ghost dragging its chains along a deserted beach. "Tell me."

"The first thing you need to know," Irene begins, fortifying herself with a sip of coffee, "is that Emma's family had money." Her voice, so like Grandma's with every Yankee vowel flattened as though by a clothes mangle, carries me back into the past—mine, not Emma's. I'm five years old, sitting on Grandma's lap and enveloped in a world where anything can happen, and magic is real.

IRENE

The first thing you need to know is that Emma's family had money. And with money came expectations. They couldn't just marry their daughter off to some car mechanic or office boy, not in 1951. Her people came from Newport around the time of the Depression. Everyone whispered that they were 'old money,' but nobody really knew where it came from. Like those Spanish doubloons that sit for so long at the bottom of the sea that all their markings wear away—that was the Godfrey fortune.

But maybe, just maybe, they weren't quite as rich as everyone thought. Why else would they give up Newport for Little Compton? We didn't even have a theater back then. And the Godfreys weren't what you might call big spenders, either. Kept a hired girl for the house and gardener for the grounds, but a place like that really needed a whole staff. Old Mr. Godfrey was a bit on the cheap side. There's a story that he used to give his wife a bushel of peaches for her birthday every year—because he fancied peach jam! So there she'd be on the front porch, mashing away at his peaches, for days. She was a nice woman—rather faded looking, but nice. He was a bastard.

I think they both put their hopes in Emma. A family that's lost its fortune can still trade on its name for a while, if they have enough ready cash to keep up appearances. All Emma had to do was marry well, and they'd be flush again. So the Godfreys sent Emma to Lincoln School and made sure she went to all the debutante dances at Pawtuxet Hall, where the boys from the prep schools came down to mingle with the townies. They sent her on expensive trips to Europe, and Mrs. Godfrey would scan the passenger lists on sailing day and tell Emma exactly who to sit next to, who to talk to. She never lacked for nice clothes, either, and when she was sixteen her father gave her a convertible—that same one in the picture. In fact that was the day we took the picture: July 17, 1950. The day we first met Teddy.

Teddy? Oh, he wasn't what they had in mind at all. He was a local boy, and his father ran the tuna boat Trixie Gale *out of Galilee. Nice people, the Johnsons. They were dead by then, though; Teddy was an orphan. And Teddy was—well, you saw him. Teddy was gorgeous. They met at Bailey's Beach. Emma went too far out that day, she was always doing that. Showing off a little. Not to make us feel bad, you understand, but just because I think she always felt a little bit apart. Her parents didn't like her going to the beach, showing her legs. They were scared she'd get too brown and look like a farmhand. Plus there was a low crowd around Bailey's Beach—low by Godfrey standards, anyway. "Not quite nice," was how Mrs. Godfrey described it. But it was a fizzing hot day, and it was Emma's birthday, so she did as she damn well pleased. We filled up a hamper with jam puffs and lemonade and parked right on the sand. You could do things like that back then, nobody cared.*

But Emma, as I said, went too far out. You remember we always told you to wait an hour after lunch before swimming? And you thought that was just your old aunties being silly? It wasn't. Emma got in the water and rather fancied swimming out to Bishop Rock. It was a flat calm day and the rock looked ever so close. So she started to swim. It was all right at first, and there in the water Emma felt far away from her family, and very clever. But then she got a pretty far ways out and realized the rock wasn't as close as she thought. Too late to turn back. Best to just make it to the rock and rest there for a bit.

We were watching from shore. She looked okay. I even saw her wave to us, and like a fool I waved back. She kept waving, and I remember Maxine saying, "Isn't she silly, waving like that? She needs her energy to swim." It was Constance who finally realized what was going on. "She's drowning!" she cried, and began running towards the water.

But the lifeguard had seen Emma too. He threw himself into an oncoming wave and made for her, great brown arms cutting through the water. By now the whole beach was watching. When he reached her they gave a great cheer, and did it again when he finally came ashore, carrying her.

It was Teddy, of course. He looked like Poseidon that day, seawater glistening on his perfect chest with his hair all tousled and damp. He laid Emma across the backseat of the Pontiac and gave her mouth-to-mouth resuscitation. That's what it looked like, anyway. But I'm pretty sure she was awake by then. Didn't seem to mind, though. When he was sure she was all right, Teddy offered to drive us home. Emma was the only one with a license, so we said yes. He drove right up the driveway to your Grandma's house and that's where the picture was taken.

Oh, yes, Emma was fine. Sometimes I wonder if she staged the whole thing, got out there in the water and started splashing around until he noticed. She did things like that. But then I remember how frightened she looked, how her hair was tangled with seaweed and her makeup all smeared, and I think, Who'd want to meet their future love like that? So I just don't know. I reckon it doesn't matter anyway. She met him, that's the main thing, and after that day he started *coming over regular. To check on her, he said. Well that's one way to put it.*

Mr. and Mrs. Godfrey weren't at all pleased. They were indebted to him for saving her life, of course, but those kind of debts don't run very long. When Teddy came a third time, with a bouquet of geraniums from his own garden, Mrs. Godfrey greeted him with a cold smile and Mr. Godfrey suggested he might enjoy a walk back to the barn. Once they got there Mr. Godfrey sat him on a bale of hay and began explaining certain facts. The Godfreys were an old and venerable family. They had social position. They remained extremely grateful for the young man's heroic actions, but now that Emma was fully recovered, his attentions were no longer appropriate.

Now I only have Emma's version of this story, so you'll have to take her word on what happened next. According to Emma, Teddy Johnson waited until Mr. Godfrey ran out of steam. Then he drew a checkbook out from his back pocket and said, "How much?"

"I don't understand," said Mr. Godfrey.

"I think you do," Teddy answered. "You say your daughter has certain expectations. I figure that means money. Well, it's a hard world, and I don't blame her, or you. So if I need to pay a premium to take her out to the movies, I'd rather just pay it now. Up front. What figure did you have in mind?"

Mr. Godfrey looked very offended. "I think you need to leave now," he said coldly.

Teddy looked at him for a moment, then back at the house with its peeling paint and sagging porch. He wrote a number on the check, tore it off and handed it to Godfrey. "That about cover it?"

I guess it must have done, because Old Man Godfrey never said a word after that. Teddy really was wonderful.

He courted Emma in a gentle manner that was old-fashioned even then, brought her flowers and candy, sat with her parents in the front parlor, played backgammon with them. He gave them all gifts. Not expensive, flashy gifts, but thoughtful ones. Emma got a fan, her mother a tortoiseshell comb, her father a leather saddle for his favorite horse. Mr. Godfrey liked the saddle (he sold it to Bud Timmons for three hundred dollars) but he wondered how to hurry things along. I'm just guessing here, but maybe he figured the family coffers might not survive Teddy's unhurried courtship. Finally he chose a warm September day to invite the lad into his study for a chat. Mr. Godfrey gave Teddy a glass of port wine, told him to sit down and asked what his intentions were with Emma.

Conversations like that hadn't quite gone out of fashion yet. A few years later Teddy and Emma might have gotten a flat together in Greenwich Village or joined a commune, but it was still 1951 and there was little Teddy could do except declare his love and solemnly propose marriage to Mr. Godfrey. That is, I mean, he proposed to marry Emma. Mr. Godfrey gravely accepted on her behalf, and the two went out to share this news with the women.

Was Emma happy? I'll say she was! I've never seen her happier. I'm sure they talked about marriage loads of times before Mr. Godfrey sprang it on them. Teddy was…well, he was ecstatic. But that's the Johnsons all over. Once they want a thing, they get it, no matter what. He'd finally gotten Emma, and no couple was better matched. We passed that whole fall in a kind of daze. Constance took Emma to Boston to buy her trousseau. The Godfreys had their whole house painted and the porch lifted to get ready for the reception. Some said Teddy paid for it, but I never knew for sure. Emma was radiant. We all were. It was the same year that I met Phil, and your Grandma her dear Mike, so we were to be three June brides together. Constance was already married then. Oh, his name was Everett. He doesn't matter.

Now in the normal course of events a fall engagement would be followed by a June wedding, but you know 1951 was not a normal year. All the boys were being called away to Korea. Phil went into the medic corps, just like that M.A.S.H. *show. Your grandpa was in the Navy, on board the* U.S.S. Kearsarge. *He left a bun in the oven, though, and that was your dad. It felt so strange, like we'd just finished off one war and here we were in another. Everybody was vanishing. They had to stop the Pawtuxet dances. And in the spring of '51 Teddy got his letter. Report to the divisional commander at Fort Dix, etc., etc. Well it wasn't exactly unexpected, but Emma was heartbroken. I've never seen her like that, before or since. Keening. Said she was sure Teddy was going to die, that they had been too happy and now God was punishing them. It's a Puritan town, remember, and those sentiments still crop up now and again. I won't say many of us didn't feel the same way, to be honest.*

On a sunny morning in early May, Teddy caught the ferry to New York. We all came up to Fall River to see him off. Emma was dry-eyed by then; she'd gotten herself together. That day she wore a pretty white dress with blue forget-me-nots and a handkerchief over her hair. She kissed Teddy on the cheek, told him to do his duty, and waved as the ferry left the dock. There was a smile on her face. I think she was there after the rest of us left.

Not long after, the first letter arrived. It was dated July 1, 1951, and postmarked Biloxi. Emma read Teddy's letters aloud. He wrote about the drill sergeants, the mess halls, waking up before dawn, and carrying fifty pounds of gear on his shoulders. He wrote of his love, and his unshakeable faith that God would reunite them soon. I suppose Teddy might have gotten a furlough to come back and make it official, but somehow this never happened. His letters were full of love and optimism, unperturbed by the delay. Mr. Godfrey, on the other hand, never forgave Harry Truman. When Teddy's check ran dry and another failed to appear, the creditors finally figured out there was nothing coming. The Godfreys had to sell their house and rent an apartment above the Texaco station. Mrs. Godfrey died not long after; she was never a strong woman. But Old Man Godfrey could still be seen there into his eighties, pumping gasoline and cursing his fate.

And Emma? It was hard for her, of course. She took a long trip to the Carolinas to some health spa—come to think of it, that must have been when she had the baby. After that she moved in with me and Phil for a while. I helped get her a job at Shepard's, at the cosmetics counter. She was still a very beautiful woman. Lots of men asked her out. She wouldn't have any of them. Emma belonged to Teddy, it was as simple as that.

The letters kept coming, all through '51 and '52. Sometimes two or three a week. Emma got promoted and ended up running the department all by herself. She moved into the little house next to your Grandma's and started fixing it up. I think she wanted to make a home for Teddy, once he came back. If he came back. And maybe bring back the baby, too. Well, she was lucky in one way: Teddy wasn't killed. At first he was a sapper, which meant laying fuses along the enemy lines or throwing grenades into concrete bunkers known as pillboxes. It was dangerous work. He was at Pork Chop Hill, and Kumsong. Then they transferred him out to a desk job at command headquarters in Seoul. And the war ended. But Teddy didn't come home.

There were reasons, of course. At first they needed him for the transition, and Emma told us how he was working as adjutant to a very powerful U.S. general, arranging meetings and hosting diplomats from all over the world. Then he was assigned to General Waller's staff, and given the rank of Captain. From Seoul he went to Paris, then Istanbul. The letters still came, every week.

At some point, though, people began to wonder. By 1960 Emma wasn't a young woman anymore, the war was long over, but still Teddy never came back. Though his letters continued to arrive without fail. Every week, like clockwork. It was uncanny.

What did they say? None of us ever knew. Emma never talked about them, not after the war ended. The house that she bought for Teddy started to look more feminine. She put out nasturtiums and painted the living room pink. She called herself a spinster, and, I'm sorry to say, the word suited her. She started wearing gingham dresses and gave piano lessons. On Sundays she played the organ at the United Congregational. Eventually, she went away to Kingston and came back with a degree in oceanography. Shocked us all. But she was damn good at it, no question. Best wreck-finder in New England, knew all about shifting sandbars and tidal currents. We brought her in sometimes to work with us at Wrecking and Salvage, whenever there was a boat that went missing.

We never asked about Teddy, but others did. It was very rude. They talked behind Emma's back, too. Why had Teddy abandoned her? Had he married someone else? Or perhaps (and this was whispered very quietly, indeed) he had never meant to marry her. Perhaps he was one of those 'gentlemen bachelors' that kept pug dogs and lived in Provincetown. But, if any of these were true, why did he still write? That was the mystery. Those letters kept coming right up until last week. No, they've stopped now. So I guess he knows she's gone. But now you see, dear, why none of this could have anything to do with poor Emma's death. Teddy loved her, in his fashion. And I'm sure he never knew about their child. We certainly didn't. What—you think he came back after all these years and brained her in her own kitchen? Nonsense.

You know, in a way I envy her. She loved a man that never aged, never changed, never lied or betrayed her. Not like my Phil. They had a whole life together—well, not actually together, but you know what I mean. Isn't that beautiful? Really, isn't it?

Chapter Five

On Friday afternoon the phone rings. Grandma answers.

"Yes! Yes! Who? No, there's no David here. Hold on." I am frantically waving my arms. "What do you want? Can't you see I'm on the phone?" She turns her back to me. "Yes, of course I'm sure. I live here, don't I? A message? For whom? No I *don't* want to meet you at the Armstrong House. Nobody's lived there for dog's years. There's a funny couple that bought it now. I dunno, funny. Like butter wouldn't melt in their mouths. What? Oh, for heaven's sake, all right. If I ever meet anyone named David, I'll give him your message. Good-bye!" She slams down the phone. "Some people!"

It seems incredible that it took only a casual suggestion by Aunt Constance to result in an invitation to dinner, but so it was. When I finally spoke with Marcus Rhinegold, the voice on the other end was effusive, delighted. Yes, yes, by all means, do come. Dinner at eight. Be happy to have you.

But that night I wonder if I've been the victim of some elaborate practical joke. The Armstrong House is dark and shuttered when I arrive. No one's lived in this place for a long time. The yard is parched and bare, with piles of sand and bits of construction material strewn about. Several of the windows are broken. The house, with its heavy gray stone and mansard roof and single ocular window staring down at the driveway, looks like a summer cottage for the Addams Family. At last the door opens to a cavernous dark within and Marcus Rhinegold emerges. "You're on time!" he cries, surprised.

"I was under the impression I was coming to dinner."

"Not here!" He looks horrified at the thought. "We'll eat on the *Calliope*. But Miss Heckman—Constance—said you'd like one last look at the old place."

In truth, I don't. I remember this house when the Cavendishes lived here. They were a nice couple with a son my own age, Peter. We went to Moses Brown School together, until he fell from a swing in his senior year and shattered his spine. Then came a terrible year of braces and wheelchairs, plasma bags and oxygen. But the big house, with all its stairs and narrow passageways, defeated them. They bought a raised ranch in Woonsocket and spent a small fortune widening the doorways and putting in ramps. Just before they could move in, Peter caught an infection and died. I went to the funeral. I don't know where the Cavendishes went after that. They might have stayed, but they had already sold the house to some land trust that was planning to turn it into a high-class rest home. By the time the trust got all its approvals, it was 2008, and the economy tanked. The firm went under and the house has been empty ever since. I never had the slightest interest in going inside after all that. But it seems rude to say so.

Rhinegold hands me a flashlight and we enter together. It's a week before Halloween and this has all the markings of a D-grade slasher flick. There's plastic sheeting on the floor. Mirrored walls catch the light from our flashlights and reveal us looking momentarily horrified. The rooms are vast and empty. "This used to be the ballroom," Rhinegold tells me.

Actually it was the front parlor. The walls are lined with oak wainscoting and red silk, with a great marble fireplace that the Armstrongs brought over from a castle in Ireland. The floor is parquet laid out in hexagrams, which may be why Rhinegold thought it was for dancing. But I look to the corner of the room and can almost see the hospital gurney, the oblong bag dangling from its hook, and hear the steady shush of the ventilator. "They put him in here so he could look out at the sea."

"What's that?" Rhinegold asks, confused.

"Nothing."

The bottle of wine still dangles from my hand. "That looks great!" Rhinegold says, taking it from me. "Shall we try it?"

"Here?"

"Upstairs. There's a great view of the ocean from the balcony. With a moon on the water, you can't miss it."

I could tell him that I spent my whole life with that water and that moon, but I don't. I'm beginning to get a sense of this man. He is very rich and very lonely, and unaccustomed to making new friends. I follow him upstairs. The French doors to the balcony are thrown open and the room is, as promised, filled with moonlight. He takes me out to the parapet. "Isn't it wonderful?"

It is. A clear night in late October, with a harvest moon hanging low and fecund over a perfectly calm bay. The air is just cold enough to be bracing. "I'll be sorry to tear the place down," Rhinegold says, "But at least I get to keep the view."

The moonlight frames his face in profile as he looks out to sea. Up close, he's younger than I thought. It's a patrician face, startlingly handsome despite the gray at the temples.

"Should we have some wine?"

"Yeah."

We open it with Rhinegold's penknife and drink it from the bottle, a cheap Chianti that makes us both gag a little. "Very nice," Rhinegold chokes, with tears in his eyes.

Through the French doors I catch sight of his yacht glittering in the harbor below. "She's a beauty."

He smiles. "She is that. We've been all over the world, Alicia and me. Biarritz, Alexandria, Tortola, Monte Carlo... Hell, the whole boat is full of crap we bought along the way. Astrakhan rugs, Benares brass tables, you name it."

"And then you came here. Seems an odd place to land, after Biarritz and Monte Carlo."

"I got tired. Can you understand that? Tired of feeling like I was being chased. Finally I realized there really wasn't anyone there." He takes another swig from the bottle. "When I was a little kid I was in an orphanage in Bensonhurst. That doesn't matter. We never really got to go anywhere, just back and forth from one big brick building to the other. I never saw anything of the world except Nostrand Avenue. Except this one time. I must've been about twelve or thirteen. That summer they sent us up to Montauk on the ferry. One day in early June. I'd never been on the water before. The Sound was a little rough, and some of the kids got sick. But I didn't. I stood right on the bow, leaned over the rail. I'd never seen so much sky before. It was beautiful."

His face is lit with a smile and looks years younger. For just that moment I can see the tough little orphan kid, his face a hard kernel of fierce joy.

"Then we got to Montauk. There was a bus waiting for us right at the pier. They took us down to the beach. The bus passed right through this little town, and I want to tell you, it wasn't anything like I'd ever seen. The houses were all painted white with flower boxes in the windows. And each family had a house all to themselves! Incredible. Instead of a supermarket they had a little grocery store with baskets full of flowers out front. People didn't hurry down the street; they just sort of ambled. Even the kids. We pressed our faces up against the glass and stared. By the time I got to the beach, I didn't give a damn about the water. I just wanted to go back to that town, and disappear into one of those little white houses, and hide until they never found me again."

"I guess you finally did."

"I guess so." But he doesn't seem sure. Then, suddenly, the mask is back in place. Marcus grins, slips an arm over my shoulders. "I'm really glad I met you, David. I hope we get to see more of each other." He's close enough for me to smell his cologne, something fruity with a tang of cinnamon. His hand hasn't moved. "That's a pretty tattoo," he murmurs, staring at the green tendrils that peek out of my open collar. "Is that a tree?"

"It's antlers."

"I'd love to see the whole stag."

Several things are becoming clearer. I edge backward, letting his hand fall to his side. "Shouldn't we be getting down to the boat? Your wife will be wondering where you are."

"No, she won't."

"But dinner…"

"It's okay." He leans and whispers urgently into my ear. "I told her not to expect us till nine. It's only seven-thirty now. We have lots of time."

"No, really…"

"There's a bed in the other room, David." His voice is almost hoarse with lust, but his eyes are pleading. "I had my staff make it up. If you…you know…want to use it."

"Marcus." I'm horrified and angry with myself at the

same time. And very, *very* angry with Billy Dyer, who should have known better. I'm only five-foot-five, with spiky brown hair, blue eyes, and long eyelashes. My face never quite lost its babyish roundness. The term, in certain circles, is *twink*. "Marcus, don't think I'm not flattered. I am. But I don't think that's where this night is headed."

There's a long moment when we just stare at each other. "Oh," he says finally. "Yeah." Doors are closing all over his face. "Did you think...did you think I was...Nah, I'm married! Jeez, I just meant in case you were tired or something!"

"I think I should probably go."

"No!" Rhinegold looks around desperately, as if there were a magic talisman on the floor that he could pick up and erase the last five minutes. "No, we've got dinner waiting! Alicia made us a terrific Jamaican jerk chicken. Well, she didn't make it, exactly, the chef made it, but she ordered it, which I guess is the same thing..."

He's babbling now, his eyes still searching the sky, the darkened house, anywhere except me. Neither of us wants to go to Alicia or the jerk chicken, but there's nothing we can do. He can't rescind his invitation without admitting it was a ploy, and I can't do anything but pretend it's real.

•••••

The *Calliope* is a stunner. Mortified as I am, I can't help but stare. Long and white and lovely, with a saloon made of solid teak and a stubby little funnel that pokes up from behind the wheelhouse. Every light is ablaze, casting a warm glow. "Wow," I breathe.

"Isn't she something?" Rhinegold gets a bit of his confidence back. "Built as a sub chaser during the war. Solid mahogany inside and out, with big Chrysler diesels that lift her clear out of the water. She'll do forty knots if she's pushed."

"I didn't know they made sub chasers that looked like that."

"Aww, well, I added a few improvements." He grins, his good humor almost restored. Like most men, he takes refuge in machines. Especially his own. "The deckhouse, that actually came off a pilot boat. And all the trim is new. The whole interior had to be gutted as well, and the hull fitted for deep-sea travel. She's got a huge gas tank now, in what used to be the depth charge storage. I can go all the way from here to Florida without refueling."

I try to look impressed as he reels off the statistics. But I get the feeling we are both waiting for something. Finally a shaft of light appears. "Marcus? You guys coming inside, or what?"

"Yeah, honey." But for the longest moment neither of us moves.

Dinner is every bit as awkward as you'd expect. Rhinegold points to various objects around the room and tells stories about them. Alicia is wearing a tank top and sweatpants and looks bored. The jerk chicken is brought in by a steward. It is very good, and I say so. "Oh, I didn't make it," Alicia avers at once.

"Alicia can't even boil water," Marcus adds.

I don't know what to say to this, so I nod and smile. Alicia goes back to staring out the window at the darkness. Rhinegold picks up a wooden figurine and turns it over in his hand. It looks African and vaguely sinister. The expression is disdainful, as if it resents being touched. "Picked this up in a market in Marrakech," he says. "The vendor claims they ward off evil and increase virility…"

"So," Alicia cuts in, staring hard at me, "did you enjoy the fifty-cent tour?"

"I...yes."

"Did Marcus show you everything you wanted to see?" Her eyes are blazing now, and I suddenly realize Alicia is drunk.

"Yes, I think so."

"How's the view from the bedroom?"

"Alicia," Marcus interjects, "why don't you go ask Consuela if dessert is ready?"

"I don't—"

"Go check." His voice is hard suddenly, brought down like a fist on the table. Without another word Alicia gets up and leaves. "Sorry about that," Marcus mutters. "She drinks too much. It's always been bad, but I swear it's gotten worse."

"She doesn't like Little Compton, then?"

"I thought she would. She's always nattering on about country life. Grew up in some godawful town in upstate Jersey. I figured she'd be glad to escape it, but wherever we went was never as good as Bumfuck, New Jersey." He sighs, shakes his head. "And now we can't even leave."

Alicia reappears. "Dessert's on its way." Her voice is flat, dead.

"Thanks, hon."

Now we are all looking around the room, as if a new conversation topic was tucked like a prompt card somewhere in the rafters. My eye alights on a buxom mermaid carved of oak and stretched alluringly over the fireplace. She is, rather incongruously, wearing spectacles and holding a writing tablet. "Where'd you pick her up?" I ask.

Marcus chuckles. "Stands out a bit, huh? No, she came with the place. They carved her right into the lintel above the wardroom door when this was still a sub chaser. In fact, she gave the boat its name. Ever heard of Calliope?"

I have, actually. Calliope was the writer's muse, whispering verses into the ears of Homer and Aristophanes. She was also, according to some legends, a gorgon that allowed her prey to write on until their magnum opus was complete. Then she would eat them. I let Rhinegold tell me all this and try to look surprised.

"They named all the sub chasers after figures of mythology," he finishes. "This one was part of the C-Class: *Calypso*, *Callisto*, *Calliope*. The *Calypso* and *Callisto* were both sunk during the war. I like to think the goddess Calliope looks after this boat, maybe puts in a good word with Neptune."

"Poseidon," I correct.

"Oh, well done," says Alicia sarcastically, giving me the slow clap.

"So," I say, in what I hope to be a casual tone, "I noticed you both at the funeral. Were you friends of Emma's?"

"Never met her," Marcus answers. "But it sounded like she was a local character. Seemed like the right thing to do to pay our respects."

"Oh, I thought perhaps you chose Little Compton because you had family here."

"No," says Alicia sharply, "We don't know any of these people."

Not long after that the dessert comes, a limp pear tart with burnt crust and something gelatinous on the bottom. I wolf it down as fast as I can and then, without actually leaping up from the table, start to make exit noises. Rhinegold puts on a face of polite regret, but I can see relief etched at the corners. Alicia barely looks up. She remains at the table as Rhinegold walks me through the saloon. "Sorry," he murmurs again.

"For what?"

He simply shrugs. We are on the aft deck now, and the wind lashes salt against our cheeks.

"I had a great time," I assure him, feeling absurdly like

a teenager letting down their date gently. "Thank you for dinner, and for showing me the house."

He nods, looking out to sea. "Guess I'll see you around, then."

"Yup, definitely." I give his hand a good, masculine pumping, and go down the ladder. Someone has thoughtfully brought my Corolla around. The seats are already warm. As I turn around toward the driveway, I look into the rearview mirror and see Marcus Rhinegold staring after me. Like Gatsby, he raises his hand.

One minute later, I realize I left my coat in the saloon.

The saloon door is still open when I climb back on deck. My coat is draped over the chair just behind it, and I think I can just grab it and go. But even as I reach for it Alicia's voice—bored, languorous, disdainful—murmurs, "So, did you suck his cock?"

I jump, and the coat falls from my hands. But she is still in the dining saloon, and the door is ajar. I can hear the clink of ice cubes.

"I don't know what you're talking about," Marcus growls back. "I doubt if you do."

"So precious." The ice cubes rattle again, and by the sound of it she has just drained her glass. "You look peaky, though. Guess he didn't put out after all. Sickening for you. Well, there's still that Starbucks kid in Warwick. You can send the car to pick him up if you don't feel like a drive."

"Alicia…"

"*Call me by name*!" she hisses back, suddenly furious. "You owe me that, at least, you miserable faggot fuck. One bit of honesty. One thing about our marriage that isn't a total sham."

A sigh. "Okay. Crystal. It's been a really long day, and we don't need to go through this again right now."

"Don't we?" She laughs coldly. "Don't you think you've put me through enough, without bringing your butt boys back home and making me eat dinner with them?"

Marcus doesn't answer. I can imagine the look on his face, the same hopelessness I saw in his eyes when I told him I wasn't interested.

"You think this is easy for me?" she goes on, her voice getting higher. "Wearing these clothes? Dyeing my hair? Playing the dumb cunt every time we go out? You think I like it?"

"No."

"We could be in Monte Carlo right now, you know that? Or Brazil, with all the brown ass you can lay your hands on. Why the *fuck* are we here?"

"You know why." For the first time his voice has an edge to it. "It's the same reason you can't just divorce me and go off with any of the fifteen guys you've had on this boat since we left Marseilles. It's why as much as you hate me, as much as you loathe the very sight of me, you still can't pick up the phone and call Anthony. Don't pretend like you haven't thought about it. I have. I think about it all the time. But you see, I can't leave you either, my darling dearest. Because we'd be dead within a week. You know it as well as I do. And so here we are manacled together on our own little slave ship for all eternity. Or at least until the house is done."

"What am I supposed to look forward to in that?"

"Your own private wing. And doors with locks on them."

"So I'm just supposed to sit in this frigging New England sinkhole and rot?"

Marcus chuckles. It's not a pleasant sound. "To be honest, love, I don't care what you do. The choice is yours. But you'd have rather a hard time keeping clear of the Molinaris without my checkbook backing you up."

Now it's Alicia's—Crystal's—turn to be silent. Treading as softly as I can, I drape the coat over my arm and tiptoe toward the aft deck. The ladder creaks with every rung, but the boat creaks, too, as it rocks against the jetty.

Chapter Six

I figured Billy would want a complete account of the evening's events, but days pass without a word from him. "I expect he's busy, following up leads," Irene says serenely. Yeah, right, I think. He's probably already regretting the fool's errand that sent me out there, and too embarrassed to ask about it. Of course, the embarrassment between us exists on several levels.

"You could always call."

But I won't do that. None of this was my idea, anyway. There are no further messages from the *Calliope* either. Marcus Rhinegold has retreated back into his mahogany-lined shell. I give the Aunts a general picture of the night, minus a few lurid details, and let it drop. I don't think Marcus Rhinegold murdered Emma. In fact, I don't think anyone did, and I have a sneaking suspicion the Providence Police Department feels the same. With no news, life slips back into a familiar rhythm. Halloween brings the fog, a great wet blanket pulled up to the chin. The harbor vanishes. Boats emerge like phantasms trailing long streamers of blue-white cloud. Mast lights hover like fireflies. Little Compton becomes an island, as remote from the world as Greenland's coast. I spend most of the day in my room staring at the walls. They are the same shade of bubblegum pink; the pictures still sit on the dresser in their chunky resin frames with teddy bears and balloons. My closet is full of clothes I will never wear again but Grandma refused to throw away, even when she could still remember why. I don't want to know what's under the bed.

Tonight the Laughing Sarahs come over to help Grandma hang the plastic witch on the door and light the jack-o-lantern that Constance carved. On the newel post in the hallway is a soup tureen full of Mars bars, Twix, Snickers, and Milky Ways—whole ones, not miniatures—for kids that will probably never show. Grandma used to have a reputation as the best giver on the block; the big bars were her idea, not mine. But then last year she became confused and tried to shoo the trick-or-treaters off her porch, waving a broom and screaming for the police. I doubt they'll come back.

Irene's been volunteering at the Methodist Home again; she's dressed as a gypsy. "Care to he-arr your fortune?" she asks in her best Zoltar voice.

"Not really. I don't think I want to know."

She laughs as if this were a joke. Aunt Constance is in the kitchen brewing cider. The smell of cinnamon fills the house. There are caramel apples on the dining room table. I eat two without even thinking about it, lick the goo off my fingers. "Those are for the kids!" Irene admonishes.

Grandma has been strangely quiet all evening. She sits in her rocking chair by the fireplace, the same spot where Captain Barrow occasionally appears, and stares at me. "Happy Halloween!" Irene shouts at her, every time she passes by.

But Grandma's eyes are fixed on me alone. "Excuse me," she says, rather coldly, "but do I know you?"

"Of course you do," Constance calls from the kitchen. "That's David, your grandson."

Her brow wrinkles as she considers this. Finally she rejects it. "Where's Rosalie?" she asks.

Irene hears, pulls a face. Without a word she goes into the kitchen and closes the door. "Rosalie?" I repeat, sadly.

"Yes. My granddaughter. Is she dead? She's dead, isn't she? *What have you done with her*?" Her eyes are starting out of her head now. She tries to rise up from the chair.

"Relax," I tell her soothingly. "It's okay. Nobody's done anything. She's fine, Grandma, I promise."

"Stop calling me that," she hisses. "I ain't your grandma. What have you done with my girl Rosalie? You tell me now. Is she gone? Did you take her away? Tell the truth!"

Now the tears come. But they are mine, not hers. "She's not dead, Grandma."

"You married her, didn't you? You married her and carried her off and strangled her someplace. Stole the jewels right out of her ears, like Bluebeard. And now you've come to get the inheritance."

"She's not dead, Grandma," I repeat, more firmly. "She's here."

"What? What are you talking about? Where?" She looks down at the floorboards, as if this were a Poe story.

I take a deep breath. This just never gets easier. "*I'm* Rosalie. I used to be. They gave me an operation a few years ago and I'm David now."

Grandma looks at me in disgust. "What the hell are you talking about? What did you do with my little Rosalie?"

"It's true, Grandma. I'm serious."

Her eyes search my hairline, my jaw, my chest, hunting for any sign of her lost granddaughter. Finally she sees the splash of freckles on my nose. Her expression softens. "Rosalie? Honey? Are you in there?"

"Yeah, Grandma. She's still here, but she's a boy now. Can you understand that?"

She frowns. We can both hear the determined sounds of pots clanking in the kitchen; the Aunts are putting on a good show. "Well, yeah, I guess so. Rosalie never liked being a girl much. Her momma made her all these little pinafore dresses that she wouldn't wear. She'd put them on and then go roll in the dirt out back."

I remember those dresses. "And then you made me a pair of overalls out of sailcloth, and told Mom that if I wanted to roll around in the dirt, I needed the right equipment."

A smile lights up her face. "That's right! I did! Huh, guess it's my fault then."

Now we are both laughing. "So are you…okay with this?" I ask.

Grandma thinks for a moment. "Sure," she says finally. "I always wanted a grandson. And you're as handsome as any grandma could ever ask for." She pats me gently on the shoulder. "Whatever you look like, whatever you want me to call you, you'll always be my precious little Rosalie. I'll never forget that, I promise."

"Oh, Grandma…"

We embrace, and Grandma goes to help the Aunts get dinner ready. I sigh, but not from relief. I'm glad it went well, of course, but it won't last. A few days later—or hours even—Grandma will be back to wondering where Rosalie is and who this strange man is living in her house.

I know something she doesn't.

We've had this conversation seven times.

• • ● • •

The Aunts are back. We are sitting around the dining room table, waiting for the trick-or-treaters. But it's nearly ten at night and nobody's come. "Ah, to hell with it," says Aunt Constance, and goes into the hall. She comes back with the bowl of candy and a Snickers sticking out the corner of her mouth like a cigar.

"Shame to let it go to waste," Irene murmurs, reaching for a Twix.

"You're getting fat, Irene," Grandma tells her baldly.

"Shut up, Mags. Here, have a Milky Way."

"Now what?" I ask. "Should we watch a movie?"

"They're showing *Hocus Pocus* on Fox," Irene offers. Constance gives her a withering look.

"When I was a girl," Grandma muses, "we used to spend Halloween down at Briggs Marsh with a campfire, drinking hot cider and telling stories. The rule was it had to be scary, or about boys."

"You know any of those kind, David?" Constance asks me. But there is a twinkle in her eye.

It's Halloween, and I'm feeling festive. "Grandma," I say, dragging out the tape recorder, "tell us about the people that used to own this house."

She scoffs. "You know that story better than I do." But she looks pleased I chose her.

"I know it, but the Smithsonian doesn't. Come on." I put in a fresh tape and slide the machine under her nose. The Sarahs make encouraging noises. Grandma is flattered, pretending to be cross. But these are the kinds of things she remembers now. And Irene is right: these are the next to go. I press play, and the gimbals start to turn.

MAGGIE

You've heard this story a hundred times. It's about the Robies, the family that owned this house long before your Great-Great-Grandpa William bought it. They were nice folks. Damn shame what happened to them.

The Robies were a Southern family, from a little town just downriver from Memphis. Roaring Ford, Fording Road, something like that. Anyway the place is gone now, so what does it matter? The Mississippi swallowed it up—that happens sometimes.

Colonel Robie was a cotton planter. Had a big plantation house he inherited from his daddy, who inherited it from his *daddy, and so on, back since the American Revolution or thereabouts. Colonel Robie wasn't really a colonel. They just called him that because he was rich and well-respected. His first name was something silly, like a girl's. Evelyn, I think. No, Hillaire. Hillaire Robie. That's it. His wife was a pretty little thing named Eunice. That's her above the fireplace in the library. George Healy painted that a few years before the war—the Civil War, that is. That was actually painted in this very house. If you look close at the background, you can see the bookcase in the front room.*

The Robies came north every May and didn't return to Tennessee until Christmastime. A lot of wealthy Southern families did that before the War. It got pretty hot down there in the summer, especially with no air conditioning and all those petticoats and vests they had to wear. The richest families built summer homes in Newport, which is how the Vanderbilts and Astors got the idea later. See, they were just copying the Southerners. That big place on Bellevue Avenue—Kingscote—was built for another Southerner named Noble Jones. Newport was quite the place in the 1850s. People thought the air was healthier here. When I was a girl there was still a special pushcart at Easton's Beach just for wheeling invalids into the sea. They'd splash around until someone pulled them out again. Don't laugh, it's true. I wouldn't tell you anything that wasn't true. People even thought fog was good for your skin.

Well, the Robies must have thought so, anyway, because

they skipped Newport and found someplace even foggier. This house had been sitting alone for some time after the last of the Barrows died out, round 1830 or so. Colonel Robie saw it from his boat when he was out sailing one day, and asked if it was for sale. So that's how the Robie family came to live at Barrow House.

Besides the Colonel and his lady, there was also a daughter, Isabel. I wish we had a picture of her, but she must have been something because it seems like everyone wanted to marry her before she was even sixteen. The society papers were full of it. Miss Isabel Robie went to a dance today, Miss Isabel Robie visited the polo courts, Miss Isabel Robie dispensed soup to the needy...you get the idea. But don't think she was some mincing little violet. From all accounts, Isabel was a spitfire. She rode a horse like a man, one leg on each side, and was the first woman in Newport to play tennis when it became a fad. There was a grass court over on America's Cup Boulevard—still is, I think—and she played a doubles match with three young men, all vying for her hand.

The Robies loved Little Compton, and began spending more and more time here. They built that second wing that comes out the back, just for their music room and servants' hall. It must have been very gay. They kept their house in Tennessee, of course, which Colonel Robie ran through an overseer that he cabled every week. Did he have slaves? Of course he had slaves, what plantation owner didn't? What does that have to do with anything?

Well, you know what happened next. The Robies came up to Little Compton in late March of 1861. Isabel would join them in a couple months. She was at a convent school run by the Ursulines in New Orleans. But in the spring of that year some damned fool named Beauregard fired on Fort Sumter, and pretty soon everybody was shooting at everybody else. The Robies were trapped. They loved Rhode

Island, but they were good Southerners, and Colonel Robie was passionate about states' rights. He wanted to go right back to Tennessee and join up, but he couldn't leave Mrs. Robie alone in hostile territory, and it was too dangerous to bring her with him. It was a sad time for them. Most of their Southern friends melted away, and the local society that had welcomed them before turned cold and hostile. Colonel Robie made no secret of his Rebel leanings. He even tried to hold some kind of fundraiser here, inviting his Tennessee friends over. Eunice played "Dixie" on the pump organ and Colonel Robie passed round the hat for the gallant defenders of Southern liberty. Then the police showed up and tried to throw everyone in jail. Colonel Robie paid them a hundred dollars and they left.

But it must have been lonely for the Robies, all the same. And there was the problem of Isabel. She was still in New Orleans, and New Orleans wasn't looking any too secure that summer. The city was right at the mouth of the Mississippi River, the very first place the Union would attack. Isabel was still only sixteen. Mrs. Robie wanted her home…in Little Compton, that is. So Colonel Robie sent a telegraph to a man he knew in New Orleans, a steamboat captain by the name of Henry Bilodeaux. Bilodeaux ran the Peninsular and Delta Consolidated Fruit Company, which hauled bananas and other fruits from Central America. There was no refrigeration in those days, so a ship had to be fast enough to get from Cartagena to New Orleans before the fruit rotted. The General Kearny *was a very fast ship. She was a steam packet with sails fore and aft and those big paddles on either side that look like Ferris wheels. The* General Kearny *was not a passenger liner, but Colonel Robie was a rich man and he wanted his little girl home. He commissioned the* Kearny *and hired Captain Bilodeaux himself to pilot her.*

That wasn't all. Colonel Robie was a good Southerner,

as I said, but he wasn't a fool. He didn't know how long this war would last or what would happen once it ended. He knew the time was soon coming when he wouldn't be able to telegraph his overseer, and the Union gunboats were stopping all Southern ships anyway. His cotton plantation was doomed. So Colonel Robie did the only sensible thing, which was to sell everything he owned and convert it into hard cash. Not scrip, but gold coin. It was minted with the Confederate stamp, but Robie figured he could melt that down if he had to. And he encouraged his other Southern friends in Newport—there were a few left, apparently—to do the same. Captain Bilodeaux was their agent. They sold their estates and amassed a pretty pile of gold, which was supposed to ride them out through the war. Now, this took time. Months, in fact. But the Ursulines were taking good care of Isabel, and Colonel Robie knew it would still be a while before the Union got around to capturing New Orleans. They were still trying to end the war in Virginia.

Finally, by December, everything was in place. Captain Bilodeaux loaded about thirty cases of gold pieces onto the General Kearny. He gave Isabel his own cabin, while he bunked with the First Officer. She thought it was a grand adventure. The Robies had always come north by way of the Mississippi, disembarking in St. Louis and taking trains the rest of the way. It was her first time on a big steamer.

The General Kearny left New Orleans about a week before Christmas. She hauled up Union colors once they were clear of the Gulf and ran along the coast as fast as her engines could go. Captain Bilodeaux was a clever man. He didn't try to evade the Union gunboats that intercepted him. Sailed up right under their lee as pretty as you please, and handed them a fake cargo manifest that said the Kearny was carrying cotton to the Union mills in Pittsburgh to make wadding for muskets. He even had some bales of cotton loaded on top *of the gold to make it look more convincing. Anyway, they let him go. By Christmas Eve the* General Kearny *passed a few yards east of Cape May light, and turned to starboard to clear Long Island.*

It was bitterly cold. A nor'easter passed over them near Hatteras and coated the ropes with a veil of ice that glittered in the sunlight. Isabel thought it looked like a fairy's barge. She had never felt winter, and every morning she came up on deck wearing the captain's spare boat cloak over her shoulders. He gave her a spyglass and set her to watching for Union commerce raiders. But he wasn't really concerned. This far north there wasn't any danger.

But Captain Bilodeaux wasn't as clever as he thought. Because it turns out there was a spy on the docks in New Orleans, and he reported back to General Benjamin Franklin Butler of the Union Army that a ship had just left harbor carrying a whole cargo of gold coins—which was just what the Union needed. There wasn't enough time to contact all the patrol boats, so instead General Butler found out where the Kearny *was headed and wired ahead to Boston. By the time the ship passed Long Island there were already three Union gunboats waiting for her in Narragansett Bay.*

Captain Bilodeaux had told the Robies to expect him on Christmas Day. They spent the whole afternoon up in the widow's walk, gazing out at the sea. You can see every ship that comes into Newport or Providence from up there. All day long they waited, and all day long there was no sign of the General Kearny. *Finally, just as the sun was disappearing into the sea, Mrs. Robie saw a trail of smoke on the horizon and called down to her husband. Colonel Robie came rushing up the stairs with his telescope. Sure enough, it was the* Kearny. *She had made good her pledge, and was steaming triumphantly into the bay with sails set and flags flying. And she was moving* fast. *"Isn't she a grand old buster?" Colonel Robie said to his wife, who agreed.*

But then Robie saw something else. A little ways behind the General Kearny *were three more trails of smoke. Now, to his horror, he saw why she was moving so fast. The Union gunboats had cornered her like hunters with a stag, and she was fleeing them as fast as she could. Captain Bilodeaux still had a chance. The sun was almost gone, and once night came it would be near impossible to see the* General Kearny. *He could drop ashore at some inlet somewhere, unload the gold and Miss Isabel, and then turn tail and slip back out into the harbor. With any luck, and with his sails stored and his engines running soft, he might sneak right past them into open sea.*

That was the plan, anyway, and for a while it looked like it might work. The General Kearny *was the fastest thing on the water, and the gunboats never had a chance. The sun set, and the ships disappeared. You couldn't even see the trail of their smoke in the sky. Colonel and Mrs. Robie rejoiced. They were sure the* Kearny *would get away. And so she might have done.*

But then, just as the stars began to shine over Narragansett Bay, there was a sudden burst of orange light. It was as if the sun changed its mind and rose again out of the sea. Colonel and Mrs. Robie saw it and wondered what it could possibly be, until a moment later when the sound of the explosion reached them over the waves. The red and orange flames flickered against the sky for a long moment, then settled into the horizon and disappeared.

Who knows what happened? Maybe Bilodeaux clamped down on the safety valves to get just an extra knot or two of speed. Maybe the bunkers were empty, and all the coal dust ignited. Or maybe the Kearny *was just going too damn fast, straining her boilers past their breaking point, until finally a little hole opened up no bigger than a thumbnail and the whole ship was blown to pieces.*

That was the end of the General Kearny. When the gunboats caught up with her, all they found were a few bits of broken wood and a seaman, alive, a cook's apprentice. He'd been in the rigging when the explosion came and was blown right clear. They say he was stone deaf for the rest of his life. Well, after the Union boats took him on board and cleaned him up, they did a few circles, looking for the cargo. But it was all metal, wasn't it, and would've gone straight to the bottom. Funny thing, that. The ship went down within sight of shore, in shallow waters, but they never found the wreck. The Army Corps of Engineers was out there for months, dredging away. They wanted the gold. But the old bay fooled them, moved the wreck around, carried it out to sea maybe. They're still looking. Was just a couple years ago a crew came down from Woods Hole. They used the same sonar scanners that helped them find the Titanic, but no luck. It's almost as if Captain Bilodeaux is still down there, keeping the gold safe until the ghosts of the Confederacy come to claim it.

But that did little good for Colonel Robie. He watched on Christmas night as the sea claimed his fortune and his daughter, and it would be cruel to say he was more upset by the former than the latter. Either way, he was ruined. Mrs. Robie went stark raving mad. They had to commit her to Bellevue. But Colonel Robie was made of stronger stuff. He didn't fall apart all at once, but piece by piece. They say he spent weeks down at Fogland Beach after the explosion, combing the sands. Hour after hour, day after day, even when it was piercing cold and the sand was covered in snow. God knows what he was looking for. But the sea gave him nothing, not so much as a coin or bit of china. Certainly not his daughter. And so, once he was sure nothing else would come to him, he threw a rope over one of the beams and hanged himself. Right in this parlor.

Some will tell you he's still down at Fogland Beach. I've

never seen him myself but a good friend of mine, Elsie Butler, did. He was tall and very thin, walked with a stoop and wore a hat pulled over his eyes. His clothes were black and sodden from years of tramping the dunes. You couldn't see his face, she said, because he was looking down at the sand.

But I have seen the light, of course. Everyone has. Some people mistake it for the Palatine Light, which is not the same thing at all. That was a German ship that wrecked off Block Island in the 1730s, and if it's still burning there, it is no affair of mine. But the General Kearny *is real enough. You can see her yourself. Go down to Fogland Beach on Christmas at sunset and look out to the sea. Bring a good heavy coat and some coffee—you may have to wait a while. The spirit world doesn't know from Daylight Savings Time. But if you wait long enough, and it's a clear night with not too much haze, you'll see her. A red-orange ball of fire blazing away, marking the spot where the* General Kearny *went down. It'll glow for a few moments, just as it did then, and then will be gone.*

Of course it's all true. I wouldn't say it if it wasn't true.

Chapter Seven

The fog lasts for three whole days and nights. Then on Sunday it's gone with the daybreak. Pastor Paige preaches a sermon about clarity emerging from chaos, and Grandma falls asleep with her mouth open. It's only eleven-thirty but I can already tell this is going to be one of her bad days. She wakes up angry, frustrated. The coffee is too bitter, the eggs too runny. On the plus side, she has finally accepted my presence in the house. But she thinks I am some kind of hired hand, a throwback to the days when the Hazards had a cook, a gardener, and a parlor maid. Now she gives orders in a peremptory voice and looks furious when I don't rush to obey. This morning's fight begins over pantyhose. She wants to put them on herself but the flimsy gauze ensnares her feet and winds itself around her ankles. "I can *do* it," she insists, as I help her up from the floor. Without a word I disentangle her, straighten out the hose, and start guiding it up her legs. "Stop that! Stop that! What are you, a pervert?"

Next come the clothes. Grandma decides she would like to wear a frilly black bathing suit from the Eisenhower administration. "It's a cocktail dress!" she insists. "And don't tell me it's too racy. I know the Caldwells are going to be there tonight."

I don't know who the Caldwells are, or care. I pull the bathing suit from her hands, more roughly than I should, and hand her a tartan jacket and skirt. She hates these now, though it used to be her favorite outfit. The tartan is from the Lynn family, which we are related to in some obscure way. Hunter green with a vein of scarlet. She wore it with a frilly blouse, high collar, and a Wedgwood cameo at her throat. Grandpa called her "The Duchess." But that was a long time ago.

An hour and a half later she is dressed, a near-perfect facsimile of Grandma. But her temper hasn't improved. Dr. Renzi says church is good for her; it calms her nerves. She remembers all the old hymns, and can recite the paternoster with her eyes closed. Familiar surroundings are a comfort also. The United Congregational smells like every church in New England, regardless of age or denomination: a unique amalgam of flowers, floor wax, dry rot, cleaning fluid, stale air, and deodorant. Grandma is happy here. She pats my arm as I hand her the hymn book, and for one moment there is a flash of recognition. She knows who I am. But then one of the Dufresne kids starts to whisper something to his sister, and Grandma turns around like an unbound Fury. "How *dare* you? This the day the LORD hath made, you little shit!" Mrs. Dufresne claps her hands over her son's ears and hustles him off to the fellowship hall. I know I'm going to hear about this later.

We come home to a house filled with gray light. Grandma announces she is going to "make lunch," a varied project that sometimes produces food, other times a random collection of household objects piled on the plate. But today she seems particularly determined; from the upstairs bathroom I hear pots slam and dishes rattle. I peel off my clothes and turn the shower knob all the way hot. I remember this room better than my own apartment: faux-marble wainscoting like blue cheese, pink shag carpet and a matching plush pink toilet seat cover, a family of Technicolor ducks marching in formation above the towel rack, all lit by a glorious confection of chrome, nippled bulbs and frosted glass suspended on a brass pot chain. Even the same bar of Yardley soap on its tray. Grandma's been threatening to redo the bathroom for thirty years. Now I guess it'll stay as it is.

Lost in the past, I catch sight of my reflection. It is like one of those ghost movies. Candyman, Candyman. My eyes are set in a face that is not my own, above a body I barely recognize. How I hated the sight of all that bare, white, peachy-soft skin! But now I've concealed a good part of it: shoulders, arms, midriff, all hidden under the protective camouflage of ink. Sometimes my tattoos remind me of who I am, like crib notes written on the sleeve. Except these are on my skin, and each is a memory. The antlers Marcus saw, for example, belong to a stag on my left shoulder, flanked by four books representing knowledge. It comes from a fountain in Rome, the *Fontana Dei Libri*, tucked into an alley near the Church of St. Ives. The church was just around the corner from my *pensione* when I was a graduate student. Nobody knew about the fountain—it wasn't in the guidebooks, so tourists just passed by like it didn't exist. Each afternoon I came with a pile of books and whiled away the hours on a small stone bench. My clearest memory was of an afternoon in late August with Marcus Aurelius in my lap. His *Meditations*, that is.

> *I have seen the beauty of good, and the ugliness of evil, and have recognized that the wrongdoer has a nature related to my own—not of the same blood or birth, but the same mind, and possessing a share of the divine. And so none of them can hurt me.*

How comforting those words might have been to the girl that stood shivering in front of this mirror, slathering on cold cream, wishing she could wash off her own skin along with the makeup. Now the man that stares back really is me, and it's this room that has become a lie. I gaze wonderingly at my perfect face until steam fogs up the beveled mirror.

Candyman.

By the time I come down it is almost an hour later, but Grandma is still hard at it. The mixer is revving out of control, and it sounds as though she is trying to extract a baking tray from under a tower of pans. There is an almighty crash. "Grandma?" I call out, worried. Silence. I'm taking the stairs two at a time, thinking of Aunt Emma buried under her cookware. Then I pass the front room. Grandma is fast asleep in her chair.

The kitchen door stands partly ajar. The light is on, the mixer is still running. As I put my hand on the doorknob it stops abruptly. The light bulb on its chain is swaying back and forth, like someone has been playing maypole with it. The mixer is empty and cold. All the cupboard doors are closed, the pots and pans innocently silent. And yet on the center island, just under the swinging light, is a plate with two pastrami sandwiches and a pickle. The pastrami I recognize from the fridge; the pickle I've never seen before in my life. Someone even drew up two glasses of milk; there is frost on the rim.

"Thanks," I tell the Hired Help, and bring the drinks and sandwiches into the living room. Because really, what else am I supposed to do?

• • ● • •

In the afternoon Grandma watches her shows. Or at least she thinks she does. Real television upsets her. She doesn't know any of the characters, and plots seem needlessly complex. "Who is *that* guy?" she asks, pointing at the protagonist of a sitcom she has been watching for three quarters of an hour. "Have I seen him before?" Commercials drive her mad. "It used to just be pasta sauce and laundry detergent. What the hell is ProMaxium?" Actually, she has a point. But after about a week of this I began sneaking DVDs into the machine. Now she watches *Matlock* or *Golden Girls* and falls happily asleep in her chair. She has just nodded off when there is a knock on the door.

Billy Dyer is standing on our front porch, arms folded across his chest. He is wearing his hat and his gun and looks very uncomfortable. The Dufresne woman must really have raised a stink. I bring him past the front parlor, where Grandma is gently snoring, to the little office in the back that used to be Grandpa's. It still has his old sporting prints on the walls, Currier and Ives foxhunts with fat-bellied horses, and a bookshelf covered in maritime registers. The room is so redolent of masculine energy it almost breathes tobacco. Against one window is a big partner's desk with a green-shaded lamp. Billy and I sit across from each other. "Look," I tell him, "you know Maggie is funny in the head. I'm sorry she snapped at the Dufresne kid, but if you were there…"

"I'm not here about that."

"Something to do with Emma, then? Did they find Arabella Johnson?"

"No, no." There is a crack along the wooden surface of the desk that looks like a dried riverbed. Billy stares at it. "Actually it's about that rich fella over on Fogland Point. Rhinegold. He say anything to you that night you had dinner?"

"Quite a bit. You didn't seem very interested."

"Oh, well, I've been busy..." He runs a hand nervously through his hair. "The thing is, David, he's gone. Vanished on Halloween night. Been missing three days now."

Whatever I expected, it was not this. There is a long pause, punctuated by the Waterbury eight-day clock on the opposite wall. "How?" I finally ask.

"Had a big fight with his wife, apparently. Dunno what it was about, she's not talking, but the neighbors heard them screaming pretty fierce."

"Neighbors?" I repeat incredulously. "There isn't anyone near that place for miles."

"Picnickers on the beach," Billy clarifies. "That's what they say they were doing, anyway. Chances are they were probably toking, but who cares? Anyway, they heard her storm off the boat and drive away in that fancy Mercedes. Not long after, Rhinegold raises the anchor and slips out into the bay. That's the last anyone saw of him. Just after one in the morning."

"Crew?"

"All ashore, over in Newport at some Halloween party at the Red Parrot. He gave them the night off."

"And the boat's just...gone?" I ask. "What about GPS?"

Billy nods. "Should have kicked in the moment he got out in the bay. But that's the funny thing. The tracker went dead. The boat just disappeared into the fog."

"Could he have disabled it?"

"Sure, if he wanted to. But he still couldn't beat radar. There was a crowd of ships passing up and down the coast that night. Two tankers, a bunch of freighters, even the *Norwegian Dawn* out of New York taking leaf-peepers up to St. John. They all kept records of radar contacts. Nothing. Well, almost nothing."

"Almost?"

Billy traces a finger absentmindedly along the crack. "We had a patrol boat out that night. For the drunks, you know. There's always a few that go out and get so liquored up they can't find their way home. At about ten p.m. they heard a big boom and saw something orange up ahead. Turned the boat around and went for a look. But you know, the fog. They kept passing over where they thought it was, but there was nothing there. Must have been ten, fifteen leagues offshore. Captain figured it was some idiot shooting off flares."

Or the *General Kearny*, I think idiotically. But, no, that was Christmas. "You think he brained Emma and tried to make a run for it?"

"Looks that way, don't it? But there's not a mite of evidence. Still, I figured there might be some chance he let something slip, or that wife of his. Alicia."

"She's not Alicia, she's Crystal from New Jersey. And I have a feeling Marcus Rhinegold is not Marcus Rhinegold. Dunno who he is, but you might start with looking at orphanage records in Bensonhurst from about thirty years ago."

There is nothing else for it but to tell him the whole story from the beginning, which I do. After about five minutes we both study each other in silence. I can hear Grandma's snores from the other room. "So," Billy says heavily, "you think that when you guys were on the balcony together... when he offered to let you use his bed...that he was... making a... pass?"

"That wasn't a pass, Billy. It was more like a head-on collision."

His brow furrows. "A *gay* pass?"

"That's what they generally call it when one man propositions another man."

Now the crease between his eyes is so deep you could stick a pen in it. "So he didn't know that you're a…I mean…"

I try to repress a sigh. "The word is *trans*, Billy. Or FTM, if you prefer. Female to male. Transsexual. Take your pick. And no, to the best of my knowledge, he had no idea. I didn't tell him. The whole thing was excruciating enough as it was."

"Yeah, I bet." He's not thinking of Marcus now, but of our last conversation, the day before I left for graduate school. The day I broke his heart. "But you don't like men. Anymore."

Useless to try to explain. Not again. "Just to be clear," I ask, "do we think this is a wreck at sea, a fugitive, or a homicide?"

"Damned if I know." The phone in his pocket buzzes. He excuses himself and goes out onto the back porch. I can see him through the window, pacing back and forth, wreathed in the fog of his own breath. After a few moments he comes back in. "You said something about the Molinari family, right?"

"Yeah. Marcus was afraid of them. Thought they were after him. Does that name mean anything to you?"

"No. They're not local. But I ran it by the staties up in Providence. The sergeant there knew it right away. Big outfit, based in El Paso. Trucking, some gambling, women. Mostly drugs and illegals. They pack them into the trucks and hustle them across the border. Pretty rough bunch. But they also happen to be the largest stakeholders in a local business. Any guesses as to which one?"

"Allie's Donut and Tack Shop?"

"All—no, smartass, Ocean State Building and Loan."

Ah. Plundergate.

"And something else you said checks out, too," he admits.

"There's no record of a Marcus Rhinegold anywhere, no birth certificate, no social security number. But the captain just got a call from Boston. They're sending down two FBI guys tomorrow. It sounds like your Rhinegold, whoever he is, was one of theirs. They don't sound too happy. I'm figuring maybe it was them that sent him to Little Compton in the first place, and it all has something to do with the Building and Loan scandal."

For a moment I envision a group of vectors—the local police, the state police, the FBI, the Molinaris—all converging at Fogland Point. And Crystal, of course, roaring back down the driveway full of drunken recrimination. Oh, Marcus, I think, I really hope you made it to Mexico.

But somehow I kinda doubt it.

• • ● • •

That same afternoon a news van rolls by, then another, and another after that. By six the whole wharf is covered with camera crews, sound booms, and newscasters pointing to the empty harbor as if it were magically about to produce Marcus Rhinegold. The missing yacht is a big story, and even the stations out in Boston and Cape Cod have picked it up. On the way to dinner I pass by the crowd and catch fragments:

"Coast Guard officials continue their search for the *Calliope*, but officials tell us there is little chance..."

"Yacht was registered to a corporation called Oceanos Holdings. There is no record of any such company, and no information about its alleged proprietor, Mr. Marcus Rhinegold..."

"Mrs. Rhinegold continues to remain inside her home on Fogland Point and has refused all requests for comment.

The local police tell us they cannot rule out the possibility of foul play…"

"Sir!" A microphone shoved into my face. "Do you have any thoughts on the recent disappearance of Mr. Rhinegold and his yacht?"

I am clearly meant to play the role of Local Character. "No comment," I growl. But at the end of the pier they've struck gold. Batty old Mrs. Thurman is standing there in her pink bathrobe and curlers, holding court. "Oh, yes," she tells them magisterially. "I think it's shocking, absolutely shocking. Worst thing to hit this town since Hurricane Andrew."

"Do you have any theories yourself on what might have happened?"

She looks at the reporter with scorn. "It's perfectly clear what happened, young man. Bennett's changed suppliers. They used to get their clams from Legal Sea Food, and those were very good, nice strips with plenty of meat on them. Best clam strip dinner in town, and reasonable, too. But Dan Fogle is cheap. Everyone knows this. So now he gets his clams from Associated, and they have bellies in them. Do you know what a clam belly tastes like? Do you?"

The reporter looks at her for a moment. His microphone has gone slightly limp. "But what about the disappearance of Mr. Rhinegold?"

"Rhinegold?" Mrs. Thurman repeats, much mystified. "Rhinegold? Never heard of him. But I'm not surprised he's gone. Won't be a soul left in this town, if Fogle keeps jacking his prices. Let me tell you…"

It's no better at the Boy and Lobster. The place is a local dive, with nothing going for it except a decent shepherd's pie on Wednesdays and a total absence of Grandma, which has become an attraction. I left her with a carton of

Brigham's coffee ice cream and a TBS marathon of *Murder She Wrote*; that gives me at least a couple hours. The Boy and Lobster has a few nets strung on the rafters and a grimy brass binnacle in the corner, but otherwise is no different than any other bar. Usually on a Wednesday night there's only a handful of patrons. Tonight it's packed. There are a few familiar faces: Wally the Postman and his wife are regulars, though tonight she's put on a spangled black vest and covered her arms with rhinestone bracelets. She's three gins in and already becoming expansive. Wally stares into his ale and looks sour. At another table sit Aunt Irene and Aunt Constance, sharing fish and chips. They wave me over.

"What's with the crowd?" I ask.

Constance grimaces. "Everybody wants to talk about that damn fool Marcus Rhinegold. Guess this is the only place to do it."

She's right. From every corner of the room that odd name echoes back, like a grotesquery of Wagner's water maidens: *Rhinegold*, *Rhinegold*, *Rhinegold*. "I didn't think it was that big a deal."

"Mysterious millionaire goes missing? Hell, they'll eat it up for days."

"Billy Dyer came to see me," I tell them without preamble. The two women exchange a look. Constance snorts into her beer. "Not about that. Well, I hope not. He wanted to ask me about my dinner with Marcus."

"Finally!" Constance exclaims.

"Was there really that much to tell?" Irene wants to know.

They both seem elaborately casual, which is Yankee for caginess. "Yeah, I guess I didn't say much about it," I admit. For the second time that day, I tell my famous dinner party story, and this time leave nothing out.

"Always knew that wife was a bitch," Constance grunts after I've finished.

"She was very sweet to us at the wake," Irene objects. Aunt Irene likes to think the best of people.

"I'd love to know what they fought about that night." An older man with thick glasses and a long gray ponytail, whom I've never seen before, turns around in his chair and says earnestly, "Yes, that's what I'd like to know, too."

"And what about that Starbucks kid she mentioned?" his wife adds. Her thin, nervous face is free of makeup, and her hair is tied into two long pigtails, one over each denim shoulder. "I wonder if the police have been up to talk to him?"

"Have we met?" I ask faintly.

"Barry Rosen," he says, offering a chapped and calloused hand. "This is Renee. We're snowbirds, here till Christmas."

"You've got that Chris Craft down at Jackson's Point," Constance says intelligently. She recognizes people by their boats.

"Have you been listening to our whole conversation?" I ask.

"Certainly," Barry admits, unabashed, "and it was very interesting. I, for one, had no idea Marcus Rhinegold was gay. That certainly adds a new dimension to the whole story."

"Marcus Rhinegold was *gay*?" someone else bleats. "How do you know?"

"He made a pass at this fellow here," Barry explains to the room, gesturing at me.

"I'm not sure what that proves," Wally the Postman snarls from his corner. "You don't know who you're talking to there, Rosen."

"Careful, Wally," Constance says evenly.

"It's okay, Aunt Constance." Raising my voice slightly, I add, "Wally just misses trying to stare up my skirts, like he used to. Still hanging round under the bleachers at the junior high, Wally?"

The bar whoops with laughter, and Wally retreats to his beer. "What was that about?" Barry asks. Aunt Irene whispers in his ear. "Oh! How very rude."

Now we have been absorbed into the general conversation. Various theories of Marcus' disappearance are launched, hover tremulously in the air, and get shot down. Dr. Renzi wonders if the *Calliope* might have headed north instead of south, perhaps even been hauled into drydock. "What good would that do?" someone asks. Dr. Renzi shrugs, buries his nose in a whisky sour. A man in a heavy blue overcoat suggests the yacht might have been swallowed up by a larger tanker. "You know, like in James Bond?" Someone else says Aliens. Mrs. Wally makes a grand gesture, sweeping her gin and tonic over the room, and takes the conch. "It's all about insurance," she declares. "He took the boat out and blew it up. Now he can collect the insurance on it."

"Wouldn't he have to show up to collect?" Aunt Irene asks, with admirable patience.

"I don't know how these big finance guys work, but he'll find a way," Mrs. Wally answers inscrutably.

Gradually, three theories coalesce. First, that Marcus somehow managed to escape undetected, perhaps with outside aid. Second, that he was coerced into taking the yacht out by someone already hiding on board, who then murdered him and sank the *Calliope*. Third, that he was a victim of Forces Unknown. The consensus of the reasonable favors the first hypothesis; Mrs. Wally, having reluctantly abandoned her insurance scheme, becomes a late if passionate adherent to the third. "There's funny things happen in fog," she declares.

"It's odd," I whisper under my breath to the Aunts. "Nobody seems to be connecting it to Emma."

Constance shrugs. "Why should they? Far as anyone knew she was just a silly old maid who reached for the wrong pot. The rest is something Billy cooked up."

"So you don't think Emma was murdered?"

"No. I don't. And certainly not by a twit like Marcus Rhinegold. For all we know he could have stolen the Robie gold and be on his way to Mexico."

Unfortunately Constance raised her voice slightly at the end, to be heard over the sudden squawk of the television, and broadcasts her theory to the entire bar. There is a moment of complete silence.

"I thought that was just a legend?" one youthful voice pipes up.

Blithely unaware of what she is about to unleash, Constance grunts, "Real enough."

"Yes that's quite true," a well-dressed man with silver hair chimes in. "There is no question of the ship's sinking, or her cargo. They've been looking for it for years."

"And Rhinegold must have found her."

"How would someone like Marcus know where it is?" I ask, in spite of myself.

"He wouldn't," Aunt Constance answers. "But he might have known someone who did. They say the Patriarcha family's been sniffing around here, sending divers down, running sonar scans. I wouldn't be surprised if Rhinegold cottoned onto it somehow, and decided to make a killing himself. So to speak."

"Steal the gold and make a run for it," someone else breathes, entranced.

"You saw inside the *Calliope*, David," Irene reminds me, "Did you ever get a look down below?"

I didn't. But I remember Marcus' words: *The whole interior had to be gutted as well...She's got a huge gas tank now, in what used to be the depth charge storage.* Plenty of space for a stolen hoard. "Isn't this all a little fantastic?" I ask.

"What part?" Constance answers tartly. "The gay millionaire, the crazy blonde, the vanished yacht, or the Mafia?" When she says it like that, she has a point. "But if that's what it is, he's long gone, and the gold too."

"What makes you so sure?" Renee Rosen asks.

"Stands to reason, don't it? Why would he leave before he did the job? No, he got the wife and crew out of the way, disabled his GPS, loaded the gold onboard, and made for open sea like Jack Robinson. The fog covered his tracks. He's in Cuba by now, you may lay to it."

"But what about radar?" I remind her.

Constance waves an airy hand. "There's ways to get around that."

"I'm not so sure," Barry interjects. "That boat was too big to be missed, and too fast to be mistaken for a fishing boat or some such. And even if he made it out, satellites would pick him up sooner or later. Nobody can really disappear once they're on open sea. If he was out there, chances are somebody would have found him by now."

"I don't think..."

"But that means the yacht could still be here!" Mrs. Wally cries shrilly. She teeters on her barstool and waves her glass for emphasis. "He could have wrecked in the fog!"

"Don't you think we might have spotted him sitting out there in the middle of the harbor once it lifted?" Constance reminds her acidly.

"Plenty of places it could have gone aground without nobody seeing," Wally the Postman offers, coming to his wife's aid. "Coves, inlets, and what not. You should know that, Constance."

Constance slams her drink down on the bar. "Don't be daft, Wally. Either he's underwater or he's gone to Cuba."

"But don't you think it's worth a look?" Mrs. Wally insists. "There might be a pile of money on the *Calliope*. And salvage rights, if there's nobody left onboard." Nobody alive, she means.

"I'll tell you what," Wally says, sliding off his barstool and thrusting out his chest importantly. "I'm gonna take *My-T-Fine* out there tomorrow and have a look-see. Just as soon as I get done with my rounds."

"That's not a bad idea," Barry agrees. "I might go out too."

"And me," someone else adds. Pretty soon the whole bar chimes in.

"You're all fools," Aunt Constance sighs.

"Maybe so, but you'll look a pretty big fool yourself if one of us comes back with the treasure. And what about New England Wrecking and Salvage then, huh?"

"It might not be such a bad idea, Connie," Irene offers. Another chorus of agreement.

"All right, all right," Constance says resignedly. "If we're going to do this, let's do it right. Divide the bay into zones, and each person cover their square. That way we don't miss anything, or go over the same ground twice."

"How do we know you won't just take the gold yourself?" Mrs. Wally demands querulously.

The bar goes quiet. "You calling me a thief, Alice?" Constance's voice is barely above a whisper.

Mrs. Wally's eyes flutter around the room, refusing to meet hers. "I'm just saying we need to be fair," she answers, rather shakily.

"Okay, then. We'll all rendezvous back at the pier and inspect each other's boats. That do for you?"

"Yes. Yes, Constance. Sorry, didn't mean anything by it."

"Of course you didn't." But Aunt Constance's gaze still rests on her, thoughtfully.

•••••

The next morning dawns bright and clear. Cirrus clouds chase one another across an azure sky. The armada is scheduled to depart after breakfast.

Aunt Irene's blue pickup and Constance's ancient Oldsmobile are both parked at New England Wrecking and Salvage, but the office door is locked. Sometimes they're out back in the boatshed, stripping down an old trawler. But no, the barn doors are wide open, the interior cavernous and empty. No business will be done today. The rest of the town is the same: Dykstra's General Store is shuttered; the Sunoco station's pumps are unmanned; the *Clamdigger*'s presses are silent. Even the post office has run the risk of felony by posting a small note on the door: "CLOSED DUE TO INCLEMENT WEATHER."

I find Constance down at the docks, surrounded by a large crowd. Her iron-gray hair is even more frizzled than usual and she is holding a clipboard. "Okay, Perkinses. You get Square 11, from Horseneck Beach to the *Hilda Garston* wreck site. Mulligans? Are you here? Yes, okay. You're Square 15, from Corvan to Cuttyhunk Island. What do you mean, where is it? Didn't you bring a map with you?"

Aunt Irene is nearby, serenely handing out sandwiches. She gives me a cheerful wave. "Great day for it, huh?"

"Christ, Irene. The whole town is here."

"Well, I guess everybody wants a piece of that stolen treasure." She winks.

"You don't actually believe Marcus is out there, do you?"

"Of course not. Connie's right, he's long gone. But it's fine weather and the swell is slight, so what's wrong with a little boating holiday?"

She's got a point. Little Compton is not a large town, and once the tourists leave, there are few distractions. The scene at the pier has a distinctly carnival air. Parents bring their children and pack coolers. A few of the boats sport jolly rogers from their mainmasts. Mrs. Wally shows up wearing her interpretation of a yachting costume: navy blue spandex, white rabbit cape, and a sailor hat. "Ahoy there!" she calls gaily, weaving unsteadily down the dock. "Woot, woot!" It is only seven-thirty in the morning.

As the boats start revving up their engines, Pastor Paige appears. He is in a black cassock and blue velvet stole. A silver cross thumps on his chest. He climbs up onto a bollard and spreads his arms, embracing us all. "Oh, Lord!" he cries, like Father Mapple, "bless this day and these boats, who go out into your mighty waters in search for lost souls! Guide their prows, Dear Father, and let that which is lost be again found! As it was written in the Book of Jonah, when the Lord Jehovah said to Ammitai…"

"Does anybody want these last two sandwiches?" Irene calls over him. "They're liverwurst but they're still pretty good."

And so it begins. By the time Paige has regained his thoughts, the little fleet is already nosing out into the bay. "May God go with you!" he shouts hurriedly, and clambers down from the bollard.

I always thought Aunt Constance odd for recognizing people by their boats, but now I realize she might be on to something. You can tell a lot about people by the kind of boat they own. *Joya*, the Karibandis' forty-foot Matthews inboard, is seventy years old and looks like it could have been built yesterday. The teak rails are freshly varnished, the brass glitters, even the ropes are coiled and clean. Nearly the entire cabin is converted to a galley, with two stoves and a big refrigerator; Mr. Karibandi has a hibachi on the stern. The boat feels happy, and loved. Dr. Renzi and his wife arrive in *Bigtime*, a giant Sea Ray with white leather cushions, drink holders, airhorns, a shortwave radio, loran, a television set, and a bimini top with fishing poles arcing out like a lobster's antennae. It looks like it has never seen water. In contrast, Wally the Postman's *My-T-Fine* is something of a legend, the ugliest boat on the sound. It began life as an O'Day day-sailor with a stubby little cabin at the bow, to which Wally affixed an ungainly plywood deck for his wife's topless sunbathing. The brass is tarnished, the brightwork flaked. Beer cans roll from port to starboard. A mold-speckled American flag droops at the stern.

Then, of course, there's the *Eula May*, Aunt Constance's baby. She's a decommissioned minesweeper, seventy-two feet long with twin diesels, a central pilothouse, and a long, narrow mahogany hull. *Eula May* is smart, fierce, and very fast. Constance painted her battleship gray and hung a red duster off the jackstaff. She's never actually fired the anti-aircraft gun, but the rumor is she keeps it loaded, just in case. Truth be told, if men sometimes look like their dogs, *Eula May* looks a great deal like Aunt Constance.

"Are you guys going out, too?" I ask Irene.

"Sure. Connie's got the *Eula May* all fired up. This many boats in the water, somebody's bound to make a mistake. A tow would pay the light bill. A proper wreck keeps us till December."

That's a jolly thought. But of course Irene is only planning ahead. Still, looking out over the ragtag fleet, I cannot help but think of Aunt Constance and Aunt Irene as big carrion birds flying overhead, circling, circling.

•••••

When I get back to the house Grandma is awake, dressed, and standing on the back porch with binoculars pressed to her eyes. The fleet is scattered across the bay. She watches each sail as it passes. "Funny sort of day for a race," she comments.

"It's that missing yacht, the *Calliope*. Mrs. Wally got everyone stirred up and now they're out looking for it."

"That woman's a fool."

I couldn't agree more. "Caught it on the news last night," Grandma goes on. "Bunch of nonsense. The boat's gone over. I should know, I saw it plain myself the other night."

"You—what?"

Grandma nods, looks very satisfied. "She's different now. A ghost. Anyone with eyes could see it. All blacked out and draped in bunting, like a funeral cortege. Her keel doesn't touch the water, just glides over it. She passed right by here like the *Flying Dutchman*."

Her voice is calm, almost uninterested. "When was this?" I ask, as casually as I can. But I should have known better than to ask for specifics. A cloud passes over her face.

"What was it? Last week? No. Couldn't have been that long. But she'll be back, of course. Dead ships never rest, everyone knows that. Her and the old *General Kearny* be doing the patrols together from now on." She laughs, looks out to sea again. Talk of wrecks has awakened something in Grandma. She's alert, almost chipper. "Did I ever tell you about old Sylvanus Hazard, the first wrecker in the family?"

She has, many times. "But what about the *Calliope*?" I press. "Did you see anyone on board? How late was it?"

Grandma frowns. "What on earth are you talking about?"

"The ghost ship. The one you saw the other night. Like the *Flying Dutchman*."

"Oh, yes." She nods. "That'll be old Sylvanus. Not a chance he'd rest easy. He's still on the hunt for Puritan souls. Not too many to be had nowadays, I expect. The *Marylee's Revenge* will search the coast, and find nothing but Italians and Irish." She chuckles, as if this were a good joke.

"Grandma..."

"Have I ever told you about Sylvanus Hazard?" she asks again. I can see she's not to be deterred.

"No," I sigh. The tape recorder is still on the dining room table. We sit on either side of it and I insert a fresh cassette. "Tell me."

MAGGIE

It's no wonder you turned out the way you did, love. Hazards have always been a queer bunch. Always running against the current. Sometimes they work it out by getting as far away from Little Compton as they can get. Your father is one of those, and Great-Uncle Charlie, who ran tea clippers for the Black Ball Line. Others just stay round here and raise hell. Your Grandpa, God rest his soul, was like that. Either way, they're not a contented lot.

Just look at Aunt Constance. Yes, she's actually a relative, didn't you know? Her mother was Fanny Hazard, who was your Grandpa's cousin. Constance got the worst from both sides of the family. Goes through husbands like Kleenex, but none ever satisfies. And she's a wrecker, too, like all the Hazards. She's more a man than most of them.

Sylvanus Hazard was the first. He came over from Braintree round about 1680. Stupid name for a town. The family settled there sometime in the 1660s when Sylvanus was just a boy, so he couldn't have been more than twenty-five or so when he made his break with them. They were proper Puritans, of course. His father, Silas, was a farmer with a big house and three barns and a seat on the Town Council. His mother, Abigail, was one of those dreadful pious types that beat her son raw with a birch rod and then prayed over the wounds. So maybe it wasn't a surprise Sylvanus finally had enough of them. Or they him.

Sylvanus was a surveyor, the man they send out into the forest to see what parts of it might be good for crops. Part of his job was dealing with the local tribes and buying land from them. Yes, I said buying. That whole string of beads thing is nonsense. Puritans might not have been good for much, but they paid cash. Anyway, these trips took Sylvanus away for months at a time and, with no postal service, the family wouldn't know if he was dead or alive until he came home again. Lots of surveyors didn't make it: disease, unfamiliar territory, and, of course, the odd scalping did for quite a few. But Sylvanus was lucky. He not only came back with his head, but a young Pequot that he took for his wife. Her name was Marylee.

Now this was shocking enough, but still worse was the little bundle Marylee carried in her arms. The couple had a child, a son. Sylvanus named him Moses.

The Puritan community was horrified. Pequots were devil-worshippers, everyone knew that. And they had no respect for traditional family roles. Pequot men took multiple wives. Pequot squaws prostituted themselves among the tribe, even committed incest with their own children. That was what the Puritans thought. Sheer nonsense, of course, but it explains what came after. The Braintree Council, the same one Papa

Silas sat on, met at once to deal with this crisis. Silas persuaded them that Sylvanus was not to blame: he had been bewitched and ensnared by this monstrous native creature.

It was just before first light when the men came. They turned their collars up and pulled the brims of their hats down low. Silas broke into the house and, none too gently, woke Sylvanus. He was lying with the devil Marylee, both naked, covered in lustful sweat. Silas threw a cloak around his son's shoulders and had three men carry him out of the house and bind him to a thick poplar tree. Marylee and Moses were locked in, the door barred and the windows shuttered. Then the good citizens of Braintree set fire to the roof. They gathered in a circle around it and prayed earnestly, loudly. But the sound of their prayers could not disguise the screams of the people inside. Sylvanus watched as his home disappeared in a column of fire. Only when it was reduced to ash did his father loosen the cords. "Now you are free," he told him, kissing him on the cheek. "Praise God and fear His holy name."

For the next few weeks Sylvanus moved like a ghost through the town. He stayed with his parents, since there was nowhere else for him to go. The other Puritans, believing he had been freed of a terrible curse, treated him kindly. They bore him no ill will. So it was all the more shocking when they came to the Hazard house one morning and found Sylvanus gone, along with a chest full of gold that had been the bulk of his father's fortune. Both Silas and Abigail were lying in bed, their wrists bound to the bedposts and their throats slashed. More horrible still, their scalps were mounted with iron tacks above the hearth.

With a chest full of gold Sylvanus had no difficulty arranging passage, and for a fugitive on the run there was really only one place to go. That was Rhode Island. Roger Williams founded the colony as a haven for dissenters and anyone else Massachusetts was glad to be rid of. There was an old rule that any renegade who made it across the border would be absolved of his crimes, for Rhode Island refused to let Massachusetts put any of its colonists to judgment. Naturally the colony became overrun with every kind of rogue. And some truly kind people like Quakers and Jews, but that's another story.

Sylvanus had just enough money left to buy a small cottage on Block Island, and a boat. He called her Marylee, *and had a mind to earn his living at fishing for the cod. This he did, for a while. But when he sailed out past the cutwater he could not help but notice the big, fat Indiamen coming in and out of Boston, swollen with spices and silks and gold. One came so close it nearly cut the* Marylee *in half. Sylvanus cursed them out, but came back into harbor brimful of ideas. He raised a second mast on the* Marylee, *turning her into a sloop, and fitted a broad centerboard that would cut through the water like a knife. He cleaned all the fish guts out of the hold and stocked it with gunpowder and shot, stolen from an English brig that had grounded itself off Prudence Island. On the bow and stern he fitted two brass tenpounder cannons, with another two bronze pieces on port and starboard. Then he stripped down the decks, tore out bulkheads, made the ship much lighter and faster. And finally he fixed a new figurehead to the prow: a Pequot maiden holding a flaming arrow of justice. He called his new ship* Marylee's Revenge.

There were lots of pirates sailing out of Rhode Island at this time, and Sylvanus wasn't better or worse than any of them. But he was cruel. If the crew of a captured ship were Moslem or Hindu or even Catholic, he let them go unharmed. Yet if they happened to be Puritan, he showed no mercy. Especially preachers. He cut off one's ears and grilled them right in front of him. Others he lashed to the mainmast and pelted with broken bottles until they bled to death. Sometimes a kind of frenzy took him, which no amount of blood could sate. He slaughtered whole ship's companies, taking hours at it, making each watch as his brethren were slain in front of him, reveling in their anguish. Even his crew was afraid of him at moments like this. In Boston he came to be known as "Demon" Hazard, and there was a fifty-guinea reward put out for his head—a pretty price in those days.

Now this sort of thing couldn't go on forever, and it was really only a matter of time before Sylvanus found himself dangling from a gibbet. But the governor in those days was Peleg Sanford, and he hated Puritans even more than Sylvanus did. Peleg was grandson to old Anne Hutchinson, she who'd been kicked out of Boston for having views on the Holy Trinity and a tongue like an adder's. Peleg was a fine, worldly fellow who kept a good table and didn't mind pirates on principle, so long as they spent their money in the town and kept their thieving to Massachusetts. But Sylvanus' wild ways had begun to attract attention from other colonies. Letters were written. Finally, even the King sent round a note politely asking Governor Sanford to do something about the pirate Hazard who called himself a devil from Hell.

So Peleg invited Sylvanus to supper, and after pipes and brandy, he put his hand on the young man's shoulder and told him, "My lad, I've every sympathy for thee, and none for those pious bastards across the sound. But they're fixing to stretch your neck in Boston, and there's nought I can do to stop 'em."

Sylvanus Hazard shrugged and said he expected as much, and it didn't make any odds with him either way.

"Now, now," the governor objected, shaking his head, "that's no way to talk. Had your fun right enough, ain't ye? Made 'em pay dear for what they did to your poor wife and son. But you're a young man still, not thirty yet. This is no kind of life. There's no future in it."

Sylvanus looked warily at the other man and asked, "What d'ye suggest?"

"Marry, for one. Plenty of fine girls in the town, some of them Pequots, if that's your taste. Have yourself a child and teach him how to reef and steer and hunt the cod."

Sylvanus shook his head. "I'll not go back to fishing."

"Did I say that? But this pirating business has to stop." Peleg brought his hand sharply down on the table. "Stop, d'ye hear? I'll not have any more damned letters on't. There's easier ways to pluck feathers out of Puritan backsides, and you're a damned fool not to have thought of 'em already."

Almost against his will, Sylvanus was interested. "Such as?"

The governor leaned back in his chair. "There's a convoy coming on the morrow evening. Raw silk and calico, three ships in all. Owned by some fellows in Boston, but I hear the captain's from Bombay, by way of London. How much you figure a Hin-doo captain would know of our waters? He'll be looking for lights and markers, same as anyone on an unfamiliar coast. Lights and markers, you read me?"

Sylvanus did. The next day he sailed Marylee's Revenge *out into the bay and began moving round the buoys that guided ships down the coast. Captains bound for New York from London usually took their soundings off Narragansett and looked for the light on Block Island to keep to starboard. But Sylvanus funneled them right into the bay, and had his men light a bonfire on Fogland Point to make the Bombay skipper think it was Block Island. He laid the markers to lead to Scilly Island, which wasn't no more than a cluster of rocks shaped like a crescent moon. Funny thing, though, it had a hidden entrance, like Ali Baba's cave. Think of a croissant with overlapping ends. From a distance it just looked like solid rock; get close, and a channel appeared. Like a big fat fly waiting in a spider's web, Sylvanus hid in the harbor till he heard the crash of timbers, then sailed out bold as brass and offered to rescue the crews. Those poor fellows thought he was their savior. But once he ferried them to shore, he and his men came back and picked the convoy clean. It was a good racket, and he kept it going. Sylvanus married Peleg Sanford's daughter and, by the time he drowned during a winter gale off Cape Newland, he was a wealthy man, well respected in the town.*

That's how we got the name "wreckers": not for salvaging ships, but wrecking them in the first place. It made good business sense. Like a fella that owns a body shop cutting down all the stop signs in town. I don't think you need to be so judgmental. Those were rough times, and men did what they had to do to get by. The crews weren't harmed, and many of them were richer for the experience. Found Jesus, you might say. The ships were insured. The men that owned them, the bigwigs in Boston and Newport, lots of them were slave-traders. It's true. Or smugglers. So I guess you could say what Sylvanus was doing was kind of like scamming the Mafia. Dangerous? I'll say it was! But profitable. It was he that built the family fortune and passed the trade on to his sons. And they passed it on to theirs, and so on, right until your Great-Great Granddad William decided to become a banker. He was the first Hazard to graduate from college. His father was devastated. The same day William got his degree from Brown, old Elias got roaring drunk, went down to Dowsy's Pier and set his boat on fire. Burned it right to the keel. "There's none of the Hazards will ever go to sea again," he said.

But he was wrong. William worked for the Greater Providence Savings and Loan, but his son Ezekiel was a captain for the old Fall River Line. And his *son, your Grandpa Michael, was something else altogether. Mike was a hard man. I loved him like hell, but he was a hard man. It was him and your Aunt Constance that started New England Wrecking and Salvage. He never said it had anything to do with family tradition. He didn't need to. Hazards were wreckers, always had been. And Mike knew boats better than anyone. That was back in the early fifties, when the big barges started coming in and out of Fox Point up in Providence. Now I won't say Mike moved buoys around, and I won't say he didn't. But he was lucky. Luckier still in '54, when Hurricane Carol came. You never saw anything like that in your life. Boats thrown clear on top of houses, piled up at their piers like cordwood, wreckage strewn all the way from here to Pawtucket.*

It was a bonanza. We filled the whole scrapyard in two weeks, lived off it for years. Those were good times. You might say there's a bit of Sylvanus in all the Hazards. Good and evil, rage and comfort, wrecking and salvage. We became wreckers to have the power of gods on Earth: choose what to save— and what to destroy.

Chapter Eight

The fleet has come back, dejected. I get a full report from Aunt Irene that evening. Two groundings, one man overboard, and a blown Evinrude, but no sign of Marcus Rhinegold or the *Calliope*. "Not like we were expecting any," she adds, though I detect a note of wistfulness.

"Are they satisfied?"

She collapses into a chair. "God, I hope so. Most of them, anyway. Wally's wife is still shooting her mouth off that the boat's out there somewhere. If you ask me that woman is unbalanced."

"She's just bored. Nothing to do here, so why not hunt for buried treasure?"

"Well, either way, she made poor Wal go out again after the rest of the fleet came back. I drove by the piers at sundown and he still wasn't back."

"Hope he's okay."

"Do you?" She gives me a conspiratorial glance. "He probably relishes the chance to escape her for a few hours. And don't worry about what he said at the bar. He's just an asshole."

"It's okay, Irene. I left Little Compton and came back a man. I figured there'd be a fair amount of comment."

She chuckles. "If you ask me, most people feel proud to have you here. Between you and the Karibandis, we're almost cosmopolitan."

The floorboards above our head creak; Grandma is rolling in her sleep. From the kitchen comes the sound of a ladle banging gently against a stockpot. The Hired Help has not produced any more sandwiches, but several times I've left dishes in the sink and come back to find them dry and spotless in the cupboards. I'd like to pay it a wage, if only I knew how.

"Did you have a nice day?" Irene wants to know.

"Grandma's been telling me about Sylvanus again."

"That old chestnut! Hope you recorded it this time."

"Yup. Got right to the part with Grandpa and the Hurricane of '54. She always fades out after that."

Irene nods understandingly. "We were all young, and happy. Your Grandma, especially. She was so much in love with Mike. Then."

That last syllable holds a lot. I remember Grandpa Mike: a thin, gray, taciturn man who chainsmoked Marlboros and put them out in the cup of his hand. He didn't have much time for children, still less for girls. He came home from the scrapyard, ate his dinner in silence, watched Letterman, smoked again, went to bed. He didn't say thirty words to me in fifteen years. My impression of him was of a volcano—ancient, seismic, dormant but not extinct. Lung cancer made him thinner, grayer, quieter. Then one day he was gone.

"I know you don't have lots of good memories," Irene continues, as if she's read my mind. "Hazards are a hard bunch. Mike needed someone like your Grandma to soften him a little, and your dad really needed Sharon. That was a love match, those two. He brought her back to Little

Compton when you were about a year old. But then Sharon died in that horrible accident. Once she was gone, that part of your father just dried up. I don't think he's ever gotten over it. And you looked so much like her, David, when you were a little girl. Her eyes, the shape of her face. Sometimes it was uncanny. At first I think it hurt him to look at you, see Sharon there. But later, when you were a teenager, it was different. He couldn't wait to get shore leave, just to see you. To see that part of your mom that still survived.

"Now you understand. When you became a boy, it was as if she died again."

•••••

That night I dream of boiling seas and breakers like black jagged teeth. The schooner is on the rocks, and the animals in their pens have gotten loose. Wolves chase chickens across the deck, and then the ship heels over, and chickens chase the wolves. Marcus is at my side on the quarterdeck. He laughs. "That's the funniest thing I've seen tonight."

Hands like white spiders on the taffrail. Men are climbing up the side of the ship.

"Were you expecting guests?" I ask him.

No, he shakes his head. "This is a private party. You go tell them to get off."

I take a belaying pin with me to beat them back.

"We are here to rescue you," my father says. But he is holding a bloody knife in his hands. "You're my precious little girl."

I wake to the bedroom blue and soft. It's not yet dawn and the house is totally still. Even the Hired Help must be resting. I pad softly downstairs, the oak floors cold under my feet, wrap myself in an afghan and take a mug of tea out onto the back porch. The ribbon of sea stretches like a broad smile, but off to one side the Sakonnet light flashes its endless warning: *Danger...danger...danger*. Mast beacons from the lobstermen answer back. The scene is quiet and sad and beautiful, and always changing. A gray mist settles slowly on the dark water and frames it against the sky. There is a moment when the two shades become one, and the sea becomes vapor, a hanging cloud between Little Compton and Aquidneck and Jamestown and Misquamicutt. We might all be islands now, adrift and floating in this endless firmament. But then the first light comes, pink as any newborn, and the sea retreats into its dark hollows. And just like that, the day begins.

We keep an old Cape Dory down at Dowsy's Pier. Her name is *Pretty Jane*. She technically belongs to my father, but he hasn't sailed in fifteen years and probably never will again. The last time was when he tried to teach me how to tack and I ended up slicing my own forehead with the boom. Eight stitches. Dad stopped trying afterwards.

Grandpa said he was a fool to attempt it in the first place. "She needs a man's touch, Andy," he growled, speaking of the *Pretty Jane* with more affection than he ever showed his wife, or me.

A week later Dad was back on his ship, the *USS Tuscaloosa*, and from then on our conversations grew increasingly rare and awkward. Once I asked Grandpa if he'd take me out, but got such a look in reply that I never asked again. He kept that boat spotless, though. Or rather, I did. Grandpa smoked his cigarettes while I sanded all *Pretty Jane*'s brightwork and varnished it, beat the dust out of her cushions, pumped her toilet and scrubbed down her decks.

"It's your dad's boat," Grandma explained, since Grandpa never explained anything. "And it's a daughter's job to look after the things her father loves." I don't know who's been caring for the *Pretty Jane* now, but the fiberglass hull is still clean and tackle neatly stored.

It's a matter of only a few moments to free the stern lines and cast off, loosen the sail, and turn her bows towards the bay. I feel like a pirate taking his first prize. The early morning breeze catches the canvas and pulls it taut, and *Pretty Jane* plunges joyously into her first wave. The tiller bucks beneath my hand, but I grip it firmly and bring us round to the wind. We were enemies once, but we're allies now. The boat leans over to starboard and shows her fat white bottom to the shore. "Hey, Grandpa!" I call aloud. "Fuck you!"

It is full dawn by the time *Pretty Jane* hauls up past the Little Cormorant. South is Schuyler Ledge, where cod once ran thick as walls; east is Dolphin Rock and the wreck of the old *SS Portland*, a passenger ferry bound for Boston that went down in a famous gale in 1898, with all hands. The coastline retreats into the horizon, nothing more than a blue-green smudge. The compass on the deckhouse tells me I'm heading east by northeast, a course that might take me to Martha's Vineyard or even Nova Scotia, if I felt like it. Poets have dribbled a lot of ink about the freedom of a sail and a star to steer by, and I won't add any more. But I will say that the wonder of it is less about absolute control, which would only excite a megalomaniac, and more about the limitless expanse ahead. I could put into Aquinnah on Nantucket Island by lunchtime, or pass it by and keep on course for Chatham. There's no fuel to run dry, no engine to overheat. If the compass gets wet I might end up in Greenland, but why worry?

There is that annoying sound, though. Clinking, like coins in a jam jar. Every time *Pretty Jane* rolls, I hear it, and it's beginning to get on my nerves. Why the hell would Grandpa keep a jar full of pennies on a boat? I put it out of my mind, stare out to the horizon, take a deep breath. Ah, the open sea. How many years has it been? Can't count that cruise to Hawaii. But here we are: the fresh breeze, the green waves, the rolling deck. And Marley's chains, clanking away nearby. After a while I can't take it anymore. The hatch is still open, the cabin empty and mocking. Two blue plastic cushions and a pump toilet that makes eager sucking noises if you get too close. Gray carpet. And that damn clinking.

I put a rope round the tiller to fix her course, and duck into the cabin. The chop is heavier, the sound louder. It's coming from under the seat cushions. I pull them back to reveal…

Bottles. A case of Bacardi to starboard. Another of Dewars Single Malt, to port. And a third, tucked up into the bow, of empties. Hello there, Grandpa. Between Emma's cake and Grandpa's hooch, this week has been a regular feast of the dead, but the sun is high, it's past noon and like any good pirate, I'm thirsty. Time to splice the mainbrace!

Yo, ho, ho, and a bottle of rum later I'm rolling more than the *Pretty Jane*. Course is northwest by…something. It's okay, though, because the shoreline is off to port and Dad is here to guide me home. "Keep an eye on the headsail, Rosie. When it starts to luff, the boat wants to turn. Then pull the line taught, and she's yours!" Stand by to come about. Come about, ay!

Grandpa was definitely onto something here. Drinking yourself into a stupor at a bar is humiliating, and doing it at home is just sad, but on a boat in the middle of the sound, you are the master of your wobbly universe. I feel like Captain Kidd as I reach for the Dewars.

"Oh quarter, oh quarter, those pirates then did cry,
Blow high, blow low, and so sailed we!
But the quarter that we gave them—we sunk them in the sea,
Coming down the coast of High Bar-ba-reeee!"

I don't know where the song is coming from. Maybe I heard it on a movie, maybe Dad sang it when I was a little kid, maybe the mad ghost of Sylvanus whispers it into my ear. I can feel them now, the Hazards. Lost ships prowl the depths beneath *Pretty Jane*'s keel. The Cape Dory swings almost on her beam ends, and Grandpa's stash scatters about the cabin. The sea is kicking up a bit. Not a storm, not even a squall. Just a fresh breeze. A few whitecaps. Good weather for catching Puritans. Another bottle and I'm on my feet, reeling, crying, screaming out to the hollowed shell of the world:

"*Sylvanus Hazard, you crazy shit, I wanna join your crew!*"

My only answer is the gulls, mocking as they wheel overhead. Sky and sea are flat, featureless, empty. No, not empty. In the distance, a sail. No bigger than a pocket handkerchief. The handkerchief becomes a table napkin, a bedsheet. It's coming this way. Gliding fast across the water, *Marylee's Revenge*, summoned up from below. I can see her black bows, the Indian maiden pointing her sword toward me. And Sylvanus standing white-faced and furious, with Marcus as helmsman. Yes! Yes, come on! Come get me, you bastards!

The sail flattens out against the sky as she turns, coming broadside. Then she turns again, tacking clumsily. My vision clears a little; euphoria becomes an ache behind my eyes. It's not the *Marylee*, of course. A dun-green hull with a stubby little cabin tucked into the bow. It's the

My-T-Fine, and Wally is drunk at the helm. "Hey, Wal!" I call out, wincing at the sound of my own voice, "Your missus is gonna be all kinds of pissed when you get home!"

He must have heard, because the *My-T-Fine* veers a point to starboard. Her bows are turned toward me now, and closing fast. Dangerously fast. He's not changing course. Suddenly we are jousting knights, the Tea Party versus the Green Party. "Watch that thing! What the hell—?"

The son of a bitch is actually trying to ram me. I push the tiller away and bring her round, just in time for *My-T-Fine* to sheer across my starboard flank. There's an ugly squeal of fiberglass, a heavy thud. His hunched form is at the tiller, bundled up in a camo hunting jacket, cap pulled low over his eyes. He doesn't even turn to look at me. "You're an asshole, Wally, you know that?"

No answer. The *My-T-Fine* goes on a few more paces and then the wind catches her, and she's all aback. Wally lets the lines go. Two boats pitching up and down like corks in a bathtub.

"What the *fuck*, man?"

There's a dent in my teak rail and two of the bumpers were sliced right off. *Pretty Jane* wallows a bit and I'm thinking, How long after the *Titanic* hit the berg did they actually notice she was going down? No sense risking it. I pull back the deck hatch and peer into the darkened hull. Green water sloshing around, and a gaping, hissing noise. The fiberglass is cracked. Damn.

My-T-Fine is still there, bobbing placidly a few yards away. Wally is looking determinedly at the horizon. "Ok, Wally, you sank my battleship. Now I need a tow."

Something wrong. Maybe he knocked his head against the boom. Hope he did. I bring the *Pretty Jane* alongside as gently as I can, her bow nudging *My-T-Fine* like a horse looking for sugar. Wally pays no attention as I bind us fast and come aboard. The face under the cap is gray and pinched, eyes squeezed shut. It looks as though he's spilled a thermos full of coffee down his front. His right hand is on the tiller, his left hangs slack at his side, palm up. Beer cans on the deck, a half-eaten sandwich sodden in bilge. Smell of urine, and something worse. He's not just drunk, but dead drunk and passed out. Dumb bastard. A man could get hurt like that. I clutch the mast to steady myself and wait for the world to settle back on its axis. It does, slowly.

Only then do I see them. Three little holes, a perfect vector: one in the back of Wally's jacket, one in the splintered teak deck, and one—a gaping, gushing keyhole—right under his chin. I called for one dead man and the sea sent me another.

Above our heads the gulls laugh, and laugh.

Chapter Nine

It's a pretty procession we make, the corpse and me sharing *My-T-Fine*'s tiller, with *Pretty Jane* wallowing along behind. By all the evil luck in the world, the day has turned warm and half the town is down at Dowsy's Pier, watching as we limp to shore.

"Well!" calls out a cheery voice. It is Renee Rosen, one half of the singular couple I met the other night at the Boy and Lobster. She is standing on the dock with arms akimbo. "That's a fine picture, I must say! Looks like old Wally's picked up a supercargo." She peers down into the boat and her face darkens. "What's wrong with his—"

"For God's sake, shut up," I hiss furiously. "You've got a phone? Call the police department. Tell them I found Wally Turner, and he's dead."

"Dead?" She still hasn't moved.

"Murdered."

The word sounds ridiculous, as if I were Professor Plum in the billiard room with the candlestick. But by now Mrs. Rosen has taken stock. "I should get Barry," she whispers. "He's up at the clubhouse."

"Get whomever you like," I whisper back, "but get the police first."

"Barry will know what to do," she muses, just as if I haven't spoken. She's still staring at the body. "We'll need..."

"The *police*."

"Yes, yes. Of course."

Nevertheless she comes back a few minutes later with Barry Rosen in tow. He is in tennis shorts and a Members Only jacket. But he has already assessed the situation. "This man is dead. Shot right through the throat. Somebody ought to call the police."

A crowd is starting to gather. The Boy and Lobster sits just above the pier, and people are coming out to take a look.

"Is that Wally's boat? Good God, is that *Wally*?"

"Drunk as a skunk, it's a wonder he made it back into port."

"Looks like he hit that other boat, though."

"What's that all over the front of him? Puke?"

"Somebody should tell his wife."

Apparently somebody has. Mrs. Wally appears on the dock, weaving unsteadily in high heels. Her face is a brilliant crimson. "*Wal!*" She is almost shaking with anger. "You dumb, *dumb* son of a bitch. You're coming home this instant!"

"Stop her," I whisper fiercely to Barry. "Don't let her get any closer."

He moves, but is too late. Mrs. Wally is leaning over the *My-T-Fine*. "Wal?" A sudden intake of breath that seems to last forever. "Get her out of here!" someone yells, but her mouth is open, a perfect round red O. Renee Rosen takes her arm, someone else tries to pull her back. But she breaks free of them all and falls into boat. Screaming, screaming, tearing through the November air, and all pretense is gone with the sound of ugly grief.

• • ● • •

Here, at last, is officialdom, in the form of Billy Dyer and his notebook. He takes me aside almost at once. "You've been drinking," he informs me. Accusingly.

"I'm fully aware of that."

"What were you doing out there, anyway?"

"That should be obvious, Billy. I was getting drunk."

He sighs. "I could cite you. Operating a vehicle under the influence. I could lock you up for that."

"Oh, shut up and get me a hamburger from the clubhouse. And some hot coffee. Black. Two sugars."

Amazingly enough, he does so, and we sit on two bollards staring down at the *My-T-Fine*, waiting for the Tiverton police. Billy sent the crowd home and taped off the area. Renee took charge of the widow—strange to call her that, but true enough—and now it's just us, and Wally. "How'd he look when you found him?"

"Pretty much like he does now. Any idea how long he's been gone?"

He shrugs. "I'm no coroner. But well over a day, by the looks of things. That lets you out, anyway."

My stomach gives a nasty jolt. "I never thought of that!"

"Didn't you?" He smiles a little sadly. "I'll tell you who did. Mrs. Wally—Mrs. Turner, I should say. She asked me when we were going to lock you up."

"*What?*"

Billy sighs. "It's just shock, Rosie. None of us are acting normally right now."

That must be true, since he is too tired to realize what he just called me, and I'm too tired to correct him. "I'm not a murderer, Billy. I don't even eat red meat."

He looks up, startled. "Really? Is that new? 'Cuz I remember you used to do a really great steak *au poivre*..."

"What about the bullet?" I ask, cutting the flow of reminiscence.

"Weird angle. I figure the shooter stood about four feet above the victim. That means a dock, or a bigger boat, or—"

"Or someone standing on the *My-T-Fine*'s stern," I finish.

"Yeah. Could also be one boat riding the crest of a wave, while the other dipped down. So, all kinds of scenarios."

"What was that smell?" I ask in a whisper.

"Bodies often void themselves after death. Something about the sphincter loosening."

A wave of nausea fills up my gullet, and I choke it back down. "There's something else. His sails were both set, and he was going at a damn good clip."

"Like he was trying to run away?"

"Exactly. Not hard to imagine a boat chasing after him, putting a shot across his stern. Still doesn't answer the question of why, though. What if he found the *Calliope*? But that's crazy. And even if he did, why would Marcus…?"

Billy winces at the name. "I don't think I'd be surprised by anything that guy did," he growls. "You should hear the FBI boys talk about him."

"Oh? Tell me."

He raises an eyebrow. "That's police business."

"Never bothered you before."

Billy opens his mouth to make the obvious retort, closes it again. We are like diplomats after a civil war, trying to find the peace, trying to find the lost common ground. "Tell me about Marcus Rhinegold," I press him again.

"We're still trying to figure out the early part. Don't even have a real name yet. But once he shows up in Texas, that's pretty clear. He started working for the Molinaris when he was about fifteen. Told them he was a runaway, gave his name as Kevin Wales."

I ponder the name for a moment, but it suggests nothing.

"They found him in Texas," Billy goes on. "Got picked

up in Austin for rolling drunks on State Street—that's the first record we have of him. But after that he drops out of sight, doesn't emerge until about a year later. By then he's in El Paso, working construction. That was his cover. He'd take his truck across the border all the time, supposedly looking for crew. In reality he was the Molinaris' point man with Mexican law enforcement. You know, the guy they send over the border to smooth things out, hand out bribes. Pretty soon he's the chief negotiator for the whole Molinari family. Kind of like an ambassador, or a secretary of state. They sent him in to deal with rival families, or the drug barons in Mexico."

"Sounds dangerous."

"Hell, yeah. Then the Mexican police started getting tough, blew up one of the Molinaris' pipelines, and the gangs started fighting against each other. But the Molinaris kept sending him out, like a canary into a coal mine. Marcus must have figured he was gonna end up dead sooner or later. So the next time they sent him to Mexico he packed two suitcases full of records and took a connecting plane right to Washington. Turned himself in at FBI headquarters with enough info to indict half the family, and six other families besides."

"Jesus."

"That's the story the FBI tells. They leave a lot out, though: like the yacht, the fancy wife, the new name. My guess is Marcus was planning this for a while, and probably in contact with them the whole time. He cleared out a bank account, dropped off the files, took the new identity courtesy of the United States government and set off on his yacht as Marcus Rhinegold, wealthy dilettante. The FBI probably told him the North American coast wasn't too safe, and he was glad to keep away. For a while. Dunno why he came back. Chances are, it probably killed him."

"What about the wife, Alicia? Where does she come into it?"

Billy looks satisfied. "No mystery about her. Her real name is Crystal Gronkowski. Born and raised Secaucus, New Jersey. Worked in one of the brothels the Molinaris ran on the border. My guess is Marcus offered her a better life if she became his—what do you call it?"

"Beard," I supply automatically.

"Yeah, that. But then the next thing you know he's a fugitive—a very rich fugitive, but whatever—and she's chained at the ankle. She had no income without him, and he couldn't let her go for fear she'd blow his cover. Must have been hell for both of them."

Poor Marcus, I see his cockeyed destiny. A smart kid with no advantages, but a deep and cynical understanding of human nature. How could he rise? Not by any usual means. So he let the Molinaris claim him—or think they had. But all the while he was stockpiling, trading on his charm, waiting for the day to free himself from these wretched goombahs and strike out on his own. "Could he really still be out there?" I ask aloud, looking toward the bay.

Billy shrugs again. "It's a clear, sunny afternoon, and we've had a patrol boat out all day. Not to mention the initial search. Even used a helicopter, then. He's gone."

"But think about what that means, Billy. If it wasn't Marcus who shot Wally, who the hell did? And what about Emma?"

He looks up at me. "What about her?"

"Do you still believe she was murdered?"

"I think so. But I'm no closer to proving it. All I've got is a frying pan and a witness that thinks, maybe, Rhinegold's car was there."

"You've got more than that," I remind him. "You have

two dead bodies and a missing person. That's a hell of a lot more than a little old lady lying under her pots. You know, I never really thought she was killed—not before. It seemed so, so *unnatural.* This is Little Compton. Nothing happens here for two hundred years, then Marcus Rhinegold shows up in his sub-chaser yacht and all hell breaks loose. There has to be a connection."

We stare at the bay in silence, each wrapped in our own thoughts. It's only just past four but the sun has already dropped low on the horizon. The Tiverton police are taking a long time to come. "I'm sorry I didn't invite you to the wedding," Billy says abruptly. "Debbie wanted me to."

I'll bet she did, I think to myself. I'll bet she played that scene a hundred times before the mirror. Clutching her bridegroom's arm with one hand and her meringue of a dress in the other. "Oh, David, we are both so *happy* for you! You make such a handsome *man*!" I may have changed, but she hasn't. Debbie Antonelli has been a bitch in high heels since elementary school. "It's okay," I tell him, "I wouldn't have gone anyway."

"Yeah, that's what I figured. But I just wanted you to know there's no hard feelings. I was angry then. I said a lot I shouldn't have. But now when I look at you, you know, you're different and all, but I can see it's really you. Like, the *real* you."

From Billy this is quite a speech. I wish he had said it then. But I can hear the question hovering at the back of it. "I was the real me then, too, Billy. Just inside the wrong body. But if you're wondering if I actually loved you, the answer is yes."

He gives a slight shudder, but his body leans toward mine. "But you don't like guys."

"I liked you. Attraction and love are two different things.

I wish I could say I was wildly attracted to you. I should have been. You were dead sexy—you still are. I thought I was going crazy. I loved you, I wanted to be with you, but I knew I could never give you what a woman should. There was something missing. I'm sorry, I wish I had known enough to tell you before it was…"

I don't know how to finish the thought. Billy does it for me. "Too late. Yeah."

On the night before I left for grad school, Billy drove me over the bridge to Newport. We had dinner at the Black Pearl—lobster and French fries—and then he took me down to the rocks at Rugged Point. And proposed. So, yeah, I should have come out to him a bit earlier. We said a lot to each other that night, but not the right things. Too much was left behind, a trunk full of memories and neither of us has the key. "So when we were talking earlier about Marcus Rhinegold," Billy says slowly, "was it like that for us, too? Was I your beard?" He chokes a little on the word.

"Oh, God, no." The suffering in his face is terrible to see, and for one moment I want to take it into my hands, like I used to. I stop myself just in time. "Look, I don't know why we're having this conversation with a dead body ten feet away, but since we are, you need to know: what I felt for you was real. You weren't some trophy to convince my family. I loved you. I truly, truly did. If that had been enough…" Again, the words carry themselves to a dead end. I take a deep breath and try again. "It's not enough, though. When I looked at you then, it's like how you're looking at me now. Can you understand that?"

But he is looking at me now in a way that I hadn't expected, and suddenly we are too close to each other. I can feel his breath on my neck, catch his scent, familiar and sad. L'Homme. I bought it for him for Christmas one year.

He still wears it. His hand is on my knee, and dead Wally is rocking gently below us.

"David…"

A blaze of sirens comes to the rescue: the Tiverton police are here. "You'd better go talk to them," I tell him.

Billy leaves me without another word.

• • ● • •

There are several reasons why getting blind drunk before noon is a bad idea. One is that it leaves you the entire rest of the day to sober up and enjoy the hangover, without the merciful interval of a night's sleep. But not even a masochist would add a corpse and six hours of grilling by the Rhode Island State Police. By the time I get home I'm carrying my head in a wheelbarrow. And of course Grandma is waiting to tell me all about her day, which involved a quick trip to Paris to have chicken salad sandwiches with General de Gaulle. "He was very polite," Grandma insists. "Not snooty like the French. He asked about you."

"That's nice of him."

"But he thinks you need to clean your pores better."

By now I'm literally pawing the bathroom cabinet for aspirin, of which we have exactly two, one of which slips through my fingers, bounces off the rim of the sink, and lands next to the toilet. I swallow it anyway. Grandma's voice drones through the door.

"…they say you can only bring one carry-on but that woman had three suitcases *and* a potted plant and they let her on, me I just had that coloring book you always liked and a couple bags of groceries but the main thing is they make you watch the movie whether you want to or not and they keep the library locked…"

Finally I put her to bed with two Benadryl and a hot water bottle. Then, because all I want is sleep and silence, Aunt Irene calls, full of news. Arabella Johnson, Emma's long-lost daughter, has been found. In a manner of speaking. "Died in a car crash back in '77," Irene announces breathlessly into the receiver. "Somewhere in Brooklyn. They found the death certificate. So that's that."

There is a sharp pain behind my left eye that throbs with every word. "The cousins will be thrilled."

"Yes," she sighs. "Mr. Perkins already told them. But there might have been a child born out of wedlock in 1974. Bill Perkins is looking into it. It's tough going, apparently. Arabella sounds like a drifter. She was in some New Age compound in Bensonhurst, where they have committee meetings on who washes the dishes every night—"

Aunt Irene prattles on. No one's told her about Wally yet. Aside from the headache it's strangely comforting hearing about this domestic little mystery, like watching one of those old movies where the characters swan around sipping martinis and solving missing wills and no one knows there's another World War waiting for them in a couple years. "*Don't kid yourself, friend,*" Nick Charles tells his high-living chums, "these *are the good old days.*" Too right, Nick. Even as I'm half-listening to Irene, I'm thinking of one of Grandma's favorite games when I was a kid. I called it The Death Star. She could tell you how any actor—big or small, male or female—died. We'd be watching *The Thin Man* and she'd sigh and shake her head slowly. "William Powell," she'd say, "heart attack. But you know, he was ninety-one!" As if living to see the second Reagan inaugural was a kind of victory, as if Powell was somehow less dead than poor Adrienne Ames: "Cancer at thirty-nine! Could have been a big star!" Still, I think Grandma derived a certain smug satisfaction from outliving her favorite actors. She hovered like a deathwatch beetle above their movies, counting down the fallen with each late-night viewing. "Oh, Karl Malden," she'd sigh, as we watched *The Streets of San Francisco*, "he just died." Olivia de Havilland was a sore trial for her.

"Irene," I break in finally, "there's something you need to know." In a few short sentences, I tell her. The line crackles with static.

"That dumb, *dumb* son of a bitch," she breathes finally.

I nearly drop the phone. Irene customarily uses words like "fudge" and "jiminy."

"Jeez, Irene," I say finally. "I didn't like Wally either, but that's pretty cold."

She sighs vastly, sending a sibilant shriek up to the satellite and into my ear. "Why couldn't he have stayed home? What the hell was he doing out there?"

"Looking for Marcus. I wonder if he found him."

"He sure found something. Oh, damn. You say you actually ran into the body? On the water?" There's a pause as she considers this. "That must have been pretty horrible. How are you holding up?"

"Not great," I admit, shivering a little. It's just after ten. I'm wrapped up in a blanket on the couch, dreading the hours ahead and wishing I hadn't used all my Ambien on a stupid head cold last month.

"Want me to come over and sit with you a bit?"

It's tempting, but I tell her no. The days when I could curl up in someone's lap are long past. "I'll just make myself some tea."

"Jasmine!" she insists, "not English Breakfast! That's got caffeine in it."

"Okay, Aunt Irene."

After another five minutes of solicitous advice, she hangs

up. The house settles itself to sleep. I can hear Grandma snoring upstairs, long soft percussions of air. A log in the fireplace cracks, sending up a shower of sparks. Absent-mindedly, I wad up some newspaper and toss it onto the flames. The headlines curl at the corners:

"State Comptroller Denies Knowledge of Payola Scam… Two Dead in Nighttime Collision…Johnson and Wales University Breaks Ground on New Test Kitchens…Mysterious Millionaire Vanishes on Yacht…"

You don't know the half of it, I think to myself. How about "Local Bigot Sails to His Own Demise"? Or "Heirs Sought for Recluse's Fortune"? Or even "Little Compton Native Found Buried Under Her Own Cookware"?

What if it's all one story?

Wait, what? I think I must be falling asleep, because it suddenly seems absurdly simple: Emma, Marcus, her money, his yacht, and poor old Wally sailing between them like the ferryman on the River Styx. All one story. Yes, of course it is. Because this is Little Compton, and nothing ever happens here. If everything is happening at once, it must all be connected. I don't know whether this is genius or delirium tremens. What would Hercule Poirot do? Think logically, little gray cells. Start at the beginning. What happened first? Marcus Rhinegold arrived in the harbor.

No, that's not right. First Emma Godfrey fell in love, and had a child, Arabella. Start with that. She left the child and came back. Teddy Johnson wrote to her but never returned. She grew old. She died. And Marcus Rhinegold, alias Kevin Wales, came to Little Compton. Again, not quite right. Marcus came before she died—in fact, just before. At her funeral he stood too close to the grave. Which would make sense if he was in some way…

Oh. I guess it was genius, after all. *Évidement*!

Now I've got the phone in my hands and I'm frantically dialing. It rings, and rings, and rings. No one is picking up at Irene's. I call Aunt Constance. Ring, ring, ring, nothing. The shop, same thing. I can feel a panic attack coming on. It's after eleven, where the hell are they? My fevered mind instantly conjures up all kinds of scenarios: a car flipped over in a ditch; Aunt Irene lying broken and twisted at the bottom of her stairs; a sudden, sharp pain in Constance's right arm that travels to her heart. Stop it. They're old; they're probably asleep in bed. There's only one number left for me to call. "*This is Chief Bill Dyer,*" his voicemail informs me, "*I am unable to answer my phone at the moment. Please leave a message.*"

"Billy? It's David. Look, I'm sorry to call so late, and I don't want to get you in trouble with Debbie…"

"David?" Billy's voice breaks in, hoarse and concerned.

"Oh, damn," I whisper under my breath. "Hey, I'm really sorry to bother you, but I think I might have come up with something. Something important. The two crimes are connected. Well, that is, Marcus' disappearance may be connected to Emma's will, which isn't exactly a crime, but you were right, she was *definitely* murdered…"

"Huh? What? Are you okay, what's wrong?"

I realize I'm gabbling into the phone. Deep breath, start again. "Billy," I say slowly, "Marcus Rhinegold was Kevin Wales. *Wales*. And Emma Godfrey had a daughter named Arabella Johnson. Get it, *Johnson and Wales*."

A long pause. "Debbie's in the other room," Billy informs me. "And I gotta get up at five tomorrow. Whatever this is, can this wait?'

Probably, but it's too late now. "I think Arabella had a son, and I think it was Marcus. Billy, what if Marcus Rhinegold is Emma's grandson?"

I can hear Debbie in the background. "*It's her, isn't it?*" No, Debbie. It's a him, now. But then Billy's voice comes down the wire, interested. "That would be something, all right. Got any proof?"

"Just the two names. And Mr. Perkins thinks Arabella had a child in 1974, which would be just about Marcus' age. The child was born in Bensonhurst, Irene said, and Marcus himself told me that's where his orphanage was. It would explain everything. Why would a man on the run from the mob come to Little Compton? It never made sense. But if he had a rich old Grandma who could be ushered into the next world..."

"But we still don't have any proof he *was* her grandson," Billy objects. "And even if he were, how did he know about her will? Or her fortune? There's too many loose ends there."

"Sure," I agree. "But look at it like this. Let's say he did know. And his money was running out. So he comes to Little Compton, makes a big splash as Marcus Rhinegold, waits for her to peg out. But she's a tough old lady. Could last another ten years. So...a fortunate accident."

I can hear him writing. Suddenly he stops. "That doesn't make any sense," he tells me.

"Which part?"

"Any of it. If he came here to cash in on her death, he'd have to reveal himself after the funeral. Which would instantly make her death look very suspicious."

"He might have killed her, got scared, and taken off," I offer. "That would explain why he vanished."

"Without the fortune, but with his skin? Yeah, I suppose it's possible. Still pretty thin, though."

I know he's right, but the idea is too good to give up. "Can you just check to see if he's her grandson? There's gotta be a DNA test for that."

He thinks for a minute. “Yeah. Yeah, I’ll do that. We got some of his hair off a hairbrush in the wife’s car. That should be enough.”

“You’ll do what? What are you gonna do? Are you seeing that THING again?”

“I gotta go,” Billy says abruptly, and hangs up.

I’m wired now. ‘The Thing’ goes into the kitchen to make some eggs. The Hired Help is now amusing itself by swinging the overhead light gently back and forth.

“If you get the chance,” I say to it, “would you mind asking Aunt Emma if she was murdered?”

The light abruptly goes still. It’s an answer, but I’m not sure to what.

Chapter Ten

The excitement of discovering a body and a missing heir on the same day is not the sort that can be sustained for long. Laws of equilibrium require any such event be followed by a long period of torpor. On Thursday my EBT card arrives, a reminder that I am not, after all, a budding detective, but an unemployed adjunct professor living on the charity of the State of Rhode Island. I celebrate by taking Grandma out for hot dogs and clam cakes. We get home in time to watch Jimmy Fallon, whom Grandma loves because she thinks he's Red Skelton.

On Saturday I coax the ancient red Corolla across the Mount Hope Bridge into Providence, watch a Meryl Streep movie at the mall, and wander around downtown for a few hours. It hasn't changed much; it never does. For a few drunken years in the nineties Providence was going to be the next Cape Cod. They flooded the Water Street ditch and turned it into a Venetian canal, complete with flickering torches and gondoliers. Some big chain bought the old Masonic lodge on Park and reopened it as a boutique hotel. The mayor launched his own line of spaghetti sauce. Then the economy tanked, the hotels left, and the mayor went to jail for racketeering. The city is like a bud that just barely opened before frost set in. Now half the buildings stand empty, and the carefully restored facades along Weybosset Street have begun to chip and flake. The canal looks like an abandoned amusement park ride. A couple of shrouded gondolas rock dismally at the sidings.

This is all making me feel my age. I used to find it funny when Grandma and her friends got hopelessly snarled on the name of some restaurant or department store that had been out of business for thirty years. Now I know how they felt. To remember is to call the thing back into life, however falsely, however fleetingly. They agonized over Tilden Thurber and Roscoe's Deli because if they didn't, if they allowed those places to disappear into history, it would be as if that part of themselves was gone too. Staring at blank stretch of windows on Westminster Avenue I say to myself, *That's where the old Providence Savings and Loan used to be*, and the thought makes me indescribably sad.

The phone buzzes in my pocket. "You were right," Billy tells me without preamble. "The DNA checks out. Marcus was Emma Godfrey's grandson."

"Jesus."

"That's not all. As soon as we told the FBI, they turned right round and said they already knew. Typical. We have to give them whatever we find, but they don't give us shit. Anyway, it turns out Marcus hired a private detective agency in Somerville to find his long-lost granny. That was over a year ago. They found her, and one month later Marcus arrived in Little Compton."

"I wonder how he even knew to look for her?"

"Dunno. Maybe his mother said something before she died? He told you the truth about that orphanage, by the way. FBI confirmed that, too. But he was only there for a couple years." He pauses for a moment. "Nice work."

I laugh. "Thanks, Billy. Does this mean I get to be your deputy?"

He coughs elaborately. "Anyway, you should also know that RIPD reopened Emma Godfrey's death. They're looking at it as a homicide now."

"With Marcus as chief suspect?"

"Sure. He's not just a missing person anymore. He's a fugitive."

I feel a brief tang of pity, and then wonder at my own mixed-up emotions. Do I actually feel sorry for the man that might have killed Aunt Emma? What a strange world this is becoming. "Thanks for telling me, Billy, I really appreciate it. I hope I didn't cause too much trouble with you and Debbie."

There's a long silence. "It's okay," he says finally, and hangs up.

My next call is to New England Wrecking and Salvage. Aunt Constance answers the phone with a gruff bark, like I've interrupted her lunch. "I just talked to Billy," I tell her, "he says—"

"I know," she snaps. "Marcus was her grandson. Whoop-dee-frigging-doo."

"How did you know?" I gasp.

"You're not the only one with friends down at the station. Can't say I'm surprised, though."

"Aren't you?"

"Never made sense, him coming to Little Compton. And I saw the resemblance right away. Irene did, too."

"Damn," I whisper. "So you knew?"

"Of course not. Don't be stupid. We just thought he looked kinda familiar. Never put the two together, why would we? For all we knew, Emma never had kids, much less grandkids."

"Do you think he ever talked to Emma?"

"I'm sure he didn't." Constance was positive. "She would've told us. And even so, I could have known just by looking at her that something was up. My guess is he didn't want to reveal himself till after she croaked."

"So you think he might have...hurried her along?"

The phone whistles with static for about half a minute. "Could be," she admits finally. "But I still think they're turning up a mare's nest with that one. If he bashed her head in, why would he take off before he could collect the inheritance?"

Another voice chimes in from the background. Constance puts her hand over the receiver, but I can hear her say irritably, "Irene, what the hell are you bothering me with that for? Ask him yourself." More inaudible twittering, of a more determined nature. Finally Constance comes back on the line. "Irene wants to know if you've had lunch," she repeats in a flat tone.

I chuckle and assure her I had. Sustained chatter now. "Oh, for God's sake...She wants to know what you ate."

"Tuna sandwich." Feeling this might not be adequate, I add, "With chips and a Coke."

"Oh. Okay. We'll bring dinner over tonight." And she rings off without another word.

I can't help but smile. Was it just moments ago I was lamenting how everything was slipping away? Providence may be a ghost of what it was, and Little Compton may be rife with homicide, but when it comes to the Laughing Sarahs, some things never change.

• ● ● ● •

The days are shorter now; the sun makes a brief pass over the harbor and is gone before I've picked up the mail. One

Monday morning it seems unusually bright, and I look outside to find the yard covered with a glittering frost. The Karabandis drape their sign in colored lights, put out a tray of handmade ornaments and play Bing Crosby for the few New Yorkers that drop by. The air is tanged with wood smoke and burning leaves. Brickley's Ice Cream is shuttered, and the guardrails come down at South Shore Beach. Tiverton High plays Chariho for the Third Division football championship; Bulgarmarsh Road is lined with tailgaters in bright orange sweaters with "Go Tigers" banners flapping in the breeze. They lose, 37-0. One by one, the big houses along the coast go dark, their owners fleeing south, and Pastor Paige looks out dismally to a shrunken congregation. "Oh, ye few, but faithful." The first real snowfall comes a week before Thanksgiving. Little Compton contracts into herself, sheds tourists and summer boarders like so many frivolous leaves, until only the bare branches remain. I am one of those branches.

Like the seasons, I am changing. Yesterday I looked in the mirror and found two dandelion-fluffs of hair springing up on my shoulders. I don't know whether to be grateful or repulsed. Most people, if they think about it at all, assume that the process of altering gender has a definite beginning and end. It doesn't. It has a beginning: I was definitely a woman six years ago. But as for becoming a man, that is a process that doesn't ever really seem to stop. I've lost the curve of my hips, but kept the delicate fingers and toes. My face has gone from being a masculine woman's to a feminine man's—which is something, I guess.

Now it's Thanksgiving, and the Laughing Sarahs are coming over. The day dawns cold and clear, with a light chop on the waves. Macy's parade is on in the kitchen, but like most things it's not what it used to be. When did they replace marching bands with boy bands?

If I were looking for signs of *temps perdus*, they're not hard to find. This was always Grandma's day. She'd be up long before the rest of us, vacuuming the living room and setting out bowls of nuts, dried fruit, and hard candy. By eleven the Sarahs began to arrive, placing their covered dishes on the big oak table in the dining room. Each was an institution unto itself. Taking pride of place was Aunt Emma's famous Fried Rice with Vienna Sausages, loyally flanked by Aunt Irene's Clam Stuffies in Garlic Sauce. Aunt Constance brought fruit salad and a tub of rainbow sherbet. She doesn't cook.

Of all my memories of that day, year after year, Grandma is never out of the frame. She is always fixing someone a drink, wiping down the counters, swapping a joke with the Aunts, telling Grandpa to turn down the damn television. Grandma was not the floury-hands kind of old lady. She didn't pinch cheeks or bake cookies. She wore polyester slacks and a green eyeshade when she played bridge. She listened to Miles Davis on the Hi-Fi. But Thanksgiving was different. That day she could have leapt intact from one of the Rockwell plates above the draining board. That day everything—the house, the food, the Aunts, even Grandpa—moved in orbit around the fixed, immovable center that was Maggie Hazard.

The last was three years ago. It was memorable for a number of reasons, none of them good. Irene's husband, Phil, was at the end of a long fight with lung cancer: a flesh-colored skeleton sitting in Grandpa's old chair, staring off into space. I shuddered as I walked by him. He looked just like Grandpa. That was also the year Grandma burned the turkey, forgot to turn on the gas under the beans, and snapped at anyone that tried to help. And it was the day I came out to my father—not at the dinner table, nothing so tacky, but in the living room with Uncle Phil drooling in the corner.

Dad didn't understand at first. "What do you mean, you're a man? No, you're not." Then, once he grasped the idea, he chased me out into the yard and broke a chair leg across my shoulders.

Last year I spent Thanksgiving at the college, tucked into a corner of the refectory with a turkey leg and a pile of instant potatoes.

It's my turn now. I feel like a stand-in on an unfamiliar stage, vacuuming the rug and putting out the nuts in the same little green bowls Grandma always used. At eight I slide the bird into the oven and prep the vegetables, my hands working through a silent mime of what I remember from watching her. Irene and Constance arrive just after breakfast. They lay their offerings on the dining room table. With everything on it, it still looks bare. Irene goes up to dress Grandma, and Constance switches on the game—for old times' sake, I suppose. The old house creaks and complains. With just the four of us, it could be any day, any meal. Grandma stares indifferently at the candied yams, orange-peel carrots, and of course Irene's clams and Constance's fruit salad. None of us can think of a single thing to say. The radiator burps and whistles. I feel like we are at a Shinto shrine, offering up a feast for the dead.

"We should say grace," Irene murmurs.

"Go ahead," Constance tells her.

We eat in silence. The television is still on in the other room, playing to an empty sofa. "Jesus," Grandma says finally, swallowing a mouthful of bread, "somebody tell a joke."

Irene chuckles softly. "I know," she says. "Let's get out the tape recorder again."

It seems a safe idea. We are clearly not very good at

living in the present; the past, dusty but comforting, will have to do. The recorder is brought out and we sit around it like a Ouija board. "What should we talk about?" Aunt Constance asks.

"Get Maggie to tell a story," Irene offers.

"You heard all my stories. Can't remember 'em anyway."

"I have an idea," I tell them. The recorder light goes green. "Grandma, tell me more about Emma."

"We already told you about that," Constance cuts in, frowning.

"I want to hear it from her, though. She was her best friend. Grandma, did Emma ever tell you about her daughter? Arabella? Do you remember when she left Little Compton after Teddy went to war?"

Aunt Irene bleats, "I really don't think—"

But Grandma looks at me blankly. "What are you talking about? Teddy who?"

"Teddy Johnson. Emma's beau."

She shakes her head. "Teddy never went to war."

"This is a waste of time," Constance interjects again. "Talk about something else, for chrissake. Tell the Robie gold story again."

"I've heard that story enough," Irene snaps unexpectedly. "If you hadn't gotten the whole bar stirred up—"

"I never thought the damn fools would—"

"What else did you expect? That greedy Mrs. Wally—"

They've begun the kind of argument that can go on for hours. "We were talking about Emma," I remind them both firmly.

"No," Constance corrects me. "We finished talking about her."

"I haven't." We stare at each other for a long moment. Constance finally looks away.

"Go on, then. What the hell difference does it make?"

"Grandma," I say to her, "this is really important. Did Emma ever mention a daughter? Or a grandson?"

But there is no answering spark in her eyes. They have gone opaque. "What do you mean? I had the child, not her. Emma never had any children. She was an old maid. A silly old maid with no one to love her. That's true, isn't it? Silly, silly, old maid."

"She had Teddy," I remind her. "Don't forget those letters. They carried on right up until she died."

"That's right!" Irene chimes in. "She had Teddy, Maggie."

"If you can call that anything," Constance adds. But the two of them nod in unison.

"Bullshit," my grandmother barks. This is what Dr. Renzi calls a "behavior." She never used to swear, not even when she and Grandpa argued. But since the dementia set in, a whole new vocabulary appeared. The Sarahs look embarrassed. "More coffee, dear?" Aunt Irene asks.

"She sent those letters to herself," Grandma says, looking at me. "Teddy was dead."

There is an awkward, worried silence. Grandma's memory is usually pretty good for things more than thirty years back, and I wonder if this is something ominously new. I look at the other two, waiting for them to sigh or tap their foreheads, but they don't. They haven't moved. Something titanically heavy drops from the sky and lands on the floor in front of us.

"That can't be true?" I whisper, aghast.

Aunt Irene slumps in her chair, like a meringue gone soft in the heat. Her eyes fill with tears, and the rolls of fat under her arms wobble with grief. "It was so terrible," she says. "He died at Pork Chop Hill. They never found the body." She turns to Aunt Constance, as if inviting her to continue, but Constance is staring out the window at the darkness.

"Then what was all the rest?" I ask angrily. "A fairy tale?"

The women shrink from that phrase: Irene with a soft shudder, Constance with a derisive snort. "It wasn't our story to tell," she snaps. "You're better off not asking about things you can't understand."

"What story?" Grandma asks, suddenly confused. "Was I supposed to tell a story?"

"Emma got the telegram right after his last letter," Irene goes on, as if the words are being drawn out of her with a hook. "We were with her then. She read it, tore it up, and then read Teddy's letter again. I guess that became the reality, the rest disappeared. We waited for her to snap out of it, but she didn't. And then the letters started coming. We knew what she was doing, of course. She didn't. I think her brain sort of split in half. Part of it knew she couldn't handle his death, so it kept writing letters and sending them, for the rest of her life."

"And you knew the whole time?" I whisper.

"Everybody knew," snaps Aunt Constance. "Good Lord, I ought to recognize her handwriting. Wally knew, too, of course, but he never said a word. Which is the nicest that could be said for him."

"So you all kept on pretending?" Before I finish, I know the answer. Of course they did. The whole town did. It's the New England way.

"It just seemed easier," Aunt Irene admits.

The image is almost too good to be true. Aunt Emma, deceiving herself, deceiving the Sarahs. And the Sarahs, undeceived, deceiving her. All to spare everyone's feelings. "Poor Emma," I sigh.

For a moment we sit in silence, contemplating the past. "Of course, it might not have been like that," says

Aunt Constance. Irene looks startled. "What do you mean? Certainly it was! What else could it be?"

"Oh, come off it, prudy. You heard the rumors. There could have been another reason for sending those letters. It kept old man Avery away, and the others too. If you ask me," Aunt Constance shifts comfortably in her chair, settling in for a good gossip, "Emma might not have liked men all that much."

"Oh!"

"I wouldn't be too surprised," Constance goes on, ruminatively. "I mean, what do you want to believe? That she was so in love with Teddy Johnson that she lost her marbles?"

"Yes!" Aunt Irene cries.

"*Or* it could have been a damn clever scheme. Maybe she was never all that sweet on him to begin with. I was sorry when he died, and I was sorry for her, but come on, *sixty years*?"

"Just because you don't believe in true love..."

"Just because my Harvey ran off with that slut cousin of yours, you mean?" This is degenerating into one of their bickering matches, but Aunt Constance stops herself. Her tone becomes surprisingly gentle. "Well, you're right. Maybe Emma had the right idea. Make everybody think you're a little crackers, and they'll leave you alone. God, wouldn't be wonderful to be left alone?"

There is real longing in her voice, and Irene's, too. I can see what is going on. Faced with the riddle of Emma Godfrey, which her death has done nothing to solve, each of the Sarahs created their own interpretation. Why would a spinster send herself letters and pretend they were from an old love? Aunt Irene, a kindly and incurable romantic, turns it into a Harold Robbins novel. Aunt Constance, who has been thrice divorced and lives with three bad-tempered

Wolfhounds, sees it as a wish for solitude. Perhaps they are both right.

Having stated their respective positions, both camps retreat. Aunt Constance disappears back into the kitchen. Aunt Irene starts channel-surfing.

I look over to Grandma. She smiles, winks. For that moment it's still Grandma, the one I remember. I love these brief flickers, when she peeks through the fog of her illness and sees me again. Like all precious things, they are becoming rarer. She squeezes my knee and leans in confidentially. "They're trying to kill me," she whispers.

"Oh, Grandma...."

"Shh!" She casts an anxious glance at Aunt Irene before continuing. "I'm telling you, it's true. They know I know. I saw his body. Poor Teddy, blood everywhere. And I can't keep all my marbles in one pocket anymore."

What is this? My brain, reeling, reaches out for something conventional. "Nobody's trying to kill you. These are your friends."

Maggie snarls. "They're poisoning my food. They want to shut me up. Murderers!"

Irene's got *American Idol* on and is placidly humming along with a Gaga tune. I desperately hope she can't hear this.

Then Aunt Constance comes back in, holding a Pepsi.

"Ask her!" Maggie screams. "Ask her who she dropped into Quicksand Pond! She knows! Teddy never made it out of Little Compton alive!"

I have to give Aunt Constance credit, her hand doesn't even shake. "I think it's somebody's bedtime," she says.

"You mean me," says Grandma.

"I mean you."

"I'll take her up," Irene offers quickly. She heaves herself out of her chair, takes Grandma's arm. The two of them totter towards the stairs like old friends.

I'm left with Aunt Constance, and Grandma's last outburst. I can't think of a way to bring it up. What's the proper form for asking an eighty-year-old woman if she killed a man and buried him in Quicksand Pond sixty years ago? A terrible thought passes through me. What if Grandma is right, what if all her secrets are spilling out, what if they are trying to shut her up? The thought is ludicrous, hurtful. The Laughing Sarahs are not like that. But then I catch a glimpse of Aunt Constance's hands working themselves in her lap. Large, thick fingers, chapped and veined but still powerful. Hands that could rip the lanterns off a wreck in the middle of the bay at nightfall, or wield a tire iron to silence whoever might still be on board. Or push a body into the muck, watching the brackish water close around it. I don't know these women.

"Your grandmother," says Constance severely, "is getting funny. You shouldn't pay too much mind to the things she says. She can't keep stuff inside anymore."

I'm still trying to unpack that statement, which seems to have two contradictory parts, when she goes on, "You shouldn't have brought all this up. It bothers her. Bothers me, too, come to think of it. Whatever sins poor old Emma had, she paid for a thousand times over, so what's the use of talking about it? I'll tell you something, since nobody else will: Teddy Johnson had the loosest fly in Newport County. And that's all I'll say about that." She turns up the television, a clear signal conversation is over.

But I'm not about to give up. "You mean he cheated on her, and she…?"

Constance looks away from the set, irritated. "Shut up," she orders. She puts down her soda, thinks for a moment.

Finally she sighs. "Here's the deal. I'm gonna tell you this, because if I don't then you'll hear it from Maggie in bits and pieces, and drive me fucking crazy with each one. But after I tell you, you will never, *never* bring it up again. Not to me, not to Irene, not at Christmas, not on birthdays, not even on your deathbed. Okay?"

"Okay."

"Turn off the damn recorder."

CONSTANCE

Emma was always the toughest. Even when we were kids. And the most passionate. The things she wanted, she wanted desperately. It's a mistake, wanting anything too much. Because even after you get it, you're terrified you'll lose it again, and then in the end, of course you do. Your Aunt Irene, now, she's different. Her mother used to say she came out of the womb laughing. I don't know if that's true, but Irene's always been full up to burst with everything. She overflows. With what? Oh, you know: joy, happiness, life, all that crap. You know. You've spent enough time with her. Don't tell her I said any of that.

But Emma—Emma was hollow. She was born wanting. I blame her father: Ephraim Godfrey was a nasty, prideful, greedy son of a bitch. The kind that would think he was doing you a favor by borrowing twenty bucks, then sneer at your ingratitude if you asked to be paid back. And Miriam Godfrey—Emma's mother—was like a great big sponge that soaked up everything around it. They were a rotten pair, no question. It's amazing, if you think of it, that Emma didn't end up a monster.

I credit your Grandma. You don't know what she was like then. I wish you did; she's actually a lot like you. She was the first of us to wear slacks—no, I don't mean it like that. I just mean she was ahead of her time. Everybody wanted to be like her, even me. And Emma. Emma was so dreadful at first. Such a big showoff. Everything had to be the newest, the shiniest, the most expensive. Well Maggie just knocked the stuffing right out of her. "Why, Emma," she'd say, "that's a lovely dress you're wearing! Did you make it yourself? Oh, I see, is it from Woolworth's? Cuz I saw the spitting image of it on the mannequin, marked down seventy-five percent. You take my advice and return that dress, go buy the cheaper one and a pair of shoes to go with." And your Grandma just kept on smiling like a Buddha. Oh, Emma would steam!

A dress is one thing. A man is another. And Emma wasn't a little girl anymore. She saw Teddy and she wanted him—and that was that. He had a reputation. I know Irene left that part out. Makes a better story. But he wasn't some random lifeguard—we knew him. Hell, it's Little Compton, of course we knew him. And even then, even before that day at the beach, we knew he was bad news. Told Emma so. But it's like that necklace she brought back from Cuba. The man that sold it to her on the pier in Havana told her it was black pearls. She came off the boat waving it around, wore it every damn day. My father was an oysterman, and what I don't know about pearls isn't worth knowing. The necklace was paste. Not even a good imitation. But even after I told her, and showed her the difference between hers and the real thing, she kept right on wearing it and telling everyone it was real. Like she could change reality just by wishing it so.

That was the vogue back then. All these self-help books telling you that you could do anything if you just willed it enough. And if you tried, and failed, you just weren't applying yourself enough to the task. Fucking Dale Carnegie.

Anyway, Emma set out to change Teddy into what she wanted him to be. And he went along, at first. Maybe he actually loved her. I will say, she played her hand well. He was used to girls falling all over him. But Emma was always cool, always remote. She could talk about Nietzsche or Cubism or the Bauhaus movement. Never simpered or giggled or asked him which movie star he thought she looked like. Teddy had never met anyone like her. She made him feel like it was an honor if she deigned to smile in his direction, and the novelty of having to work for the thing, rather than it just being handed to him, carried him halfway to the altar. Not all the way, though. Because, as much as you want them to, people don't really change. They can fake it for a bit, even convince themselves, but in the end they are what they are.

I told her so. We all did. One afternoon I sat Emma down on the couch in your Grandma's parlor and said Teddy was a sweet man and handsome, but it was a certain fact he had laid everything except the North Sea cable and Emma was a fool to think any different. Why, even now he was carrying on with some bartender's daughter in Cranston, not to mention the girls he picked up round the Naval base. And those were just the ones we knew about. Did she seriously think he'd give it all up for her? What if he gave her some loathsome disease, syphilis or the clap? And what, in God's name, if she got pregnant? What then? Emma just sat there, saying nothing, smoking one cigarette after another. When I was finished she stood up, ground out her cigarette, and said, "Teddy's asked for my hand. I told him yes. The wedding's in June. So go fuck yourself sideways." And walked out. She and I didn't speak for months.

Eventually Irene leaned on me. She said not to make Emma choose between her friends and her man, because we wouldn't like the choice and then we'd be stuck with it. That was true enough. So instead we pitched in, helped her plan the wedding, picked out her trousseau, hired the caterers.

Then the war came, and Teddy was drafted. I think he was relieved. They had already set a date and booked the Congregational and hired the Knights of Columbus Hall and a six-piece band. Irene was making the cake. The thing had a momentum of its own, and if the draft letter hadn't come, I think he might have found himself married out of sheer inertia. So instead of a wedding we planned a going-away party. That was for Saturday.

I'll never forget Friday night as long as I live. June 21, 1951. That was the night Milton Berle came back to host the Texaco Star Theater. Mike was already in the Navy then, so it was a girls' night in. Me, Irene, and your Grandma sat around the old Emerson with its big fuzzy yellow speakers and screen like a fishbowl. Then the curtain went up and the band started to play:

Oh, we're the men of Texaco,
We work from Maine to Mexico,
There's nothing like this Texaco of ours!
Our show is very powerful,
We'll wow you with an hour full,
Of howls from a shower full of stars!

Just then Emma came in. She walked right through the back door, stumbling a little like she'd been chased. It was a clear, cool evening, but she was soaked to the skin. Her hair was limp around her shoulders. Her hands and arms were bright red, scalded. And there was a livid bruise just coming in under her eye. But she was eerily calm. She might have been returning from church. "Oh," she says, in this weird voice, like a piece of hollow glass, "the show's on. Did Milton Berle wear a dress again?"

"Emma!" Irene cried. "What happened to you?"

She looked from one of us to the other. "Nothing at all," she said. "Just an accident. Teddy's cleaning it up."

I'll bet he is, I thought. I'd seen this often enough. My momma, God love her, used to tell people she tripped over the rug when she was vacuuming. Happened so often one of the other wives at church seriously recommended she see a doctor for balance issues. As if they didn't know. But they knew. You just didn't talk about things like that then. What good would it do? Couldn't get divorced, couldn't make 'em stop going down to the Boy and Lobster on a Friday night. Your Grandpa—well, you know about him.

So when Emma told us it was an accident, we just took her into the bathroom, cleaned her up, and sat her in front of the television. She didn't move, didn't blink. Damn, I thought, Teddy really got her. But maybe it was a blessing in disguise. I always knew he was a bastard, and now she knew as well. Like a fool, I was already thinking about the future: Teddy would go off to Korea, the engagement would fizzle, and that would be that.

But then Texaco ended and Ernie Kovacs came on, and Emma still hadn't moved. She stared at the television screen like it was talking just to her.

"Honey?" Irene called to her, "Are you okay? Do you want something to eat?"

Emma got this weird look on her face. Like she was trying not to laugh. It was terrifying. "Why, no, thank you," she said in that same flat, lifeless voice, "I made lobsters for Teddy. They are his favorite. Boiled with some drawn butter and mayonnaise sauce. And new potatoes."

That sounded good, but I had to wonder why she was here and not eating those lobsters with Teddy. By the looks of things she'd emptied the whole pot of boiling water onto herself. Or he had. Irene and me just glanced at each other, didn't know what to say. Your Grandma went into the linen cupboard and got out a spare duvet and pillow. "You can stay here tonight," she said.

"No. I can't. I have to go home and clean up."

"You're not going back in there alone," I told her.

"I have to. Teddy…"

"I'll take care of Teddy," I promised. The three of us stood up together. Emma just shrugged. As if she weren't soaked and scalded. As if the whole thing had happened to someone else.

"Suit yourself," she said.

Well, as soon as we got to the house, I could tell something was wrong. The front door hung open, letting in every bug in Christendom. One of the lamps in the living room had been knocked sideways, and a vase was smashed on the floor. The light shone right in our faces. And the house was awfully quiet. So quiet that I could hear the hiss and pop of the burners on the stove; she'd left it on. But no sign of Teddy. "Where is he?" I asked Emma. I was beginning to wish I'd brought my twelve-gauge. Or at least a rolling pin.

"He's probably finishing his dinner. I made boiled lobster, his favorite…" She repeated the whole thing like a record. In the meantime I was looking around, peering behind doors, waiting for him to pop out like a jack-in-the-box. The living room was empty, the hallway dark. The dining room table was set for two, with good bone china imported from England and two brass candlesticks, still lit. The lobster tray was shaped like a lobster itself, with a goopy smile painted on that welcomed you to feast on his brothers. It was empty.

Then Irene screamed.

We found Teddy in the kitchen. He lay on his back, one arm flung towards the door, the other palm-upward at his side, as if he were semaphoring. He was dressed in a singlet and gray trousers, with midnight blue suspenders that Emma had given him for Christmas last year. His shirt was as wet as Emma's, and his face was bright red, like he'd just been told a dirty joke. There was a pool of blood under his head, and a dark red smear on the green formica table next to him. And those lobsters! They lay on either side, arms splayed out like his, just as red as he was. I remember thinking that was oddly funny: three corpses laid out on the linoleum.

"Emma," I said slowly, as calm as I could. "You'd better tell us what happened."

She was standing in the middle of the kitchen, looking down at her fiance's body like it was a particularly stubborn carpet stain. And in that same detached voice she answered, "I was making lobsters. They are Teddy's favorite. He likes them with mayonnaise sauce. I didn't hear him come in from work; I was at the stove, with my back turned to the door. Teddy wanted to surprise me. He came up behind me and grabbed my shoulders just as I was taking the pot off the burner. I jumped. The water went all over both of us. Teddy stumbled back and slipped on the wet floor. He hit his head. Is he...is he dead?"

"Don't worry about that now," Maggie said. She was very pale.

Irene wrapped her arm around Emma's shoulders. "You poor dear," she murmured. "You just go into the living room and sit down on the sofa. Connie, Mags and me will take care of everything. Come on, now." Irene led Emma like a child into the other room and plopped her down. Then she came back to me and said under her breath, "What do you both think?"

"It's a pretty convincing story," I whispered back, "but it doesn't explain the broken vase or the overturned lamp in the living room."

"Or the bruise," Maggie added.

Irene put her hands on her hips. "We can fix some of that. Would anybody believe the rest?"

I considered this. "Depends on how much they find out about Teddy's little hobbies."

Maggie sighed. "I don't think we can take that chance."

"The important thing," I told them both, "is to make sure she has a good story and keeps to it—"

"Teddy was having an affair."

All three of us jumped. Emma was standing in the doorway. Her eyes looked feverish. "I got a letter in the mail today. It wasn't meant for me. It was from Teddy, to some floozy he's been keeping on the side. I read it. A good-bye letter, because he's getting shipped out." Her voice was unspeakably bitter. "He lied to me. He was cheating on me the entire time."

There was a long pause. "Yes, dear," Irene told her sadly, "we know."

"I made him lobsters," Emma said once again. "I didn't know what else to do. They are—were—his favorite. But I never liked them. Did you know that? Never liked dropping them in the pot, hearing them try to claw their way out, those dreadful creaking sounds the shells make that sound like screams. I hate them, actually. But they were Teddy's favorite. And I figured—I dunno what I figured. Win him back? I don't know. But they were still on the stove when he got home. Teddy came in and took off his jacket and shirt and stood there grinning at me in his undershirt. I showed

him the letter. I wasn't going to, but I did. And he…oh, it's horrible! He laughed *at me. Called me a fool and a bitch, and said if I wasn't so damn frigid he wouldn't need to go whoring around. I came at him; he pushed me back. The lamp fell over, and one of the green jade vases broke. I went into the kitchen. He was just behind me, still laughing. And that's when…"*

"Don't say any more," Maggie said, her voice shaking.

"I threw the water at him. I don't think I meant to kill him. I don't know. But he hit his head and now he's dead." She hiccupped, tittered at the accidental rhyme. "I'm not sorry. Not even a little sorry. Everything was a lie."

Well, that tore it. All that anger—there was no way she could hold up to police questioning. Self-defense? Spousal abuse? Fuck that, it was 1951. The police chief in those days was Barry Haddam, and he used to slap his wife around so bad she wore a gardening hat to church every Sunday just to hide the bruises. Can you imagine explaining all this to him*? The essential thing was to spare Emma, to make the whole thing disappear. Then maybe, just maybe, she'd keep her head. I think your Grandma, Irene, and I all thought the same thing at once. We exchanged a glance, just one, and knew what we had to do.*

I went over and took Emma shoulders in my hands. "Listen to me," I told her fiercely. "Teddy is not dead. *Do you understand that? He is still alive, and he's going to Korea tomorrow. You made him lobsters as a farewell dinner. He ate them and enjoyed them very much. Are you hearing me?"*

Her eyes were huge. "Yes," she said simply.

"We will take care of this. All of it. You don't have to worry about a thing. But you must remember that Teddy is still alive and going to Korea. Can you remember that?"

"Yes," she repeated.

Maggie sat with her on the couch while Irene and I got busy. We dragged Teddy's body through the back door and laid it out in Irene's pickup. It was brand new then: a sky blue Dodge with white wall tires and tweed tartan seats, very smart. Oh, she was mad to have that thing bleeding all over her truck bed! We wrapped him in a tarp so he wouldn't stain the wood. Then we came back into the house and started cleaning, all three of us. Emma just sat on the couch and stared. After a while she said, "It's awfully nice of you to help out for the party tomorrow. I'm sure I don't deserve it." That was creepy, all right.

It took us about an hour to get everything back the way it was. I mopped up the blood and water; Irene cleaned out the pot and took the lobsters out with the rest of the trash. Couldn't do anything about the broken vase, but who'd miss it? It was your Grandma that had the final inspiration. Just as we were on the way out the door, she cried, "The letter! Emma, do you still have it?"

She pulled it right out of her pocket. "Don't you know it was crazy to keep it?" I told her, rather sharply. Emma just shrugged. Maggie took the letter from her and we left her there, sitting on her sofa.

It was after midnight now, which was a blessing, since there was no one else on the road. Irene drove carefully, just below the speed limit, peering out into the darkness to make sure there wasn't a Statie waiting behind every bush. Of course there wasn't. But even I was jumpy that night. There's a sharp curve at John Sisson Road, and as we took it I heard the body roll and thump against the side. That gave me a nasty turn, I can tell you.

Finally we reached Quicksand Pond. It's not really quicksand, but a long shelf of marsh that drops off into a deepish bit of water. Plover and tern nest along the banks. Nobody goes out there, and nowadays nobody can. It's protected. It wasn't so, back then, but it was still a desolate spot. The deep bit was known as "The Gut." That's where we drove that night, with mud sloshing up to the radiator grill and flying out in two giant fans on either side. We had to switch off the headlights, couldn't risk them being seen. Everything was black, and we could feel the other's body shivering as we sat together in the cab, staring out at nothing. Birds screeched and flew up as we passed, and the reeds made a hell of a racket slapping against the truck. Finally they began to thin out, and I could just barely see the flat, black sheen of water ahead. That was The Gut. Irene put on the brakes. Nobody said anything. We all got out—me, Irene, Maggie—and waded around to the back of the Dodge. I climbed up and pushed Teddy to the tailgate. Irene took his feet, and Maggie grabbed him under the armpits. I got down and helped. Together we carried him a bit deeper, then dropped him into the water. I don't know what we thought would happen. The body bobbed on its stomach for a bit, then floated right back toward us. We tried again, pushing him into the water, but he shot right up again like a cork. "This isn't going to work," I said.

"We need something to weigh him down," Maggie answered.

Well sure, we should have thought of that before. But let me tell you it's not so easy when you are actually living through something like this. I thought maybe we could put rocks in his pockets, like Virginia Woolf, but all he wore were those trousers and they wouldn't hold much. Irene remembered she had a spare battery behind the seat, and in the end we tied the battery to his chest with jumper cables and turned him loose again. He sank right enough that time.

That should have been the end of it, but we still had to make our way out of the marsh. In darkness, don't forget. It felt like forever, dodging and twisting around the reeds, feeling the whump of something unknown passing under the wheels. We were all the way back on Pottersville Road before Irene dared to turn on the headlights. Poor Irene. She parked the Dodge behind her house so nobody'd see it all covered with mud. But she needn't have bothered. I came over the next morning and saw for myself: big dents in the door and fenders, rocks as big as baseballs lodged in the wheel wells, the grill all chapped and broken like snarling teeth. We washed it off, of course, but that only made it look worse. She had to tell everyone she'd lost control of the wheel and driven it into Wilbour Woods. Irene hated that lie, for she was a very good driver.

All that was left was to tackle Emma, and we did that first thing in the morning. She greeted us same as always, put a pot of coffee on, offered us rolls. It was eerie. We sat around the same formica table. In a few short sentences, I explained what had become of Teddy, and what she had to say. Teddy was leaving for Korea today. He had asked us to cancel the farewell party, as he didn't want to make a fuss. We would all be seeing him off at the ferry later. And then, after a few months, Emma would receive a letter informing her that Teddy had been tragically killed. Whatever grief she might be feeling, she could release then. But not before, not now. Did she understand? Emma answered me matter-of-factly. There was no trace of anguish in her voice, or anger, or anything. Just said she understood perfectly and thanked us for everything we had done. "I'm sorry to put you to all the bother," she said. She offered us more coffee.

The letters were my idea. There was no family to worry

about: both his parents were dead. But there was still the rest of the town. So first we all drove to the pier in Fall River and waved good-bye to the New York ferry, just as if Teddy were on it. Then a few weeks later I went up to Providence and sent Emma an envelope stuffed with blank paper and Teddy's name on it with a return address in Biloxi. Aunt Irene left that month for Paris on the Ile de France; she posted a letter from overseas with that fancy candy stripe around the edge. We couldn't do anything about the handwriting on the envelopes, but how closely does a postman look at handwriting? I just put everything in block print and told Irene to do the same.

We only meant to do it for a few weeks, before Teddy had his "accident." Then something really weird happened. One afternoon Emma showed up at your Grandma's house, chipper as all getout. I thought, good, she's finally coming round. But then she pulls this letter out of her purse and says, "You won't believe the funny things happening to Teddy!" And would you believe it, she rattles on about Teddy in basic training, Teddy on the ferry to Busan, Teddy working for some General Whatsits. It was the damndest thing I've ever heard. The glass dropped right out of my hands. Your Grandma just kept staring with her mouth open. And Irene, poor sweet Irene, says right away, "Oh, that's lovely, Emma! How he must miss you!"

So that's how it was. I can't really explain it, except to say it was like the pearl necklace, but much worse. She created a whole reality and put Teddy into it. To this day I don't know whether she really believed in it or not. Sometimes I think she really did go crazy. That she forgot everything that happened that night. Other times I think she was just being sly. Like she couldn't trust us—us—and decided to freeze us out *by playacting. But why, why would she keep going? There was no reason for it. Year after year those damn letters kept coming, until everyone in town knew about it. Crazy old Emma Godfrey and her fake fancy-man.*

My momma always said, "The way of the transgressor is hard." *If you took a cigarette from her purse, she made you smoke the whole pack. Eat an apple from the fruit bowl without asking, you'd have apples served to you every night for a week. Like a Calvinist sort of Hell: forcing you to take a surfeit of your indulgences, again and again and again, until all enjoyment turns to ashes in the mouth.*

I think what Emma did was a kind of penance. She knew nobody else would punish her, so she punished herself. Kept sending those letters, long after it even made sense. Like that old duchess in the story that strangled her children with a handkerchief, then had the handkerchief presented to her every night on a silver salver. The letters were her atonement, and waiting for them to come, seeing them in the mailbox, reminded her of her sin.

So there it is. Maybe you say we should have left her there, brought in the police, faced it all out. Well, that's one opinion. But what good would it have done? Teddy might just as well have gone to Korea and been killed. Lots of guys were. What did it matter, really, if the Koreans killed him, or Emma did? Dead is dead. Oh, but what about justice? I'll tell you about justice. About twenty-thirty years ago some rich prick, Count Something-or-other, murdered his wife in one of those big mansions on Bellevue Avenue. Stuck her full of insulin and watched her slip into a coma. And wouldn't you know, he hires a Harvard Law professor and a team full of lawyers and gets acquitted. That's justice.

But Emma didn't have the Harvard professor. She just had us.

Chapter Eleven

Aunt Irene is coming down the stairs, her big toe seeking out one tread at a time like a snail's antennae. The arthritis has bent her knees, and she leans on the banister. When she reaches bottom she lets out a satisfied sigh. "Glad that's over."

"She's down?" Aunt Constance asks from the sofa.

"Down and out. Fought me a bit at first, but now she's sleeping like a lamb." Irene looks at us both benignly. "Did you have a nice little chat?"

"Oh, sure," Constance tells her, popping the top of another Pepsi.

Chapter Twelve

Channel 12 says a storm is coming. Grandma has been saying so for days. Her internal barometer, the last and most durable of her senses, began falling on Thursday. That morning she came into my room before daybreak, switched on all the lights, and stood at the foot of the bed like the Ghost of Christmas Past. "IT'S ALMOST HERE," she intoned, and pointed out the window.

Tony Patricola of the AccuWeather Forecast agrees with her. Outside it's a clear, crisp day, with cirrus clouds studding a perfect blue sky. But on Tony's electric map a monster is churning its way up the Atlantic coast. "We have live images from Norfolk," he says excitedly, and the scene cuts to a solid wall of white, through which pinprick beams of headlights move sluggishly. "Residents of outlying areas are warned that emergency services may be suspended, and roads may become impassable after four o'clock..."

Outlying areas. That means us. Right now everyone in Little Compton will be digging through their garages for batteries, flashlights, candles. Down at Dowsy's Pier they'll be dragging big blue tarps over their boats, tying them down with bungee cords, offering up a silent prayer that *Jubilee Jim* and *Lazee Daze* and *Auriola* will still be there in the morning. The Stop & Shop will be mobbed with frantic shoppers grabbing all the bread and milk in sight. Why always bread and milk? I have no idea. Rhode Islanders are so predictable. In New Orleans they toast a hurricane from their barstools, but here we batten down the hatches and ride it out with kerosene lamps, cold cuts, and Monopoly. The truth is, we love a good storm. There is something deeply satisfying about stocking up the pantry and deep freeze, checking the emergency generator, stacking firewood in the den. At the hardware store and the supermarket, neighbors greet each other with a kind of fatalistic exhilaration, like soldiers at the Alamo. "Big one coming this time. You paid your insurance up, Fred?" "Yeah, did you pull your boat out yet?" Old-timers will reminisce about snowdrifts that went clear up to bedroom windows, winds that could hurl a blade of straw through a sapling.

I spend the whole afternoon fitting storm covers over the windows, all thirty-seven of them. These are just sheets of plywood, once painted white but now the color of dirt, with numbers etched in the corners that correspond to a small brass tag above each casement. They used to fit snugly, but age has left them warped and frayed at the edges. Nothing fits anymore. Grandma decides to help by standing at the foot of the ladder and screaming with every panel, "*That's* not the right one! That's for the front parlor! Can't you tell the difference?" We keep this up for about four hours. The wind pricks at my eyes and the sky turns a dull gray. I can feel it coming now.

In a way I'm glad. Storms bring change, and lately I've been feeling as if the axis of the Earth had altered one degree and turned everything just a little bit on its side. Nothing is familiar anymore. The morning light strikes objects strangely, making grotesque what used to be comforting: the

Dresden shepherdess on the mantel, the old oak hatstand in the front hall. I put this to Aunt Irene, who told me it is just part of grief. What grief? I asked. "You started grieving for your Grandma as soon as you found out she was ill," she answered. She's right, of course. There are times when the house itself seems to be degrading along with her, and other times when it seems crueler that this should not be so.

But there is more than grief. I haven't been sleeping. It started the night after I found out about Emma and Teddy Johnson. As soon as I got into bed my legs felt warm and sticky, and the bedclothes chafed. I kicked them off and lay naked in the frigid air. I flopped onto my side, back, stomach. I closed my eyes and felt them rolling behind my eyelids. I tried to imagine cool grass and a riverbank, but all I could think of was Wally with his throat shot away, and the Laughing Sarahs carrying a shrouded figure out into the night. That's when my breath started coming in short gasps. The darkness of the room closed in, and I had to turn on the lights before I drowned.

It's been like that for nearly a week now. Insomnia tears ragged edges off of everything. Clothes scratch, food sours on the tongue, stair treads are not where you expect them to be. Nothing feels right, or normal. By the end of it you would trade your immortal soul just to be able to lie down on the couch, pull the afghan up over your shoulders, and sleep, sleep, sleep.

By the day of the storm I've been awake nearly seventy hours. My hands tremble against the ladder's cold aluminum. As the last cover reluctantly wedges into place, I look over and see the empty windows of Emma's house staring back at me. Her bushes have become frowzy, and the yard is choked with leaves that chase one another and fling themselves against the porch. Emma's old Buick is still there, but one of the tires has gone flat. No one is left to close the green wooden shutters, tie down the lawn furniture, protect the house from what is coming. I feel a queer pang of pity for it, which is really for myself.

Aunt Irene arrives just as the first flakes begin to fall, bringing a picnic hamper full of tuna sandwiches and a spare flashlight, because she figured Grandma's might be dead. It was. "Big one coming this time!" she announces predictably.

"Is your place okay?" I ask. Irene lives in a tiny saltbox Colonial at the edge of Briggs Marsh.

"Oh, yeah. Melvin looks pretty shaky tonight. I'm crossing my fingers." Melvin is a vast, ancient, leaf-blighted oak whose branches loom over her house. Irene's been waiting for Melvin to crash through her roof for thirty years, and won't replace so much as a shingle until he does. "There's no point," she insists. "Insurance'll just end up paying for a new one." But since Melvin's planned trajectory includes her living room, Irene always comes over to Grandma's during a storm.

"You'll be dead and buried before that tree comes down," Grandma insists, chuckling.

"In that case I'll have Bill Phillips chop it up and make my casket. If I go down, I'm taking Melvin with me."

We sit around the kitchen table, watching the sky grow steadily darker. The wind comes in gusts and spurts, rattling the storm covers and hammering on the back door like an unwanted relative. Channel 12 is already calling it the Storm of the Century, which is what it called every blizzard since the year 2000, and we still have eighty-plus years of century left. But then they switch over to the radar, and Irene gasps. Everything from New London to Buzzard's Bay has disappeared under a churning white mass with a small, black, wicked eye. Its fingers brush against the coast. "Record snowfall already reported in Foster-Gloucester... all schools evacuating immediately...police warning all non-essential vehicles to remain off the road...reports coming in of downed power lines and dangerous conditions throughout southeast Rhode Island...fires...white-outs... buildings collapsing under the weight of the snow..."

"Jesus," I whisper.

"I've never seen one that big," Irene admits, to which Grandma inevitably ripostes, "That's what *she* said!"

The house begins to groan in protest, each board and shingle braced against the onslaught. But it hasn't really started yet. There's still a patch of sky over the bay, and I can see the waves tossing up great frothy sculptures of foam. "God help sailors," Irene intones, "on a day like this."

Even as she speaks I spy the mast lights of trawlers homeward bound, heeled over against the wind. "What the hell are they doing out there in the first place?"

"Can't miss a day's catch," she answers. "It's hard times for the fleet. But they'll be all right. There's still time yet."

Outside, the world is disappearing. A wall of white moves across the bay, consuming the waves, the rocks, the last few boats still straggling toward shore. Beavertail Light gives one last faint flicker and surrenders. In a moment the entire coast is gone. It is as if the animator ran out of ink, leaving only a blank page.

The storm flings itself on us like a lunatic escaped from an asylum: crying, screaming, laughing, scrabbling at the windows and doors, begging to be let inside. The noise is immense, intolerable. I strike a match, and a moment later the red glow of the hurricane lamp throws weird shadows on the walls. From the darkened kitchen we stumble through the dining room, the hall, and finally into the den, but the sound follows us everywhere. The house has become possessed. Storm covers chatter and complain, nails squeal as the wind claws them loose. "This can't go on," Irene moans.

But Grandma seems curiously unmoved. The vagueness in her eyes is gone, replaced by a kind of knowing shrewdness that I have not seen there for a long time. "It's a good blow," she says. "It'll clear the air. Need to wash things out once in a while. Good for us all."

"Not so good for the house," I suggest.

She shrugs. "Queen Anne was on the throne when they nailed those beams together. I don't really think they waited this long just to come apart, do you?"

But even as she speaks I can hear a strange clicking and rattling. A chink of darkness tears through a storm cover; a moment later it's gone. The wind cries triumphantly and flings itself on the panes, which buckle and shiver. From the other room comes a heavy crash. It sounds like one of the doors just blew off its hinges.

"Should we go to the cellar?" Irene asks. Her face is huge and round in the weak light.

"Don't be ridiculous, Irene," Grandma snaps at her. To prove her point, she sits behind the partner's desk and nonchalantly lights another Marlboro. "I think there's a bottle in the cupboard there. Why don't you look, David?"

I give a start. This is the first time she's called me by my name in weeks. "Sure, Grandma." And there is. Johnny Walker Black Label, with about a third missing. Grandma pulls out some glasses from the desk and the party is on, in a manner of speaking.

The Waterbury eight-day clock ticks unperturbed. Irene huddles close to the lamp and leafs through old issues of *Architectural Digest*. Grandma pulls out a pack of playing cards and deals herself a hand of solitaire. "Shame we don't have a Ouija board," she muses. "This would be a heck of a night for it."

Instantly, I imagine all the ghosts circling round the house: Emma, Teddy, Grandpa, the Robies, old Captain Barrow. *Yeah, right,* I think to myself.

"What would you ask the spirits, Maggie?" Irene wonders. I'd kick her if she were close enough.

Grandma looks surprised at the question. "Why, who killed Emma, of course."

Irene's eyebrows go up. "What makes you think she was killed?"

"Don't be daft, Irene. I saw that fella hanging round her house that day."

Now we are both staring at her. "You saw someone at Emma's house?" I ask.

"Sure. He was skulking around the driveway."

"Did you see his face?"

She looks at me as if I'm a born fool. "Well, of course I did, do you think I'm blind or something? Dark hair, gray at the temples, kinda handsome. Looked very posh. Big fancy black car, too."

"A Mercedes," I say, almost to myself.

"I guess so. Why, do you know it?"

Oh, yes. I know it. "Did you see him go into the house?"

Just at that moment the window shatters, and the wind slashes through the room like a scythe. The storm is all around us. "Get the bookcase!" Irene screams. It's on the same wall as the window, and about the same height. "Help me," I say, and together, heaving and grunting, we push it over the aperture. The room quiets to a low howl. I relight the lamp.

Grandma's cards have scattered to the floor. She mutters, gathers them up, begins laying them out again. "Grandma!" I call to her. "Did you see the man go into the house?"

She looks up at me blankly. "What man?"

Irene gives a derisive hoot.

"What man?" Grandma repeats. "What house?"

The storm answers the question for her, attacking the house with a fresh burst of vigor and renewed cries. "That's the dead," Grandma says matter-of-factly.

We both look at her. "What are you talking about, Maggie?" Irene demands.

"My momma always said that a storm happens when the world of the dead gets too close to that of the living. The air pulls things down from the sky, and up from the sea. Everything is upside-down. Just at the spot where the wind touches, if you look hard enough into it, you can see the other side. And they can see you."

"Your momma had a morbid imagination, Mags."

Grandma shrugs. "Maybe so. But that don't make it any less true. You hear it? That's the sound they make when they're trying to cross back again."

"Who?" I ask.

"The ones that didn't quite make it. Sometimes you get halfway over and then just…stop. Nobody knows why. You're not in one place or the other. Like poor old Captain Barrow. Others have made it through, but wish they hadn't. It's not what they expected. So they're trying to get back also. And then there's the ones that left too much behind…"

Anywhere else such a speech would sound mawkish, but not here. Little Compton has always been not quite where it should be, a place suspended between sea and sky and land, never entirely one element or another. Should it be so surprising if it creases the envelope of the netherworld?

But Irene is a strict Presbyterian. "You shouldn't say such things," she chides. "The dead are dead, and very happy in paradise." She purses her lips.

Grandma's snort is eloquent, but she says nothing more. Her point has been made. She lays out her cards, turning them over one at a time. Softly she begins to hum to herself, then sing. The song is an old one; I remember her singing it to me as a lullaby:

A girl upon the shore did ask a favor of the Sea,
"Return my blue-eyed sailor boy safely back to me!
"Forgive me if I ask too much, I will not ask for more,
"But I shall weep until he sleeps safe upon the shore."

Irene looks up from her magazines. Her face is suffused with pity. She takes a breath to join in her own quavering alto, but just then a chink of light above the cabinet turns pale blue, then gold. Suddenly, impossibly, a ray shoots in with the intensity of a laser beam. It strikes Aunt Irene right between the eyes. "Gracious, me!"

"It's over!" I cry, delighted.

Grandma remains oblivious, eyes closed, her face rapt with the story. Irene and I are both giddy with relief. "Well," Irene says, "that wasn't so bad, was it?"

"Don't count your chickens yet," Grandma grumbles. She has not moved from the desk. Slowly, methodically, she lays down another card.

"Oh, Mags, don't be such a grouch!"

Grandma shrugs again. "Go see for yourself."

We take her at her word. The kitchen door hangs off its hinges, and the room is filled with golden light. Outside a foot of snow blankets the yard. It gleams with unnatural brightness. "My God," Irene whispers, "it's beautiful."

It is, but an odd kind of beauty, to be sure. Colors are inverted and strange: yellow sky, brown sea, and above our heads a perfectly round aperture in the black clouds through which an arc of brilliant sunshine streams down to Earth, benign and forgiving. It reminds me of those old medieval paintings of the Last Judgment. "It's the eye!" Grandma tells us. "It'll pass over for just a moment."

"Then what?" I ask, fearing the answer.

She shrugs. "More of the same." Then she takes a breath and sings softly to herself:

As though the Sea did hear her plea a vision did appear,
The drifting tip of some wrecked ship came floating ever near.
A figure there did cling to it approaching more and more,
As if to ride on some strange tide safe upon the shore.

The shingles on the house glimmer with iridescent frost like fish scales. "Well, I'm going to enjoy it while I can," Aunt Irene declares. She galumphs into the snow and throws up a handful into the air. Each crystal catches the light and twinkles, like tiny fireworks. Irene is enchanted. "Wonderful! Wonderful!"

"You look like a fool," Grandma calls from the porch. She crosses her arms.

"I feel like a girl! Come on, Mags, have a snowball fight with me!"

"Don't be an ass."

"David?" Before I can answer, I get a faceful. Even Grandma laughs.

"Oh, you're gonna pay…"

"Come get me!"

All mad together, we dance around each other like duelists. Irene's girth should make her an easy target, but she moves with surprising grace. Another ball swipes my cheek. I dodge behind one of the bushes and fire back with three well-placed rounds, but the voice that cries out is surprisingly deep.

I look up. Irene is standing in the driveway with her arms akimbo, laughing. Grandma tosses down a dishtowel to Billy Dyer, who wipes the snow from his reddened face. "I came to see how you all were doing."

"As you can see," Irene tells him, "we are bewitched. Want some coffee?"

"Yeah that'd be nice, if there's time. Gotta get back to the station before it hits again. I thought maybe you'd want to come with me?"

The police station was once the colonial armory, made of fieldstone and designed to withstand everything from a hurricane to a French invasion, so his offer is not idle. Yet I can't help but notice he keeps his eyes turned everywhere except at me. Right now his gaze is fixed on a spot just above Irene's left ear. She looks back quizzically. "That's sweet of you. Do all the old ladies in Little Compton get this kinda service?"

He grins. "Only my favorites." Still he won't look at me.

"Guess we can't say no then. Can we, David?"

"How's Debbie?" I ask him roughly.

His answer is a quintessential New England shrug, eyes downcast. "Gone to her folks up in Central Falls."

"She'll be safer there," Irene says approvingly.

"Yeah. I guess." Finally he looks up at me. "What's it to you?"

There's really no answer to that question, but mercifully Grandma interrupts. "Who's that?" she demands, pointing towards the sea.

Irene doesn't bother to turn around. "There's nothing out there, Mags."

"Don't give me that. I can see well enough for myself. Someone's missing a crewmate."

Irene sighs. "All the boats are in harbor now. Right, Billy?"

"Absolutely."

But Grandma's vantage is better than ours, still on the porch with her hand outstretched, pointing. "It's there, I tell you. Look for yourselves."

Sighing, Irene turns around. We all see it at the same time: a white something bobbing like a buoy between the rollers, only a few hundred yards from shore. "Could be a piece broke off a trawler," Billy says dismissively, "Or a lawn chair even."

"Do lawn chairs wave?" Grandma demands.

I see it too. A hand outstretched, disappearing for a moment under a fresh burst of foam, rising again.

"Oh, my God," Irene breathes, "It's a man."

"Son of a *bitch*!" cries Billy.

"Come on!" It's my own voice that answers him, and my legs that are hurtling down the rocky path towards the beach. Grandma calls out something, but whether in protest or exhortation I couldn't say. Billy struggles behind me; I can hear him panting, cursing as he trips over the stones. But I've been down this path a thousand times before. In no time at all I'm on the beach, still carpeted with fresh snow. From here the waves look enormous, great rollers forming whitecaps at their heads and crashing onto the surf with the sound of a thousand drums all beating together. Billy is shouting something, but the roar is too great. I shrug off my coat, kick off my shoes and throw myself into the breaking sea, just like it was a hot Sunday in July.

At some point hot and cold come together, and the sensation is neither one nor the other. The body sends signals of pain, but the brain cannot understand what it is experiencing. I feel as though I am running headlong into a solid wall, which instead of shattering, enters me instead, until I become part of it, a frozen piece of cinderblock in a stone monolith. I am not cold, no, because there is nothing left of me to feel anything. Yet my arms and legs still move of their own accord. I'm swimming, one hand over another, an automaton winding down its spring. The drowning man is closer now. His head breaks the surface, arm outstretched. He is turned away from me, so all I can see of him is a dense mat of black hair and a white shirt plastered against his back. "Swim towards me!" I call out. But if he hears he makes no sign.

The sea has set itself against my struggles, slapping me back again and again. Now suddenly it changes its mind, and the surge lifts me up until I am staring right down at the figure in the white shirt. We are side by side, struggling together. "Come on," I urge him, "Take my hand!"

But there is no acknowledgment. He still has not turned around. "Hey! You! A little help here?"

The current pulls us into each other's arms, and for a moment we are caught in a *pas de deux*, his unyielding body pressed against mine. The flesh is rigid as marble, and just as cold. Now, at last, he turns. Black hair gone white at the temples. A face that is not a face but a mass of gray putty gone soft over bones. Dark, empty sockets ringed with blood. The mouth is gaping. Water rushes in, rushes out. Black lips, seaweed snarled among the teeth. Marcus Rhinegold is laughing. *"I'm so glad I met you David. I hope we'll be spending a lot more time together."*

The eye passes over. The sky turns black above our heads. I know what must happen now. This is the spot where the wind touches, and Marcus has come to drag me to the other side.

Chapter Thirteen

Carols playing somewhere, the sound of bells. It must be Christmas morning. They're ringing the chimes at the First Congregational. Downstairs, Grandma is laying out the plates for breakfast. I can hear the clink of china, the television nattering in the background. Fred pours a bowl of Fruity Pebbles for Santa. Barney comes down the chimney to steal them. "*Ho, Ho, Ho, I'm hu-hu-hungry!*" The Sarahs will be here soon. Grandma will serve them stollen bread and anise drops, strong black coffee with lots of sugar. There will be a fire with pinecones dipped in Borax that light up in ghostly colored flares like the Northern Lights.

I drift along in that pleasant, warm place that is somewhere between sleep and wakefulness. There's no hurry; they'll wait for me. I shift a bit under the covers, exploring the edge of the bed with my big toe, open one eye slowly. The window is framed with frost. It's still snowing. A garland of lights flashes against the pane in twinkling orbs of yellow, blue, red, green. One bulb has worn thin, brighter than the rest, a brilliant white. It flares and disappears, flares and disappears. A warning. Shoal water near.

I writhe a bit in the bedclothes, which constrict like a python lazily contorting itself around a field mouse. But snakes are dry, everyone knows that. These coils are wet and clinging. I want to cry out, but when I open my mouth the sodden mass rushes down my throat. I'm choking, gasping, drowning in linen. Then darkness, endless and silent, the bottom of the sea where light can never reach. I'm being dragged, chained to a dead man. I have only one last lungful of air. "*Grandma!*"

"Quiet now, honey."

A hand, cool and dry, brushes my forehead. It twitches the sheet up over my shoulder and pats it smooth. The storm passes over, and the coils unclench.

"It was Marcus…"

"Don't worry about that now."

"He's dead! You've got to tell them…we were wrong. Marcus Rhinegold is dead."

"They already know. Lie still, baby."

The room takes shape around us. It is not morning but midday, and brassy winter sunlight streams through the windows. Someone has hung my clothes on the radiator to dry. My shoes are tucked neatly under the rocking chair, and a fresh pair of pajamas lies folded on the seat. Aunt Emma stands next to it, hands on her hips, looking down at me with a quizzical expression. It is absolutely her. Not a mirage, or a memory. Her glasses are perched on the end of her nose, connected with a long chain to her collar. She is wearing the old Eastern Star pin she always wore, a bit tarnished around the edges, and gray flannels. So that's it, I think, the answer to the mystery. She didn't die after all.

There is so much I want to ask her. But my mouth is dry. She helps me take a drink of water from a glass on the nightstand. "Is it really Christmas?" I ask.

She chuckles softly. "Not quite yet. Rest now, somebody'll be in to check on you soon."

I can hear the rustle of fabric as she moves across the room. In a moment she'll be gone, and I'll be no wiser than before. "Please don't go!" I cry, panicked. "If you go it won't be real anymore."

She pauses with her hand on the door handle, but her voice is already distant. "You'll be all right now. You are a sweet boy, David. I'm proud of you."

The door clicks shut behind her.

• • ● • •

When I open my eyes a second time, the chair has moved to the foot of my bed, and Billy Dyer is in it. His head is tilted back and a thin line of drool trickles down his chin. He looks as though he hasn't shaved in days. His face is pale and haggard. A uniform coat lies across his knees like a blanket. Oh, God, I think, someone else is gone. Emma is back and someone is gone. The storm has rent a seam between the living and dead. "Billy?" I croak, worried. "What is it? What happened?"

He snorts, opens his eyes. The color rushes back into his cheeks and he grins disarmingly. "Hey! You're awake!"

"Of course I'm awake. I was awake before. What's going on? What's wrong?"

"Nothing at all. Everything is great, just great." On an impulse he takes my hand. His own is damp with sweat. "You're back, so everything is fine!"

"Back?" I ponder this for a moment. But my brain feels like it's still swimming around in open sea. "Where did I go?"

He shakes his head wonderingly. "We didn't know if you were going to make it. You were totally blue when they brought you in. The doctors said it could go either way."

"Was I out for a while?"

Billy's smile fades a bit. "A little while."

Aunt Irene appears as if from nowhere, wrapped in a fuzzy orange shawl and sipping something from a styrofoam cup.

"Where's Emma?" I ask. They both look puzzled, and worried. "She was just here," I insist. "They must have gotten it wrong. She didn't die at all, Marcus did. If one did then the other couldn't have, don't you see?" I'm speaking perfectly clearly, but Billy stares at me like he doesn't understand.

"It'll be okay," he consoles. "I'm gonna get a doctor in here to have a look at you."

"Is Renzi here already? What, is he downstairs with Grandma?"

Irene shakes his head. "Your Grandma's back home, David. Don't worry. Connie's sitting with her."

"Home?" I open my eyes a bit wider. The sunlight isn't sunlight at all, but the harsh glare of fluorescents. It bounces off the white plastic console, the aluminum rails of my hospital bed. There are tubes snaking in and out of the bedspread; some of them are attached to me. "Wow," I say wonderingly. "How long has this been going on?"

Billy's gaze is almost pitying. "They brought you in about six days ago. Severe shock and hypothermia."

"Have you been here all this time?"

"We took turns. Me, Constance, and Irene. One of us sat with Maggie and another with you. I've been coming over between shifts."

I look at the two of them and feel the prick of traitorous tears. "Thank you."

"Aww, honey," Irene says, waving an arm awkwardly. She turns her face away towards the door. "I'm gonna get myself a sandwich from the cafeteria. I'll bring you back something." She leaves in confusion.

"Thank *you*," I repeat, taking Billy's hand again and squeezing it.

He looks down at our hands for a moment, then pulls his slowly away.

"Don't mention it. You're an important witness. I wanted to make sure I got your testimony as soon as you woke up. And you were talking a lot in your sleep."

"Did I say anything useful?"

"Nothing we could understand. It was pretty wild, though. Did you have nightmares?"

"Only at first. After that I dreamed of Christmas. It was actually quite pleasant. You must have kept a good vigil."

Billy's Irish blood tells on his face. He flames with embarrassment. "Oh, hell."

"What does Debbie think of you spending all your time here?" I meant it lightly, but there's still seawater sloshing around in my brain and takes a moment to realize Billy is staring at the bedclothes, silent, grim. "Oh, shit," I breathe. "I'm sorry. I didn't mean anything by it."

"S'okay." His shoulders lift slightly, then droop even lower than before.

"Want to tell me?" I ask gently.

"Nothing to tell. And you're sick."

I try to ignore the sharp edge on that word, and press again. "I'm a good listener, Billy. In fact, as long as I'm laid up here with no books or magazines or cable, I'm the best listener there is. Go for it."

"She left me. Or I left her. Either way, she's back with her folks in Central Falls."

This news fights its way through a muzzy cocoon of Vicodin and other medications, so for a moment I'm not sure whether to smile or shake my head. Finally I manage to look grave. "I'm so sorry." I hope it sounds sincere.

He takes a sip from the coffee in his lap, pushes out his cheeks like a squirrel storing nuts, until the coffee reaches a more temperate heat. I recognize the gesture; he always did it when he was contemplating something distasteful. But right now I don't know if the distasteful object is me, Debbie Antonelli, or himself. "I know you never liked her. But you need to understand. It was a rough time after you... left. The boys were ragging on me pretty bad. Saying what kind of a man I was if my woman wasn't even a woman at all..." He chokes, embarrassed.

"Go on."

"That was when Debbie started coming around. She stood up to them, all those guys. Said I was as much a man as they were, and she knew it. Well, after that I guess I kinda owed her something. She was really sweet. Came over all the time, cheering me up, taking me out, bringing dinner and eating it with me. I was grateful."

So grateful that when Debbie laid out the big seduction scene you went right along, just to prove you were as much a man as she expected. Oh, my poor Billy, what you don't know about women! "Of course you were," I say encouragingly.

"We dated for a while. On and off. I was never all that into her, if you want the truth, but—she was around. It wasn't going anywhere, though, and by last summer I'd had enough. Then she got pregnant. I don't know how, she said she was on the pill, but whatever. I guess these things happen."

"If you make them happen," I whisper.

"What was that? Did you say something? Anyway, she was gonna have a kid, and her parents are Catholic. Hell, *my* parents are Catholic. And it wasn't like you were coming back."

"Not like you remembered, anyway."

"No. I mean, yes. But then you *did* come back. And I

thought it was okay, I'd just keep my distance. Then this fucking case..."

A convenient excuse, I think. But didn't I look forward to those conversations too? Didn't I call him in the middle of the night, bursting with news of Marcus Rhinegold? Didn't I know Debbie would be right there next to him?

Of course I did.

"She called me a fag." He takes a deep breath, lets it out in a long sigh. "Right in front of my folks. My mother. My father. Can you imagine?"

Easily, but I shake my head in sympathy. "Why would she do such a thing?"

"We had them over for dinner. Dad wanted to talk about the Rhinegold case. All the details. You came up. Dad brought you up. I tried changing the subject, but he brought you up again," Billy says, making me sound like something his father expectorated onto his plate. "Debbie was getting steamed, but Dad didn't seem to notice."

William Dyer, Senior, I recall, had never liked Debbie much.

"So you told him," I press.

"Yeah. Then Debbie just exploded. Like, all over the place. Threw a plate of calamari at the wall and called me every name you can think of. Including that one. Then she stormed out. Maybe she figured I'd call her, come around her parents' place like some lovesick kid, try to win her back. Well, fuck her."

There are so many conflicting emotions in my head right now that I'm afraid to open my mouth, lest the wrong one escape. "Billy, I'm so sorry," I repeat. And I am, I really am.

That shrug again. The quintessential New England gesture, meaning all things and nothing. I put my hand on his to hold him fast. There are so many sparks flying it's a wonder the oxygen in the room doesn't ignite. "Billy," I say slowly, "why are you telling me this?"

"You asked."

"Sure, but..." These may be the most important words I'll ever say, and I'm choosing each one. "I've looked like this a long time. Even when I was calling myself Rosalie. And you were with me then. So when Debbie called you... that name...was there any part of you that wondered if you might be, y'know...?"

He looks up from his lap. There is a whiteness around his lips that was not there before. "Right," he says, but not in answer. His eyes are hard. "I gotta get back to work."

"Billy..."

"I'll let Irene know. She'll be here in a minute."

He tries to slam the door but the padded hinge defeats him, and it closes with a soft apologetic click.

• ● ⬤ ● •

The terrible thing about hospitals is how much time they offer to revisit past sins. I spend the next four unrelieved hours replaying that last conversation in my mind, deaf to Irene's attempts to interest me in raspberry jello, pictures of her nieces, or *All My Children*. Finally she gives up and leaves, and I am triumphant in my misery. At nine-thirty the duty nurse turns off the lights. Now it's just me, and the voice that I've been trying to ignore all day.

This is what I should have said. *Billy, do you remember our junior prom? That's when I decided to put on the damned dress. Grandma talked me into it for three solid hours, and once I felt that gauzy fabric falling over my shoulders, I knew it was wrong, but it was too late. She dragged out a makeup case as big as a toolbox and went to work on my face. Rouge, powder, eyeliner, dark red lipstick, each layered over the last like a kabuki mask. Finally she stood me in front of a mirror and breathed, "Oh, honey, how beautiful you are."*

The dress was a sickly shade of peach, too much like skin, that made my reddened arms and scrawny neck look even blotchier. I hated it, her, Little Compton, and everything else. But myself most of all.

You always claim you were my date that night, but you don't remember. You were with Debbie. She came in on your arm like the prizewinner at a state fair, beaming and waving and blowing kisses to everyone. And I was just standing there, near the fold-up tables with Ritz crackers and Cheez Whiz, waiting to go home. The gym was dark and claustrophobic, with a strobe light mounted on the ceiling. They didn't even bother to take down the rings or parallel bars. You were practically at my elbow by the time you realized who I was. I knew what you were thinking. We'd been best friends since preschool, but now it was as if I had betrayed you somehow, gone over to the other side and left you behind. I wanted to tell you I was sorry. I wanted to say, "This isn't me. It's just some stupid thing they make me wear. You know me." I would have said that, all of it, but you got there first.

"Wow, you look gorgeous."

Then I knew I could never go back. The rayon fused to my skin like an exoskeleton. It didn't matter if I wore that dress or overalls or anything else, even if I went butt-naked down the street. You would never see me any other way than how I looked that night, and neither would anyone else. I felt like the universe had conspired against me in some cosmic joke, split me down the middle and given me a heart and brain that went in one direction and a body that went in another. But you couldn't see inside, underneath the makeup and cloth and skin. So to this day, Billy, I don't know who it was you fell in love with: the me you saw, or the me you knew before. Because you never knew, and I could never tell you, that they were two completely different people.

I'm sorry. I should've told you then, but the truth is, I hardly knew myself. Maybe I didn't know you, either. Maybe we both stared at the other and saw the thing we thought we were supposed to have, rather than what we wanted. But that's no excuse. Not then, not now.

I should have let you go.

•●●●•

In the morning, a miracle. Billy is here. He's not smiling, and the stubble under his chin is a bit longer, but he's here. And he's got a notebook out. "I need a statement," he says.

"Modern art has killed aesthetic appreciation of beauty."

One corner of his mouth twitches. "No fooling around. Let's start with you finding Marcus in the water." Billy walks me through that whole terrible afternoon, as if he had not seen it all for himself. When we reach the part where the corpse spun around, I can't quite repress a shudder. "What happened to him?" I ask. "Have they done an autopsy yet?"

Billy frowns, displeased at being forced to answer questions instead of ask them. "Sure," he nods, "but the body was in the water for a long time. Looks like something took a few bites out of him."

"Yeah," I say flatly, "I saw that."

"No mystery about how he died, though. Lungs were full of seawater. There's a knot the size of a golf ball on the back of his head, too, so the coroner figures he might have been hit with a piece of flying wreckage and gone into the sea unconscious. No signs of burning or other contusions on the skin, but the clothes have been practically flayed off.

Again, that could just be exposure. Tentative theory: the *Calliope* exploded and blew him clear."

"Exploded? Just because of that boom you heard?"

"No. Not just that. Things have been happening." He hitches himself forward. As long as we're not talking about his sexuality, he can afford to be forthcoming. "Remember that night the patrol boat said it thought it saw an orange flame out in the harbor? Well, we all sat around a table at the station, trying to figure out what it would take to blow up a boat the size of the *Calliope*. Best thing would be to fix something to the gas tanks, right? But you'd need an incendiary, something even more combustible to get the blaze going. Not so easy to find. Except, of course, fertilizer."

"Like Oklahoma City."

"Exactly. So we started calling around feed shops. And low and behold, we got us a receipt from Allies' Tack over in North Kingstown. She paid cash, of course, but they remembered the face once I showed them a picture. Even caught her on security cameras. Twenty-six bags of fresh manure. Said she was doing a whole yard."

"She? Wait...*Alicia*?"

"Yup."

"Wow," I breathe. "Have you talked to her yet?"

"No. The Staties had a go at her after Marcus disappeared, of course, and they've been up to Fogland Point a few times since. It's their case, after all. I'm just the errand boy now."

I can't help but catch the note of bitterness, but my wheels are turning. The fever has burnt itself out, and now all I can think about is escape from this wretched linoleum cell. But I must move cautiously. "Mhmm," I say, casually, "I suppose, though, there can't be any rule *against* you paying her a visit. You could say you need to search the house."

He nods, distracted. "That's true enough. We just got

confirmation on the fertilizer purchase this morning. I'm still waiting on a warrant. The judge comes in at ten; should have it pretty soon after that."

"And if you go, and she happens to be there, you might ask a few questions…"

"Yeah, I guess."

"I wanna come!" I'm sitting upright in the bed like a kid on Christmas morning.

Billy jolts out of his reverie. "What? No! Don't be ridiculous. It's police business!"

"That's just the point. I know this woman. If you show up with your sirens and your badge, she'll clam up before you reach the porch. But if I come along it's more…social."

He is still incredulous. "She hates you, David. You told me so yourself."

"Only when she thought I fucked Marcus. I just wandered into their orbit. Imagine, she's been cooped up in that house for weeks now without a soul to talk to. Honestly she's probably dying for a good long chat." I'm completely making this up as I go, but it sounds plausible, no?

Billy shakes his head. "I don't think we can do things like that."

"*We*? What, you and the Staties? You're suddenly best buds now? It's their case, you said. Do you think they give a rat's ass what you do?"

Billy Dyer never liked getting his manhood jabbed, and I always knew just where to prod. But a decade is a decade, and his armor is thicker. He puts his palms on his knees and strives for an air of patience. "Even if that's true," he tells me reasonably, "there's gotta be rules about interrogating suspects with civilians present. It's just…not done."

"So what exactly was I doing up at the Armstrong house a few weeks ago? This is Little Compton, Billy. You couldn't even afford a squad car until last year. Think I don't remember that golf cart with the flashing lights on top?" He flinches; the golf cart is a sore point with him. I press home my advantage. "You didn't think I was too much of a civilian to go talk to Marcus for you. I was one of the last to see him alive, and the first to find his corpse. Not to mention poor Wally. I'm as much in this case as you are, and it's your fault."

"You're still sick," he says, grasping at his last defense.

"I'm being released today. In fact I was just about to start packing." Suiting action to the word, I pull myself out of bed and begin throwing random objects into my backpack. As if on cue the nurse arrives, scowling fiercely. She sees me out of bed, my white bottom gleaming like porcelain under the fluorescent lights as I struggle into my jeans. Hands on her hips, she fixes me in a there-will-be-no-breaking-the-rules glare. "Now, you're not going to be difficult, are you Miss Hazard…"

"*MISTER*." Amazingly, it is Billy that corrects her. His face is flushed. They stare at one another for a moment, and irrelevantly I think how much she, with her teased blond hair and pug-dog expression, reminds me of Debbie Antonelli. I'll bet she's a cousin. But something has snapped in Billy; maybe he sees the resemblance too. He turns to me. "Leave the rest of your stuff. I'll come for it later."

"Patients can only be discharged by the doctor on duty!" the nurse bleats.

"Official police business!" Chief Dyer roars back. "You get away from that door or I'll bring you in for unlawful obstruction of justice." When this seems to overwhelm her, Billy takes a menacing step forward. "Move your fat ass!"

The nurse jumps to one side, still holding her clipboard over her bosom like an inadequate shield. Her eyes are huge.

Gently, I take the clipboard from her trembling fingers. Sure enough, it gives statistics for "HAZARD, Rosalie." I black out the offending word and write *David* above it, adding *PhD* for good measure. "There," I say, patting her on the shoulder, "It's official. Rosalie Hazard was never here at all. And Dr. Hazard has discharged himself."

I can hear Billy chuckling in the hallway. I take his hand as we head for the door, and he lets me.

The drive up to the Armstrong house is long and lined with poplar trees. No one has swept up the leaves. The house looks much as it did when I saw it last, but even more desolate. "Are you sure she's home?" I ask.

Billy just points to the car in the driveway, a black Mercedes SLE that probably traveled in *Calliope's* hold, until ship and master disappeared.

Alicia—or Crystal—greets us at the door in a tattered pair of leggings and a purple sweatshirt with "YOLO" stenciled on the back. Her hair hangs damp around her shoulders, dark roots grown out beneath the blond, and her face is shiny without makeup. In her hand is a dirty mug half-filled with something I don't really believe is coffee. All in all, a far cry from the coiffed perfection of a few weeks before. When she sees me we both flinch.

"What the fuck do you want?"

"Mrs. Rhinegold?" Billy moves confidently into the space between us and pulls out his badge. "I'm Chief of Police William Dyer. I know you've talked with my colleagues already, but I was hoping I can ask you a few questions?"

"You're a cop? You don't look like a cop. And what did you bring him for?"

"Dr. Hazard is a very important witness. I just wanted to make sure both your stories correlate."

Alicia narrows her eyes. "Yeah. That's a great idea. You

might start by asking the good doctor here how he keeps happening on the scene when bodies turn up, like Angela fucking Lansbury. Want my opinion, he's got you all suckered."

"That's a very interesting theory," Billy agrees affably. "And let me add my condolences on the loss of your husband. It must be a terrible time for you. Grief, that is."

It is an overcast day in early December, but Alicia is squinting so much it could be a blinding August afternoon. "I'm devastated," she answers in a flat tone. "Anything else?"

"Just one little thing," I put in, countering her Angela Lansbury with Peter Falk, "How's your garden coming along?"

We both look over to the bare stretch of crab grass, already browned and covered with dead leaves. An overturned wheelbarrow adds to the effect. "Huh?"

"Better get a move on," I advise. "It'll be early frost any day now. Need a hand with the sod rolls?"

She crosses her arms. "Are you drunk or something?" That's pretty rich considering the sharp, pungent smells wafting our way.

Billy chimes in on cue. "It's such a nice yard, but it needs a bit of upkeep, doesn't it?" He looks around elaborately. "You considering any big landscaping projects?"

"Of course not. I hate this house. Always did. This was Marcus' little pet project, not mine."

"Huh." Billy strokes his chin thoughtfully. "You're gonna have a heck of a time getting rid of all that fertilizer then."

Now the silence is absolute. Alicia stares at us both. Her mouth is not actually open, but there is a slackness to her face that was not there a moment ago. It's as if the spool inside her has wound itself out. "Fuck it," she says finally. "You'd better come inside."

Billy and I follow her into the cavernous front hall. It is morning but the curtains are drawn and the lights switched off. Billy trips on the carpet edge and swears to himself.

"Couldn't pay the electric bill," Alicia calls over her shoulder. It is not an apology. "It's a bit brighter in the living room. Come on."

I make my way mostly by instinct. The living room is indeed brighter, since there are no curtains to cover the windows, and the floor is polished pine. There is no carpet, either, no pictures on the walls or books on the shelves, nothing on the fireplace mantle, save an empty Starbucks cup. A nubby blue sofa, two folding chairs, and a coffee table of indeterminate age huddle together in the center of the room and seem to apologize for their presence. "Sit," Alicia commands.

We each take a folding chair and Alicia spreads herself across the couch. There is a looseness to her movements, like an actor relaxing in her dressing room after a long performance. But her fingers drum a tattoo on the cushion. "So," she says, "the fertilizer. What's the big deal? Marcus had the landscapers coming later that week and needed it done. I did it for him. End of story."

"That was very helpful of you," says Billy.

She just shrugs.

"But you couldn't have had the chance to lay it down, all the same, right? I mean you'd need a contractor for that."

"No, I never had the chance."

"So it must be in the garage? I've got a warrant here," He makes a great business of searching through all his pockets before finally producing it. "Yup, here we go. Can you just show me the fertilizer? Then we'll be on our way."

Alicia hasn't moved, but her whole body tenses. "I don't think it's in the garage."

"No? Maybe the boathouse? Or did they just leave it in the yard?" Billy leans in, drops the polite mask. "Or did you tell the Allies' deliverymen to load it right into *Calliope's* hold? Kinda foolish, wasn't that? They remembered it at once. Why would anyone need twenty-six bags of fertilizer on a boat?"

Her face becomes even shinier. "Marcus said to put it there! I don't know why! That's what he said!"

"Oh, come on now," I interject. "You two were barely speaking the night I met you. I have a hard time imagining you doing his errands for him."

"What do *you* know about it?" she snarls.

"Quite a lot, actually. I know, for example, that the Molinari family wanted Marcus dead. And that you could have contacted them any time. Pretty simple, just one phone call—to Anthony, wasn't it?—and you're a very wealthy widow."

She pales at the name, but still manages to look incredulous. "That's what you think. Anthony wouldn't have wasted any time on me. I'd be gone as fast as Marcus."

Billy smiles gently. "That's not really true, though," he puts in. "You're very persuasive, Mrs. Rhinegold. You must have been, to get this far. You could easily have painted them a pretty picture: captive spouse, afraid for her life, loyal to them all along. Even if they didn't buy all of it, they'd be damn grateful to hear from you. Then they gave you your instructions: purchase the fertilizer, rig up some kind of explosive device, and make damn sure you were away when the fireworks started—"

"No!" Alicia swings her legs round and sits bolt upright. "That's horseshit! I never called them."

"Wifely fidelity?"

"They would have killed us both!"

"Okay, okay," Billy holds up his hands. "Let's say you're right. It doesn't change anything. You still wanted out from this life, this marriage. You didn't need the Molinaris to tell you how to blow up something with fertilizer. You just needed Google."

"I never—"

"Your husband is dead, Mrs. Rhinegold. The contusions on his body suggest he was blown clear of *Calliope* when she exploded. We know that much; it's only a matter of time before we find the wreckage. We also know that the same day he disappeared you ordered twenty-six bags of highly combustible fertilizer loaded right onto the boat. If you can't explain these facts to me, you'll very likely have to explain them to a jury."

Alicia is on her feet, furious. "I've had enough! I know my rights! You get the fuck out of here!"

"You can certainly refuse to answer but you can't really make us leave, Mrs. Rhinegold."

Things have reached an impasse. Alicia is shaken but adamant; Billy is cool, but not hopeful. "Crystal," I say softly, hoping her real name will reach past her defenses, "this isn't helping either of us. Let's just leave the fertilizer for a moment, okay? Did you know Marcus was actually Kevin Johnson?"

"Who?" she answers blankly.

"Never mind. You knew him as Kevin Wales, I suppose?"

Slightly mollified, she sits again. "Yeah. That's what he called himself. He was real wire, back then. Lots of fun. I liked him a lot."

"Did you know about his other…interests?"

Her mouth hardens, and I brace myself for a torrent of obscenity. Instead she just shrugs. "Not at first. He didn't come on like that. You know, faggy. But he was different than the other guys round the club. Quieter. Like he was thinking things out. Most of these goombahs, they come at you with big smiles and billfolds flashing, but not him. I actually went after *him*, can you believe it?" She shakes her damp curls. "What a fucking moron. I should've seen he was just scoping us out. Didn't matter which he ended up with; he took more time choosing a car than he did marrying me. But what did I care? He was on the way up, anybody could see it. I've seen marriage proposals come from three whisky doubles and a lap dance—why should mine be any less successful?"

"But then you found out about his interest in men," Billy puts in, rather bluntly.

"No. That came later. It wasn't like he didn't know how to do the job, believe me. We went at it pretty regular at first. Then it tapered off. But I figured he was just stressed. He was stressed. I tried. I actually think I loved him, then. So much, that when he came home one day, handed me a plane ticket and told me to pack whatever I needed for the rest of my life, I didn't hesitate. I followed him like a good little wifey."

"Why should he take you at all?" I wondered. "If the marriage was just a front for the Molinaris, why not just leave you with the rest of his abandoned identity?"

"Hey, fuck you!" Alicia shouts, all her rage returning at once. "Who do you think you are? Marcus might not have been the man I thought he was, but our marriage wasn't just a sham. I liked him. And I think—I know—he liked me."

"There's another reason," Billy adds. "From all I've been able to understand about him, Marcus Rhinegold was almost preternaturally careful. He planned his escape from the Molinaris meticulously; the FBI said it was the best they'd ever seen. He couldn't risk leaving Alicia—Crystal—behind, because if he did, the Molinaris would know what he was up to instantly. Not to mention she would have given them enough information to track Marcus down themselves. By taking her, he bought himself some time, and also a possible return ticket. If things went wrong, he could just fly home with her and say they were on vacation or something. She was his insurance policy."

Alicia considers this. "Yeah, that does sound like him," she admits. "He was a great one for plans. But even if that was part of it, it wasn't all. I knew him, don't forget, better than anyone. At bottom, he was a very lonely man."

"Yes," I say, "he was."

"And you know, for a while it was actually fun. We went to Paris, Biarritz, Monte Carlo, then picked up *Calliope* in Villefranche and bounced around the Med. I liked the life. It seemed almost romantic, like some movie: two exiles on the run from the mob. It was romantic, all right, but I wasn't the lead. First he started working his way through the crew: stewards, deckhands, even some engineer from Porto they brought on to fix the diesels. He had this big scene laid out for them. Drinks on the aft deck, lots of fancy talk, more drinks, then a quick tussle in one of the empty cabins. With me just a few feet aft, snoring away. Well, it didn't take that long to find out. Then, finally, I knew what my marriage was. I knew what my life had become."

Alicia looks down into her half-empty cup, considers it for a moment, puts it to her lips.

"You must have hated him," I say quietly.

"Oh, sure," she agrees. "At first. I hated him like poison. But it's not so easy to keep hating someone you see every day, all day. Not unless he's a crud or a psychopath, and Marcus wasn't either of those. I'll say that much. He was decent, in his way, and I don't think he ever meant me harm."

"You sounded pretty bitter that night."

"Of course I was. You would be, too. But don't read so much into it. I was bored, frustrated, angry. At least when we were in Europe we kept moving—but now, suddenly, we were stuck here. Stuck with me playing the role of Lady Di or some crap, and Marcus off doing little errands in the town. I thought I'd go shithouse crazy."

"Errands?" Billy interrupts, looking interested. "What sort of errands?"

Alicia shrugs again. "Some family stuff," she says dismissively. "That's why we came here in the first place. He had a relative somewhere. Thought she might be able to help him. With what, I don't know. Maybe he didn't either. By that point he was just exhausted. Sometimes I think he just wanted to rebuild that big ugly house as a mausoleum: finish it, furnish it, then blow his brains out right in the living room. He liked grand gestures."

There is a quiet kind of sadness to her now, very different from the brittle anger before. I feel like I am seeing her for the first time: not a murderous spouse, or a greedy one, but a straightforward and rather stupid woman who gave her life to a man she couldn't possibly understand. "Crystal," I say earnestly, leaning toward her, "who do you think killed Marcus?"

Her eyes widen, as if I've asked her to explain the Holy Trinity or the color mauve. She considers the question for almost a minute. Finally her lips part.

"All along, I figured—"

The doorbell trills in some dark corner of the house. With a curse Alicia stands, tripping over the table leg. "Wait here," she orders, and disappears down the hall. Billy and I exchange a look.

"This," he says, "is the moment when we hear a long drawn-out scream and a dull thump in the front hall."

At any event, we don't hear either. Instead there is the sound of muted conversation, earnest but normal, moving this way. The door opens and Alicia returns, flanked by two men in dark gray suits. Both have blond hair cut ruthlessly short and the lithe athletic step of all professional dancers and policemen. The shorter of the two pushes forward and presents his badge for inspection. "Agent Philip Slemp, FBI," he says, with a slightly Southern drawl. "This is my partner, Agent Watters. You must be Chief Dyer."

"Yup," says Billy, looking them both up and down. "What can I do for you?"

"Does Providence know you've been interrogating this witness?" Watters demands. His voice is all New Jersey tough.

"Maybe, maybe not," Billy answers coolly. "What business is it of yours?"

"Plenty," Watters retorts. "Mrs. Rhinegold is under the protection of the United States government. You had no right to question her without authorization."

"Who the hell are you to—"

"Please, Chief Dyer," Slemp interjects, raising a placatory hand. "We are all on the same side. But unfortunately Mrs. Rhinegold has been compromised. The television news broadcast her whereabouts, so now we must assume the Molinari family are aware as well. We need to protect our witness."

There is something proprietary in that statement. Billy notices as well. "You're taking her?"

"To a secure location, yes. If you wish to interview her again, and if your superiors allow it—" Agent Slemp raises his eyebrows delicately, "you may of course do so. Under our supervision."

"Do I really need to remind you," Billy says, coldly

furious, "that this is a homicide? Possibly even a triple homicide. Your interest in Marcus Rhinegold is of considerably less value than ours."

Agent Slemp actually smiles. "That may be so, Chief, but it would really be a matter for Providence, wouldn't it?" From his tone it's unclear whether he means the city or the deity.

"I don't wanna go." Alicia's voice is like that of a small child's, frightened and obstinate. She clutches herself with both arms.

"You have to, Mrs. Rhinegold," Slemp answers, turning to her. "You are not safe here. It's a very nice house, I promise."

"It's got a pool," Agent Watters interjects.

"Billy," I whisper, "is there nothing you can do? She looks terrified."

He is grim but shakes his head. "She's their witness," he whispers back. "She and Marcus were in the protection program. Technically they can move her as often as they want. The Staties will know where she is, at least."

"That's right, Mrs. Rhinegold," Slemp encourages her, "go put a suitcase together. We'll wait."

There are a few minutes of awkward silence while Alicia goes to gather her things. The FBI men stand off to one side and stare blankly at the walls, discouraging conversation. Billy punches furiously at his phone. "How the *fuck*," he growls, "are we supposed to investigate this case if our star witness ends up in Boise?"

"The Staties must have alerted the FBI about those fertilizer bags," I muse.

"Sure. And now the FBI wants her all to themselves. They don't give a shit if she killed Marcus Rhinegold. They don't care who killed him. They just don't want her talking to us."

I can't disagree, but moved by some obscure protective instinct, I don't want to leave, either. Alicia finally reappears with a pink backpack slung over one shoulder, like a travesty of a co-ed. "Okay, I'm ready."

"Great!" Watters exclaims. Slemp is already at the door.

"Well," Alicia says, looking at us, "bye, I guess."

Still confused and rather woebegone, she lets Watters guide her out to a waiting black Ford. Agent Slemp suddenly notices us again. "Here, Chief," he says, handing Billy his card, "we'll be in touch soon."

"Yes, we will," Billy concurs.

A moment later they are gone, tires crunching against the gravel. Billy and I stare at each other in the abandoned living room. "Now what?" I ask.

The warrant still dangles limply from Billy's hand. "Fucked if I know," he admits. "FBI wouldn't take her without letting the Staties know, so they must not care."

"I don't think she killed Marcus."

He raises an eyebrow. "Motive and opportunity, every time. Do you really believe she bought all that fertilizer because Marcus told her to?"

I've been thinking about that. "No, I don't believe her either. At the same time she seems more puzzled by Marcus' death than anything. What if she bought it intending to kill him, then changed her mind?"

"Oh, come on," snorts Billy. "What are the odds? One person plans to murder Rhinegold, then another steps in at the last moment? That sort of thing doesn't happen except in movies."

"I'm starting to think none of this is real. What now?"

Billy looks around the house, as if asking it."We could make a search, I guess. I had a look in here after Marcus disappeared, but the Staties yanked jurisdiction before I could see much."

This seems as good an idea as any. We take it room by room, turning over cushions and flipping through every book on the shelves. But it's poor sport. The house is nearly bare of furnishings—everything was on the *Calliope*. A sheaf of blueprints lies on the dining room table, held down with tacks. Marcus had ambitious plans for his new villa. The drafts show a long, low structure with curtains of glass that raise at each end like the wings of a bird taking flight. It's beautiful and sad. "What's going to happen to the Armstrong House now?" I ask.

"She'll sell it. All of Marcus' accounts were seized, and there's lawyers to pay. My guess is it'll go up for auction by the end of the month."

At least it won't be destroyed. Eventually we find ourselves on the upstairs balcony by the bedroom where Marcus made his ill-timed advances. I sit down on the cold marble floor, and Billy joins me. The sun is setting, throwing golden light on the bay.

"I keep thinking about that night," I admit. "What would have happened if I said yes? What did he want from me? Was it just sex, or companionship, or someone to listen to him? Would he have told me why he really came to Little Compton?"

"You talked to him for a while. Did he give any clues…I mean, how did he seem?"

"Horny." I thought for a moment. "No, not just that. Frustrated. And deeply, deeply unhappy. But at the same time there was a strange kind of hopefulness, like he believed things were going to get better and was irritated it was taking so long. I don't know, I could just be projecting onto him."

"Why?" Billy asks, leaning closer. "Is that how you feel?"

"I haven't been hopeful in a long time, Billy."

"Yeah, Irene told me about losing your job. I'm really sorry."

"It's not just that." How can I explain what I barely understand myself? "The whole time I was growing up, I only wanted one thing, and it was the thing I absolutely could not have. Constance and Irene think it's because my mom died at birth—that somehow if she'd lived I would've had a role model and not wanted to be a boy. But that's bullshit. I didn't want to be a boy. I'd have given my soul to not feel my skin crawl every time I put on a skirt. All I really wanted was to feel like I *belonged*. Imagine living with that, every day, and not being able to change it."

"I can't imagine," admits Billy.

"But then I left Little Compton, and started my transition. If life were a movie, it would have ended there. Getting out, being free, becoming my own person. But life keeps going. And what they don't tell you is this: every life, however long or short, ends in tragedy."

"That's dark."

"I can't help that. So I got the thing I always wanted. I became David. But even so, it still feels like I'm hiding. Every time I catch someone looking for the Adam's apple, or wrinkling their brow because my voice is too high, or trying to see if I've got boobs strapped in under my shirt, or a bulge in my crotch—you see, I still don't belong. I'm like that Aesop story about the bat. Neither bird nor beast. I can't cut off my wings, and I can't grow feathers. I'm fucked."

Billy looks at me for a moment. Suddenly, astonishingly, he begins to laugh.

"Oh, good," I say, affronted. "I'm glad I could brighten your day."

"I'm sorry! I'm really sorry! To be honest, I was just imagining you as a bat." The image is too much for him, and he doubles over, wheezing with mirth.

My leathery wings curl into fists. "Keep laughing and I'll punch you where it hurts. I know where they are."

"No...it's just..." He takes a breath, composes himself. "Can I ask you a question? Like a real question?"

"Sure."

"Are you attracted to guys or girls?"

My eyebrows shoot up. "Seriously? That's what you want to know?"

"For now, yeah."

I can't contain a sigh. "Sexuality doesn't work like that, Billy. I mean, not for everybody. I've had girlfriends and boyfriends, and dated them as both a man and a woman. If that makes sense."

"Not really. So you're...bi?"

"Stop trying to slap a label on it. It's not like I get up each day and match my sexual orientation with a pair of shoes. I was attracted to men when I was dating women, and vice versa. But that doesn't mean if I'm with a man I'm just marking time until the next switcheroo."

Billy frowns like he's piecing together a complicated algorithm. Finally he asks, "Why didn't you say any of this when you left me?"

That stops me cold. "I suppose," I answer slowly, "because I didn't think you'd understand."

"That's unfair."

"Is it? Maybe it is. I'd been lying to everyone for so long. The truth seemed...unexplainable."

"So instead you let me think I was part of that lie."

"No, Billy. Never that. I really did love you. If I didn't say it then, I'm saying it now."

He shakes his head sadly. "I wish you had trusted me. But I guess I can understand why you couldn't. Maybe I wasn't ready to hear it. David, do you think people can change...like, really change?"

"You're asking *me* that?"

Billy looks unaccountably embarrassed. "I never told you, but all those books you left behind at my place—do you remember?"

"I do."

"I read them. After you'd gone. All of them, can you believe it? Took forever. Can't remember most of it, if I'm being honest. But there was one poem that sounded like it was written by a sailor. You know: *There lies the port, the vessel puffs her sail: there gloom the dark broad seas…*"

"Tennyson!" I cry, surprised. "That's one of my favorites."

"It's about a king, right? But he doesn't really like being king. He wants to get back in his boat and start exploring again. Like, he's seen the world, but the more of it he sees the more he wants to see."

The lines come back at once. "*Yet all experience is an arch wherethro' gleams that untraveled world where margin fades, For ever and forever when I move.*"

"It always made me feel a little guilty, that part. I've never been much further than Boston. But I remember the rest, because once I read it, I knew that's what I should have said that night." He stares out through the French doors at the crimson sky folded over a darkening sea, points to the distant beacon of Sakonnet light and murmurs:

"The lights begin to twinkle from the rocks:
The long day wanes: the slow moon climbs: the deep
Moans round with many voices. Come, my friends,
'Tis not too late to seek a newer world.
Push off, and sitting well in order smite
The sounding furrows; for my purpose holds
To sail beyond the sunset, and the baths
Of all the western stars, until I die."

Billy's arms fold around me. He leans his face down. I turn mine up. Suddenly we are close, too close, and there is no stopping the collision. His lips are on mine and I'm thinking, *Wow, this is not like I remembered.* I wonder if he's thinking the same thing and, if so, if that's good or bad. But suddenly it doesn't matter anymore, because I can taste his tongue darting between my lips, coffee and beer and something else, something dark and warm like brandy. This time there is no surrender, no melting into a man's arms. I take his face in my hands and hold it, claim it. He understands. He doesn't want to win or conquer. We could be the first two people on Earth, or the last. Skin and bone and muscle and cartilage, hair and teeth and nail, covered with a few random bits of cloth. No titles or genders or assignations. Just two beings exploring each other, taking childish delight in each discovery. This takes some time.

When the camera pans back down we are both lying on Marcus' bed, naked, entwined in each other. "I have to believe," I say into Billy's ear, "that if Marcus haunts this place, he'd probably approve."

Billy chuckles. "He's jealous. So what happens now?"

"Dinner, movie, the usual things I guess."

"No, I mean…"

"I know what you mean." But the truth is, I don't have any answers either. Billy's phone trills and rescues us both. He rolls out of bed and rummages through the pile of clothes on the floor. "Chief Dyer," he answers, unconsciously straightening into something like a salute. "Yes… yes…what? What do you mean? Didn't you get my text? The FBI came just a few…" He looks at his phone, starts a little, "…about an hour ago. Of course I'm sure. Why…?" His voice trails off. The phone continues to nicker in his ear. Billy doesn't speak, just shakes his head slowly. He hangs up without a word. The black plastic dangles limp from his hand.

"What is it? What's happened?"

He looks down at me as if surprised to still find me there. "That was Providence. I texted them to find out where the FBI was taking Alicia. They said nobody told them they were taking her anywhere."

"Huh? How could that be?"

He shrugs. "Maybe they don't trust us. But it's still weird not to even let the Staties know."

More than weird; impossible. "Billy," I say slowly, "Do you still have that business card?"

He fishes in his pants pocket and retrieves a small square of paper. It looks official enough. Heavy cream-colored card stock with blue piping around the edge and the familiar crest with *Fidelity, Bravery, Integrity* emblazoned below. And a name: *Philip J. Slemp, Special Investigator.* The area code is District of Columbia.

"Dial it," I tell him.

Billy puts it on speaker. We both listen as the phone crackles, rings. I count six before a voice answers sharply:

"*Lucky Chen Restaurant! You want pick up or delivery? Hello? Hello?*"

Chapter Fourteen

Three weeks later, Alicia is still gone. Totally, completely, irrevocably gone. It's officially a missing persons case. "Because that sounds better than a body-at-the-bottom-of-the-bay case," Billy announces sourly.

These days are hard for him. He feels responsible for Alicia, and he's not alone. While there was no official censure from above, the fact that the Molinaris were able to kidnap her from right under his nose did not go unremarked. It was, they said in Providence, just the kind of thing a townie cop would do. He has not been removed from the case either, but that's because the case is considered closed. Alicia murdered Marcus to escape the living hell of their life; the Molinaris removed her to prevent any more details of that life from coming to the surface. Neat, easy, digestible.

"But wrong," Billy insists. "Wrong a dozen different ways. If she killed Marcus, why did she kill Wally? Or did she? And why hang around here waiting for the police to come? Why not kill him, grab a suitcase full of cash and run for Mexico?"

I've heard these objections before. Billy has talked of little else, and along with my newly acquired status of quasi-boyfriend, I am obliged to hear him out yet again.

"I know," I agree, for the fifth time. "But what can you do? He's gone, she's gone, the *Calliope* is gone, even the Molinaris are gone. What's left?"

What's left, I've tried to remind him, is the beginning of a very promising romance. His divorce is still ongoing—Debbie's fighting him for the house, the car, even his old LP collection—but we don't talk about that. Actually, we don't talk much at all. It's a companionable silence, the kind between two people who know each other well enough to enjoy the quiet. Sometimes we take his truck up to Fall River to watch the freighters come in and out, or across the Mount Hope Bridge to Newport for lobster dinner. On the afternoon of Christmas Eve, coming out of the Black Pearl, Billy hears himself called a faggot for the first time.

There are two of them, mid-thirties, bullet-headed with close-cropped hair and denim jackets. They don't shout. They just walk by and one turns to the other and says, "*Faggots*" in the same tone of voice he would use to point out an interesting bit of public sculpture. Billy is holding my hand; his fingers clench tight. "Ignore them," I whisper.

If he hears, he gives no sign. There is a hard gleam in his eye that makes his normally affable features cold as marble. For the first time since I've known him, he looks dangerous. He begins to follow. I twitter along behind, equal parts horrified and excited. I've been called faggot more times than I can count by a wide range of races, ages, genders, and socio-economic backgrounds. But one thing is certain: I never had anyone to share my outrage. The sensation is new and strangely pleasant. So it is ironic that while Billy is working himself up into a lather of righteousness, I'm drifting along in his wake in a happy daze. I have a boyfriend! Yay!

Billy tails them right to their car, a black Wrangler double-parked on America's Cup Boulevard with a Trump/Pence sticker on the bumper. Finally one bullet-head turns. There is a moment of genuine surprise, quickly followed by a reassuring appraisal. Billy is about five-eight, and slight. And there are two of them. "You want something, asshole?"

"Yeah, your taillight is out."

"Huh?"

Billy approaches the Jeep and considers it for a moment. His right foot shoots out and kicks in the light. It shatters into a dozen shards of red plastic. "That's a fifty-dollar fine."

"What the *fuck*, man?"

Now they're advancing on him, murderous. "You're gonna get it this time, pussy boy. You fucked with the wrong guys."

Billy smiles, takes a step back. "Did I? You sure about that?" He digs into his pocket and flashes his badge. "Tiverton police. How's your day so far?"

They stop, stare at him, at each other.

"Your car has Georgia plates. Y'all from Georgia? Welcome to Newport." He kicks in the other light. The two men jump a little, but seemed rooted in the ground. "You know," Billy goes on conversationally, "you really need to do some research on a place before you visit. Oh, and you're double-parked in a loading zone. That's another eighty dollars."

"You can't do that!"

"Sure I can. I can do this, too." From his back pocket he pulls out a taser wand. Both men know what it is. Now they are barely breathing. Billy taps it gently against his palm. "I can shove this thing up your ass and light you up like a Christmas tree. You want to call me a faggot again?"

"N…no."

"Are you sure? How 'bout my boyfriend here?" He jerks a thumb at me. "Got any fresh observations for him? Come on, you were so eloquent before."

"No, sir."

"Right. Well, if you say so. Here's your ticket." He pulls out his pad, scribbles something on it, hands it to one of them. "Merry Christmas."

The two troglodytes stare at him open mouthed. They haven't even gotten into their car. It's as if they've wandered into a dense forest and forgotten how to get home. Billy sketches a friendly wave and I do the same, much emboldened. But once we turn the corner I collapse into his arms.

"Oh, damn, are you okay?" He's holding me close, concerned. He takes my face in his hands. Only then does he realize I'm laughing hysterically.

"Yes," I say, still choking, "Better than okay. I just realized how much fun it is to date a cop!"

•●●●•

While I was in the hospital, Aunt Constance hired a nurse for Grandma, a sensible soul named Mariana Tipatuna whom Maggie immediately, inevitably, began calling Rosalie. I don't correct her. Mariana is Guatemalan and motherly, about fifty years old with grown children and an invalided husband in Central Falls. She moved into the guest room and visits her family on weekends. I come back from the adventure of the Black Pearl to a kitchen filled with the unfamiliar smells of achiote and coriander, and Grandma happily carving up plantains. "We're making bananas Foster!" she announces.

Mariana nods and smiles toothlessly. "Yes, yes, very good, Maggie! Slice them small, now!" She comes over to me and whispers, "It is *mole de platanos*. I make for my children all the time."

Mariana is short, even shorter than me, and almost spherical. Her hands are like paddles, and she plays marimba on old cassette tapes while she dusts and vacuums. "Is that Arthur Lyman?" Grandma would call from the other room. "That's Arthur Lyman. Mike and I saw his show at the Moana in Waikiki. Him and Martin Denny. Mike said he thought they were queers, but who cares? It was a good show. They let live birds fly around the stage." Mariana sways her hips in time to the music, unperturbed. Even the Hired Help seems cowed by her. Once while she was making *hilachas* the mixing bowl began whirring of its own accord, beating angrily against the table. Mariana turned round and bellowed, "*¡Eh, cerote, sho pizado!*" It went quiet at once. She shrugged and returned to peeling carrots, muttering, "*Pusa*. Don't make me bring in a priest."

Tonight is Christmas Eve, as I said, the real one this time. This is the night for which New England was made: candles glittering in windows, fields of bluish snow crackling underfoot, smell of woodsmoke in the air. Everything about a New England Christmas is traditional, from the carols to the ornaments (each with its own story, retold each year as it emerges from tissue paper), to Uncle Richard's plaid cardigan that Aunt Agnes only lets him wear this day, to overdone ham with the sad fringe of eight pineapple rings—no more, no less—to Lionel trains around the Christmas tree and the same stories told at dinner, again and again. We take comfort from these things. But sometimes they can also heighten the absence. When I wake tomorrow there will be no stockings on the hearth. Grandma will not be laying out plates in the dining room, nor Grandpa trundling back from the woodshed with a wheelbarrow full of firewood. The Laughing Sarahs will still come, as they always do, but be greeted with the smell of *gallo en chicha* and fried plantains. We will sit together around the dining table and reminisce about Christmases when we were whole, alive.

At six-thirty in the evening Aunt Irene's ancient Dodge rumbles into the driveway. Grandma is in winter tweeds with a cashmere shawl and a clutch of pearls at her throat. She pulls on gray doeskin gloves and adjusts a tam o'shanter that looks like a fluffy woolen bladder. I've long since given up trying to choose her clothes for her; I just want her to be warm. But Mariana is unexpectedly determined on this point. "Is Christmas Eve," she repeats. "She need look good for Jesus." Grandma, who tried to bite me the last time I dressed her, submits to her ministrations like a lamb. Sometimes I think she just does it to annoy me.

Mariana sees us off, leaving a plate of fresh *tamales colorados* on the kitchen table—traditional Christmas dinner in San Andres Itzapa, apparently—and waves good-bye before heading back over the Mount Hope Bridge to her waiting family. The trip from our house to the church is not long. Snowfall from the storm still lies heavy on the ground outside, covered with a fresh dusting from the night before. Little Compton looks like a postcard. Little knots of the faithful pick their way across slippery walks to the summoning bell of the First Congregational. Every church window gleams with electric candles, and open doors throw a pool of warm yellow light on the glittering pavement. Inside, the altar rail is wrapped in garland that perfumes the air with a sweet woodsy scent. Colored lights twinkle from the chandeliers. Pastor Paige waits in the vestibule, bestowing a smile on each of us in turn, but his eye is always on the door. There's a decent turnout of visitors on Christmas Eve—tourists or in-laws or those who have some dim memory of pageants and candle wax from their childhoods. Paige won't close the doors until ten minutes past the hour, just in case of late arrivals.

The service has been the same since I was a child. There

is comfort in that. A Bach introit is followed at once with a rousing chorus of "Oh Come All Ye Faithful"; then a quavering solo by Mrs. Elsie Featherstone (song of her own choosing, but usually "Once in Royal David's City"), then "Hark the Herald Angels Sing" (first and last verses only, thank you). Voices droning like bees in a hive. "*He was crucified for us under Pontius Pilate, and suffered, and was buried, and the third day he rose again, according to the Scriptures...*"

Change. Transformation. The very essence of our faith. Something in that, surely. Marcus and I were alike in one way at least. Both of us trying to break free from the chrysalis of our own bodies, our desires, our pasts. Perhaps that's what drew him to me, and I—though I'd be loathe to admit it—to him. Perhaps that's why he died.

But then we pass rapidly on. Pastor Paige delivers himself of a short message, allegedly on the coming of Christ but usually on the subject of Christmases celebrated by him and his dead, sainted first wife (while his second wife, Mildred, glowers at him from the front pew). "Joy to the World" is sung with the ebullience of convicts about to be released, a Doxology and collection follow in quick succession (Bach again, an air, for God loveth a cheerful giver), another reading from the Scripture, and finally it's time for the candlelight send-off. When I was little they still used real candles, with a paper tray around the bottom that never quite protected your hand from drippings. Now they're all electric, which is safer, but less inspirational. The church lights dim, the candles ignite, and we stand to sing "Silent Night." For that moment only, the ghosts of our Puritan forbears are satisfied.

In years past, Christmas Eve service would be followed by a caravan procession back to Grandma's for bundt cake and hot chocolate laced with brandy. The husbands would grow expansive, the Aunts keeping a watchful eye on them. Eventually they would sing carols, until Uncle Robert (Constance's third, and last) began substituting the lyrics with his own. These were considerably livelier than the originals, and you couldn't deny the man had a real flair for show tunes. Later, of course, we found out why.

For some reason I've never understood the evening always ended with Grandpa and Uncle Phil singing a song about dogs' assholes. Phil claimed he got it off some Brits from the America's Cup. He would finish his drink and intone mournfully, "*All the dogs once held a meeting, they came from near and far; Some came by train, some walked, and others came by car…*"

And Grandpa, wherever he was, whatever he was doing, would immediately join in: "*But before they got inside the hall and were allowed to take a look; They had to take their assholes off and hang them on a hook.*"

That part never made any sense. They took their assholes *off*? How? Why? So that, of course, one prankster dog could rush in and shout "FIRE!" whereupon all the dogs rushed to the coatroom, grabbed an asshole and slapped it on, hopelessly mixing them up in the process. "*That's the reason why,*" Uncle Phil concluded, "*a dog will leave a nice, fat bone; to sniff another asshole, 'cause he hopes to find his own!*"

Tonight Aunt Constance suggests drinks at the shop instead. Her own house is too small for entertaining, and Aunt Irene's is too far (by Little Compton standards), so the shop has become a kind of clubhouse. There's a decent-sized common room where the men once hung their fishing tackle and kept a foozball table and some playing cards. The Sarahs junked the table but kept the cards and tackle, adding a leather sofa and a few squashy, comfortable chairs. The room hasn't changed in years. Aunt Constance dispenses Old Fashioneds in chipped china mugs; Irene passes around a plate of fruitcake. Grandma is off in her own world, humming tunelessly, though I notice she makes short work of the fruitcake. Lately she has taken to watching television shows inside her head, and will occasionally laugh aloud or sigh in consternation at whatever scene plays before her. The other Sarahs move nervously. Conversation is halting, as it often is now. They don't want to talk about the past, and I don't want to talk about Marcus. We trade desultory bits of gossip that we already know, each of us wondering how long we need to keep this going before appearances are satisfied.

"Have another drink if you want," Aunt Constance says finally.

That's the signal the party's ended. It must be past midnight now, so I kiss each of them on the cheek and murmur, "Merry Christmas."

"Merry Christmas!" Grandma exclaims, delighted to know it's come around again.

"We'll see you in the morning," Irene tells her gently.

The phone in my pocket starts buzzing. It's Billy. Aunt Constance looks over my shoulder and raises an eyebrow. "Oh, shut up," I tell her, and answer, more nervously than I expected, "Hi?"

"Where are you? You're not at the house, I was just there. Where are you?"

Billy's voice sounds oddly strained. "I'm at Aunt Constance's shop down by the pier. What's up?"

"*I can be there in like five or so. Can you come outside?*"

"I'm with Grandma and the Aunts, Billy."

"*I know, I know. But it's important. Can you? Please?*"

Thoroughly mystified, I answer, "I guess so."

"*Thanks.*" He hangs up without another word.

The Aunts are still peering at me closely. Something in my expression has alerted them. "Everything okay?" Irene asks.

"Yeah. Billy's coming over. Wants to talk about something."

"Oho!" says Aunt Constance, smirking. Irene carves off another slice of fruitcake and hands it to me. "Never talk about serious stuff on an empty stomach, I always say," she confides with a wink.

It seems like only seconds before the headlights from Billy's truck flare against the shop windows. As I come outside I'm acutely aware that my sweater is emerald green with an embroidered cat wearing reindeer antlers, a gift from Aunt Irene and the least alluring garment in the Western Hemisphere.

"You rang?" I ask, heaving myself into the cab.

Billy's face is flushed and strangely excited. His eyes glitter in the green dashboard light. I wonder if he's been drinking. "That story about your old Uncle Sylvanus," he says without preamble. "The one your grandma told you. Tell it to me again."

"Huh?" I stare at him blankly. "What are you on about? It's Christmas Eve, for heaven's sake."

"Never mind that." He brushes the Holy Birth aside with his hand. "Tell me the story. Please."

Confused, angry and more than a little cold (the heater in Billy's truck hasn't worked right since the Bush administration) I repeat the story of Sylvanus and his unlikely romance. Billy listens intently, as if I'm an eyewitness to a homicide. But when I come to the end he says, "No."

"No, what?"

"There was something else. The island. Your grandma talked about an island where Sylvanus ran the ships. Remember?"

"Shaped like a crescent, with a harbor inlet too narrow to be seen. Scilly Island, I think Grandma called it. You can't see the approaches unless you're almost on top of them."

Billy's eyes glitter more than ever. "Your grandma ever tell you where this island was?"

"I think she said it was somewhere past Dolphin Rock. But she was pretty vague. And anyway, why....Oh!" Now I've seen it too.

"A secret island," he repeats, "that looks like solid rock but conceals an inner harbor. Just the place to hide a missing yacht, for instance?"

But even as he speaks I shake my head. "*Calliope's* gone, Billy. You said so yourself. Twenty-six bags of fertilizer wouldn't leave much behind."

"We have no proof they were ever detonated. For all we know they could still be inside the hull."

"Even so, Scilly Island's probably washed away. And if it did exist, what are the odds anyone alive would know about it?"

He shrugs. "Depends on who we're talking about. I've never heard of it, and I lived here my whole life. But there's people that spend a lot more time trolling around the bay than you or me." To my amazement, he opens the glove box and pulls out a folded map. "I've been thinking about it all day. Well, shit, nothing else to do, right? You see here," he says, unfurling the map on the seat between us and pointing. "There's a cluster of rocks off Briggs Point that would be just about perfect. But we searched all of them, I remember. Nothing big enough to hide a boat. Then I found this." He indicates an egg-shaped outcropping about a mile off Little Pond Cove.

"Can't say I recognize it, but the position fits. Jesus, it feels like Treasure Island all of a sudden."

"Wanna go take a look?"

"Yeah, I guess, if…But, you mean, *now*?"

"Why not?" He waggles his eyebrows humorously. "It's an adventure."

"It's Christmas Eve!" I repeat. "I've got to get Grandma home. And the Aunts are waiting for me." I look over to the shop windows and, sure enough, they are both there, Constance and Irene, faces pressed to the glass like children at Macy's window. Billy waves at them cordially. Aunt Irene waves back.

"They'll be okay," he promises me.

"But it's dark! And even if we find it, you couldn't call it in, it's too late, nobody'll be there…"

"If we find it, it'll still be there in the morning. I can call it in then."

"How will we get there?" I ask, fishing for objections.

"The police launch. It's always got a full tank of gas." Billy's enthusiasm is infectious. There's something else too, and I'd be a fool not to realize it. He's been in the doghouse ever since Alicia disappeared. If he could actually find the *Calliope* it would be a coup. The fact that he wants me along for the hunt is actually endearing. Still it's bad policy to give a boyfriend what they want without at least a token struggle. I let him wrangle me for about ten minutes before I finally, with a great sigh, assent.

Fifteen minutes later I'm regretting my decision, and just about every other one for the last three months—especially the fruitcake. The police boat is a Boston Whaler with an unheated closet-sized cabin wedged in the bow and two giant Chrysler diesels hanging off the stern. It tackles the waves like they owe it money, raising its fist and hammering them into submission. Great curtains of foam engulf the cabin, and us. My reindeer cat is completely soaked. "Can't…we…go…slower?"

Billy grins and, like all men everywhere, guns the engine. He takes us out of the harbor and turns south, running close along the coast with the Cormorant Light flashing off the port bow. The twin diesels lift us right out of the water, and the roar fills the cabin. We are reduced to making dumb show with our hands and, finally, staring out through the windscreen at the endless dark of the sea. I check my watch. 2:04. "Hey, Billy!" I scream, holding up the watch and forcing myself to be heard over the engines, "Merry Christmas!"

He grins, winks. We're banking heavily to port now, making a wide arc around Sakonnet Point. A tall spotlight casts its bluish glow over Tappens Beach; somewhere, behind the dunes, is Quicksand Pond, and Teddy Johnson. A string of gaily colored bulbs means we've reached Warren Point Beach Club, which once denied membership to Joe Kennedy and has been boasting the fact ever since. Beyond that the peninsula ends, and all that is left is open sea. Billy aims for the void. "This far out?" I ask, surprised.

"Yeah, it used to be on the old trading route," he shouts back. "Lots of wrecks out here."

I wonder how many of them were courtesy of old Sylvanus Hazard. Billy throttles down the engines, and the shapeless dark begins to assume dimension. The clouds part below a full canopy of stars. Their light is almost too faint to discern something directly ahead, blacker than the sea, whose existence can only be inferred from the slight chop of the waves as they strike against it. "That must be it," Billy tells me, unnecessarily. If there were ever a less likely place for a millionaire's yacht, I haven't seen it. There is not so much as a lobster pot or channel marker to give us bearing. Billy brings the Whaler down to a slow crawl, creeping toward the rocks. Up close, they form a definite shape. It appears to be a solid mass, rising roughly fifteen or twenty feet from the sea, with a few straggly weeds strewn along the top. The boat moves slowly along the perimeter. We are close now, so close that I can almost reach out and touch the rocks.

"Sure this is it?" Billy wonders.

"Nope. Keep going around."

Just then I see it: an aperture in the wall, curved inward so that from even a short distance it appears to be solid. "There." The narrow entrance is almost concealed by overhanging stones. Billy noses us in, and the sound of the engines reverberates off the cliffs on either side. It is grim and shadowy, like the fortress of an evil magician. "Oh, I don't like this," I mutter.

"Don't be such a girl."

I turn on him, furious, but he is grinning wickedly. Another rite of passage past; we can joke about it now. "Faggot," I whisper at him. His grin widens.

Suddenly we both gasp. There it is, the *Calliope*. After all this time, it is right in front of us.

Or what's left of it.

Clearly something terrible has happened. The yacht rides high in the water, canted over to starboard and showing her red anti-fouling paint like a wound. The main cabin is gone, along with the wheelhouse that Marcus said had been taken from an old pilot boat. But that's not the worst. Some monstrous creature has attacked the *Calliope* and left great gaping holes all along her flank, some as small as a paint can, others big enough to drive a car through. Seawater rushes in and out, making an odd sucking sound. "What the *fuck*?" I ask, amazed. It looks for all the world like *Calliope* had an encounter with a Kraken and came out the worse for it.

The Whaler is still inching forward, reluctantly, an old mare skittish around the sight of so much death. Billy brings her alongside the largest of the holes and shines his flashlight into the interior. This must have been the master bedroom, though there is little left to identify it. The walls have been stripped down to their beams, the carpet torn up to reveal bare steel. But, strangely, the bed is still there, turned on its side with pillows and sheets cascading onto the floor. Something else, a nightstand or dresser, lies denuded with its legs pointing feebly in the air.

"What could *do* this?"

Billy looks grim as he casts a line and secures it on one of the jagged boards sticking up from the hull like rotten teeth. "Come on," he says, and jumps into the void.

It's a vote of confidence; if I were Rosalie, he would have at least offered a hand. I follow his lead, but my legs come up short and I catch my shins across the broken wood. I fall heavily on the deck, cursing. Billy helps me up, and once again there is that sudden rush, the electric charge of his body against mine. It seems as if we are at once in two parallel worlds, a penny dreadful and a rather conventional—in some ways—romance. But the setting favors the former. *Calliope* is utterly dark, the only sound the gurgle of the waves passing in and out of her broken hull. It is like slow, gasping breath. The yacht is wounded but alive, and still possessed of whatever demon threw her against the rocks and ripped out her insides.

I follow the beam cast by Billy's torch. It bounces against empty corridors, piles of flakeboard, shards of glass and pink cotton-candy insulation strewn everywhere. "It's like something was trying to eat it from the inside out," I whisper.

Billy shakes his head. "Don't get so carried away. Human hands did this."

"Why the hell?"

He raises his shoulders. "That's what we need to find out. Look around." The beam rounds a corner and disappears.

It takes a while for my eyes to adjust. There is just enough light from the portholes to make out a spiral staircase, still intact even though the cabin above is gone. It opens onto empty air. Someone has laid down long planks, like catwalks, over great gaps on the deck. Yet what looks like random destruction actually has a kind of system. It's like construction in reverse, pulling up the decks and tearing down the walls, then moving slowly aft and down, deck by deck. Looking into the cavernous depths, I can just make out the engine room, still untouched. There, stacked in neat rows, are twenty-six bags of fertilizer.

The stern remains mostly intact; there's even a patio table and chairs, and a furled awning nearby. Yet a blowtorch sits beside it, silent but menacing, its greedy flame waiting to gobble up the steel beams it rests on. And something else, a silvery cylindrical object lying, seemingly discarded, at the rail. Clearly it's been here a while: one whole side is dark with brown rust. Yet the other looks almost new, untouched. Not really knowing why, I reach down and pick it up. Just a fire extinguisher. But the rust is not rust. There is something clotted on the bottom, dulling a sharp edge that speaks of blood and mangled bone.

"Be careful with that."

I look up and Billy is standing just a few feet away on the opposite end of the plank. The flashlight dangles from his left hand.

In his right is a pistol.

"Billy?"

He doesn't move. The pistol is aimed at my heart. "You're not gonna like this," he says.

I don't already. Seeing but not believing, I edge slowly away. The fire extinguisher is still in my hands. "That gun," I said, staring at it, "is that the one…?"

"That shot Wally? Yep, thirty-two magnum. No question about it."

There is a strange look in his eyes. I feel like I've never seen him before. "Why are you holding it, then? Isn't it evidence? I mean, fingerprints?"

He sighs. "It was lying in a puddle. Anyway, I think I know whose prints were on it. This is it, David. This is where it all comes out. Everything."

"And this?" I ask, holding up the cylinder.

"You don't need me to tell what that was for. You saw Marcus closer than anyone."

True, but now I'm seeing something even more incredible, like the eye of a tornado, or the volcanic cloud over Pompeii. The face of a murderer about to kill again. He is in absolute agony. His face is twisted and raw, consumed with guilt for what he is about to do. In a way I almost feel sorry for him. "Billy," I say, very quietly, "what is all this? What have you done?"

He stops, confused. He looks down at the pistol as if he can't understand how it got into his hand. "Oh, my God, no! What? No!" Disgusted, he flings it down onto the deck. "Not me! Jesus, David, not me!"

I didn't realize I was holding my breath until now. "Fuuuuck," I say, letting it out in a long gasp, "you scared the crap out of me. What did you do that for?"

"Sorry! Sorry! It's just…Oh, hell, David, don't you see what this means? Who could have done all this?"

I'm still breathing hard. "You tell me."

"I told you, you're not gonna like it. I remembered something just now. When we first started looking for the yacht, the police sent patrol boats, but the Coast Guard had a helicopter. There's no way they could have missed this place."

"So the *Calliope* wasn't here then?"

"Couldn't have been. It had to be close, though. And whoever had it knew it would be safe from us and the Coast Guard, but for whatever reason couldn't keep it in its initial hiding place forever. Which means that somewhere nearby there is a *second* hiding place, even better than this, which we all overlooked. And you know, David, there really only is one."

"Which is?" I ask, puzzled.

"Look around you. The *Calliope* wasn't attacked. Somebody was trying to destroy the evidence. She was scrapped."

He waits to let this sink in. "You mean…*Aunt Constance?*"

Billy spreads his hands. "What's the one place we didn't think to look during the initial search? The old submarine barn. I mean, why would we? Couple of old ladies and a scrap company, why would they be hiding a twenty-million-dollar yacht?"

"But I was there! Not a week after he disappeared, I came right into the boathouse and it was completely empty."

"Sure, the yacht had been moved by then."

"To Scilly Island?" I'm thinking rapidly. What was it Grandma had said? *She's different now. A ghost. Anyone with eyes could see it. All blacked out and draped in bunting, like a funeral cortege*. Shrouded, to prevent detection. Crossing the bay like a phantom in the night.

"There's something else, too," Billy goes on sadly. "Remember on the second search it was Constance who drew up the chart and assigned each person a different zone. We just thought she was being efficient. But I remember which zones everybody had, because I wanted to make sure nobody sailed into shoal water or breakers. And where do you suppose Constance was searching herself?"

I collapse into one of the patio chairs. "No," I tell him, shaking my head, "That's not possible."

"Why not?" he insists. "She kept the *Calliope* in the boathouse for a couple of days, just long enough for the search to end. But she couldn't keep it there forever; eventually you or somebody else would happen upon it by accident. So she snuck it across the bay to a place she knew nobody would ever look. But then the town got excited, and there's another search. So what does she do? Pretend to go along with the idea, then carefully keep everyone looking in the wrong direction. Who else could have been so confident no-one would ever find this place?"

"All that trouble just for an old yacht? And what do you think, she brained Marcus and pitched him overboard on the way?"

Billy sighs again. "I think so, yeah. And I think poor old Wally got curious and blundered in here while she was still onboard. So she took care of him, too."

"In God's name, *why*? Millionaire's yachts pass through this town every day. She's probably seen ten thousand of them. Why turn homicidal over this one?"

Billy is still frowning, but he cannot conceal a small smirk of satisfaction at his own cleverness. "She told you herself. The Robie gold."

"Oh, please. That's just a myth. Even if it weren't, so what? Marcus found it, Constance discovered somehow and went pirate? Does that sound likely? And if she did," I go on, gathering steam, "why would she be such a fool as to announce it in the middle of the Boy and Lobster? She had the whole town looking for the gold then!"

He nods fervently. "Exactly! Don't you see? That's just what made me wonder in the first place. Why was she so determined to put that story out there? Why get the whole town looking for gold she already stole? But in another way it was genius. How do you conceal a crime? Add more suspects! Get everyone out on the water, blundering around. Constance knew there was no chance of them finding the *Calliope*. Not as long as she kept the sector with Scilly Island for herself. She muddied the waters, literally, and sat back to watch another layer of mystery get added to the *Calliope's* disappearance. Of course," he adds, "she couldn't have done all this alone. Irene must have helped. But you know Irene; she'd go along with anything Constance did. They're closer than sisters."

"But Billy," I say, fighting to remain calm, "Think about what you're saying. You *know* them. The Laughing Sarahs, for Christ's sake. Could they really…" Really, what? Brain a man and toss his body over the side? Sure, why not? They'd done it before.

But Billy doesn't see my hesitation. "I know," he sighs, "it sounds bonkers. I don't want it to be them, God knows, but there's no doubt of it now."

"Oh, bullshit," I cut him off. "This is circumstantial at best. Constance isn't the only one in Rhode Island that knows how to scrap a boat. She could have genuinely missed seeing *Calliope* here that day—it wouldn't be hard. I still refuse to believe she'd suddenly go rogue, even over a fortune in gold. What the hell would she do with it? Put a new roof on the dog kennel? You said it yourself. These are just a couple of old ladies."

"A couple of old ladies that just lost their best friend. What if Marcus killed Emma, and Constance found out? Then it wouldn't just be about the gold. It would be revenge."

I don't like it, not one bit. But Constance is a Hazard, and Hazards are wreckers. I can almost feel the shade of Sylvanus moving amongst the rocks around us, staring down with amusement at my feeble attempt to exonerate his progeny.

Billy cannot read my thoughts, which is just as well. His hands squeeze my shoulders. "I know, I'm really sorry. But what can I do? I'm a police officer, as stupid as that sounds. I can't just ignore all this."

I pull back slowly. "But you wouldn't have to do anything unless you're sure. Are you sure, Billy?"

He is silent for a long moment. "No," he admits finally. "It's possible—not likely, but possible—that it could be somebody else. There's really only one way to be certain." I already know I'm not going to like this either. Sure enough, I don't. "We need to search the boathouse."

"Now?"

"I could get a warrant. But this is enough for probable cause. And I wouldn't like to think what they'd manage to do in the time after you warn them."

The air leaves my lungs. I honestly hadn't even thought that far, but in the time it takes me to work up a decent head of outraged steam, I realize he's absolutely right on both counts. Irene and Constance managed to strip Emma's house before the body even cooled; how long would it take them to empty out the boathouse? And, yes, of course I would warn them. Whatever else, they are family. "Well, shit."

"You'd better come with me," he says. "I'll need a witness, and if it turns out there's nothing there, we can both have a good laugh and lock up again quietly."

"And if there is?"

For the first time he looks away, down at the shattered deck. "Guess we'll have to figure that out when we come to it."

So it's to be like that. I'm now the appointed defender of my elderly aunts, against the prosecution of my ex-, tentatively non-ex, soon to be re-ex boyfriend. Merry Christmas. "Just out of curiosity," I ask as we climb back onto the Whaler, "what were you planning for our *next* date?"

Chapter Fifteen

It must be nearly four by the time we get back to Dowsy's Pier. Billy passes right by it, bringing us up alongside the boathouse with "Salty Brine's Best Littleneck Clams" still showing faintly under the paint. The office is dark; the Aunts have gone home and taken Grandma with them, probably having a good snicker about how late Billy and I are staying out and what we might be up to. The reality makes me physically sick. "God, Billy," I mutter, "can't we leave it till morning, at least?"

He keeps his eyes on the boathouse. His expression is stern. For the first time it is Chief Dyer standing before me, and he is as unsparing as any Puritan judge. "It is morning, David. And it won't get any easier then."

Christmas morning. What a sick joke. We tie up right by the giant barn doors and Billy turns to me. "How do you get in?"

"Side door, padlocked," I answer automatically.

The lock is new but the hasp is old. Three minutes' work with a screwdriver and we're in. The interior is pitch dark, but I know it better than my own house. Without a pause I reach to the left and hit the switch. These are original kliegs, which hiss and pop as they come on.

"Damn," Billy whispers, impressed.

The boathouse is a cavernous space, three hundred feet long with barrel ceilings that vault over our heads like a cathedral. The docking slip is empty and filled with gray, brackish water. Two giant gantries stand guard at the hinged barn doors. Lining the walls are the tools of the wrecker's trade: hacksaws, blowtorches, evil-looking wrenches with grooved teeth that bite into steel.

But none of that is what impresses Billy. On the wall closest to the shop, extending some thirty feet into the air, are the spoils of New England Wrecking and Salvage. Grandpa started the collection. He had a bit of book-learning, and named it the *rostra* after the broken ships' prows that once made up the speaking pulpit of the Roman Senate. There are dozens of wheels, some teak with brass studs, others polished chrome; binnacles and compasses on buckling shelves, wound with bits of rope; yards of teak decking stacked like lumber; doors with glass beveled edges and portholes lined with nickel; buckets full of handles, knobs, cleats, davits of every possible size and age. One whole section has been given to totems, figureheads and other bits of maritime art. "Tourists love that crap," I remember Constance saying dismissively. I look amongst them for Calliope, the bespectacled mermaid, but she is not there.

Billy joins me in the search. Yet once a ship has been scrapped and reduced down to her component parts, all identity falls away. There is nothing distinctive about any of this nautical detritus; it could have come from any trawler or yacht, freighter or catamaran. Stacked against the wall are dressers, bureaus, cabinets, television consoles, dining tables, and more chairs than I can count. They all could have come from *Calliope*, or any other boat.

"Okay assholes, the party's over."

The voice is familiar, the tone authoritative and confident. Aunt Constance is standing in the doorway, a shotgun in her hands. Irene and Grandma peer anxiously over her shoulder. I turn around, and they all gasp. "*David?*"

"Hi, Aunt Constance."

"What the hell are you doing here? I thought you were robbing the place. And Billy Dyer? This your idea of a joke?"

From behind her, Irene titters. "They're not burglars, Connie, they're just looking for a little privacy."

Constance considers this. "You guys sure picked a strange spot. Why couldn't you have just gone back to your house?"

I open my mouth to correct her, but Billy gets in first. "I'm sorry," he says, "It was my fault; I suggested it. How did you know we were here?"

"Silent alarm. Went off the moment you opened the door."

Of course. I was a fool to think anyone as cautious as Constance would leave all her treasures to the protection of a single lock. Billy moves forward. "We didn't mean to disturb. You can put the gun away now."

"Yes, Connie," Irene bleats, "I don't like you waving that thing around."

Constance lowers the rifle, but her expression is still puzzled. She looks back and forth between Billy and me. "Where were you all this time?"

"That," Irene interjects, "is none of your business, Miss Constance."

Chief Dyer is gone; Billy could be a bashful teenager again. He stares at the floor and scrubs his toe across it distractedly. "Sorry to disturb you ladies." Clearly there is nothing here, and he is turning red with shame. Fortunately, the Aunts will never suspect the true source.

Aunt Constance finally softens. "Well, okay. This has been quite a night. Guess we'd all better get on home, then."

"One moment," I hear myself say. My eye has fallen on a strange object tucked inconspicuously behind one of the compasses. "This tiki," I ask slowly, "where did you get it?"

Constance shrugs. "Picked it up in a flea market ages ago. Why? You want it?"

"No."

No one would, really. It's an ugly thing, with disdainful eyes and squat little arms and legs. It regards us all coldly. I take it in my hands. "They say it's bad luck to take someone else's tiki. Like stealing their spirit. You should have left this where you found it."

Constance raises the gun unconsciously. "It isn't polite to manhandle other people's things...."

I fling the idol onto the floor between us. The motion is so sudden, so savage in its complete understanding, that Constance stops dead. Her face is gray. Suddenly, for the first time, she looks old. "You don't understand. Let me explain."

"You told me yourself, Constance. There are some things you can't explain. Some things better left hidden. You should have hid it better."

"What is all this?" Irene asks, looking from one us to the other. Then her gaze falls on the tiki and she draws in her breath with a sharp hiss. Billy hasn't moved. The four of us are frozen in a tableau, and I think irrelevantly that it would make a great cover for one of those period murder mysteries, *Death of a Tiki*.

"You know what it is, Irene," I say finally. "It belonged to a young man named Kevin Johnson, Aunt Emma's grandson. He bought it on his travels. Only by then he was calling himself Marcus Rhinegold. It came with him on his yacht. And there's only one way it could have ended up here."

"We found *Calliope* at Scilly Island," Billy adds. "What's

left of her, anyway. I persuaded David to search for the rest here. We both figured it was better this way than a police warrant."

"Thank you," says Constance ironically. "Anything else?"

I nod. "We found the gun that killed Wally, and the fire extinguisher you used to brain Rhinegold. Whichever of you, that is. Just like *Clue*, right? Aunt Constance on the deck with the pistol; Aunt Irene at the fantail with the fire extinguisher..."

"David!" Irene cries, scandalized. "That's really enough!"

"Put the gun down, Constance," Billy says calmly. "Put it on the floor."

Constance looks irresolute, but keeps hold of the rifle. It's still pointed, seemingly unconsciously, at my solar plexus.

"Going to shoot me, Aunt Constance?" I ask, my voice cracking.

There is a long, ugly pause. Finally, gently, she lays the shotgun on the concrete. "That was for burglars," she says, seemingly irrelevantly. I've never heard that tone in her voice before. She sounds like a very small child.

"I understand," Billy assures her.

"*Murderers!*" Grandma screams suddenly. She elbows herself into the space between us, pointing an accusing finger at Irene and Constance. A thin line of spittle drips down her chin. "What's in here? It's Teddy, isn't it? You put his body in here and cemented it over. Tell the truth!"

Billy turns to me, completely bemused. I tap my temple meaningfully.

Irene looks exasperated. "For God's sake, Maggie, Teddy's been dead for fifty years! There's nothing in the boathouse but old junk."

"Let's see it all, then!" Grandma has become an unexpected, and deranged, ally. "I know what you're plotting, the two of you. You want to send me to the Funny Farm. You've been taking stuff out of my house and telling me it's lost. But it's not lost, is it? It's in here. Everything. My books, my photographs. All my memories. But you don't want me to remember. Cutting me off, telling everyone I'm losing my marbles. What have you been feeding me? Drugs, I bet. Stuff that makes me go funny in the head. I'll never take another bite of your food again, not if I starve to death! Lying bitches. I remember now. Emma with her brains all smashed in. You said it was an accident, but I saw you cleaning up in there! You pulled the pans down to make it look like an accident. And the letter…the letter…"

There is a sudden sharp sound. Aunt Irene has slapped Grandma across the face. Grandma gasps, chokes. It would be hard to say which of them looks more shocked. "That's enough, Maggie. You just calm down now." Each word sounds like it's been strained from a sieve.

But then Grandma sinks into a folding teak chair and begins to cry.

Irene is crying too. "Oh, Mags, I'm so sorry." She rests herself on the chair arm and pats Grandma consolingly on the shoulder. Constance moves instinctively toward them. Her face is still ashen. "Irene, take Maggie back to her place and sit with her. Go on, right now."

Aunt Irene turns up a tear-stained face. "But what about you?"

"I'll be along in just a bit."

So might someone on the *Titanic* have said it, nonchalant yet with grim eyes. But I'm in no mood for pity. "That's a good idea. I'll be back to sit with Grandma if Constance… can't."

The finality of this makes Irene wince, but she takes Grandma by the hand and pulls her gently toward the door.

"Come on, honey, I think there's still some Brigham's ice cream in the freezer."

After they are gone, Constance turns back to us. She is standing on the sloping deck, the band is playing and all the lifeboats have gone. "Let's go into the shop," she growls.

She leads the way. This room, so familiar and comfortable, now seems utterly alien. Every object—the leather chairs, old squashy sofa, faded photographs of the Aunts and of the Hurricane of '54 in their flyspecked frames—seems to have betrayed me. Or did I betray them? Constance seats herself behind the big aluminum desk she salvaged from a purser's office on the *Queen Frederica*. The glass case with Grandma's green ledgers is behind her head. She opens the drawer, takes out a cigarette, lights it. The pack are Tareytons, which haven't been made since the 1980s, around the same time Constance quit. She takes a deep drag and leans back in her chair. "Sit."

Until then I didn't realize we were still standing. Billy and I sit awkwardly. Constance takes the lid off a tin of Danish shortbread and pushes it toward us. "Have a cookie."

Since there is no proper etiquette for refusing shortbread from a murderess, we each take one. It grates on my dry throat like cardboard.

"Okay," Constance says, blowing a blue cloud of smoke toward the ceiling, "what do you want to know?"

"Everything," I say at once.

"I should warn you," Billy adds, "that you still have the right to remain silent. Anything you say may be taken down in evidence…"

I realize with something close to an electric shock that my boyfriend is reading Aunt Constance her Miranda rights. This is actually happening. "Billy!" I cut him off. "Stop that! This isn't the police station."

"I'm a police officer."

"You want to play it that way? Fine. I'm the only other witness, and I'll deny everything you say till I'm blue. And by the time you get your boys back to Scilly Island, there won't be anything left but rocks."

Billy looks stunned, like he's never really seen me before. "But that's obstruction of justice!" he protests. "You could go to jail! You could…"

"Kids," Constance interrupts, bringing the flat of her hand down on the desk. "Don't fight. I'll say all I have to say now, and later, if Billy wants, I'll say it again under oath."

This silences us both. Constance continues to regard us calmly. But her skin looks pale and mottled under the fluorescent lights. "Where do you want me to begin?"

Suddenly, madly, I think of the Mad Hatter in *Alice in Wonderland*. Constance read me the story many times. "Begin at the beginning," I tell her, "and when you get to the end, stop."

She chuckles. "Well, okay then. In the beginning, Marcus Rhinegold came to Little Compton.

"We didn't know who he was, of course. I had no idea he was Kevin Johnson, Emma's grandson, or any of that. I'm sure Emma didn't either. If he had any plans of making himself known to her, it's certain he never had the chance. Even now I don't really know what he intended. Maybe just to see her again, to have that connection with the family he lost. Who knows?

"But that's how things were. He hired us to take down the old Armstrong place. We started laying out plastic sheeting, got the caterpillar in. I don't think I exchanged more than fifty words with him that whole time, and all of it about the house. He never mentioned Emma, or anything else. So you can imagine how surprised we all were when he showed up at the funeral."

"I was pretty surprised myself," I admit.

"Well, it makes sense, now. So that's how things stood." She pauses, takes a drag from her cigarette. "Then one afternoon Marcus shows up at the shop. Oh, sometime near the end of October. He's in an absolute sweating panic. It took Irene and me ten minutes just to get him to sit down and tell us what was wrong.

"Well, the long and short of it was that he found Alicia had been making plans of her own. She bought a truck-load of fertilizer and was going to blow the *Calliope* higher than hell, or so Marcus claimed. She'd had enough of their fake marriage, enough of traipsing round the world after a fugitive. We asked a few pertinent questions, and the whole story came out: the Molinari family, Marcus' snitching to the FBI, all of it. He didn't tell us he was gay, of course. Didn't need to. We'd both seen the way he looked at you. So in the end, Alicia got in touch with the Molinaris and they put the hit on Marcus Rhinegold. How did Marcus himself find out about it? Maybe he saw the fertilizer receipts, or caught something unwholesome in the way she looked at him. Either way, he knew his days were numbered. She was going to load the fertilizer into the cargo hold and set a timer—probably a firecracker looped through a cigarette, or some such—and be safely on her way to Miami by the time the show began. So Marcus had to act fast. Which is why he came to us."

"Not quite," Billy cuts in. Constance raises an eyebrow. "Oh, I'm sure that's what he told you. But we spoke to Alicia right before the Molinaris took her. She claimed Marcus made her buy the fertilizer."

"But...why?"

I see it, too. "A classic frame-up job," I interject, placing us all in a Micky Spillane pot-boiler. "He wanted to be free of the Molinaris, and of her too. So he hatched this plan to make it appear that Alicia had set him up."

"But we would know!" Constance objects.

"Sure. But you would have thought she was planning to kill him anyway. Knowing that, would either you or Irene have lifted a finger?"

Against her will, Constance smiles a fraction. "Irene might. I wouldn't."

"Clever Marcus," Billy admits. "But please go on."

"His request was simple. Could we help him escape before Alicia got him? I said we weren't much good at smuggling fugitives. He said sure, but we were pretty good at tearing up old yachts. I admitted that was true. His plan was actually brilliant. He would sail the yacht into the middle of the harbor on a foggy night and set off an explosion of some kind, then creep back into port. Right into our boathouse, in fact. Then, while everyone was looking for the wreck, we would quietly and quickly alter the *Calliope* to the point that nobody looking at her would suspect what she was. Once we finished, Marcus would wait for nightfall and sneak out of the bay again, destination unknown. For all this, Irene and I would receive two hundred and fifty thousand dollars, each. Cash. He had a suitcase full of money, just like in the movies. Well, shit. That was the exact amount your Grandma, God love her, pissed away on the scammers. Things haven't been too easy since then. So I said sure. After all, why not? It wasn't illegal. And we were saving a life, in a roundabout sort of way. That was the line your Aunt Irene took.

"The plan went off without a hitch. You remember the fog that Halloween; it was perfect. Marcus picked a fight with Alicia and she went storming off in her Mercedes, just as he hoped. Then he quietly slipped anchor and sailed out into the bay. He waited until the patrol boat spotted him, then ducked into the fog and set off a whole case full of fireworks. Strapped 'em onto a zodiac boat and let it drift behind. Worked like a charm. The patrol heard the explosion, and Marcus turned off all his lights and tracking devices and crept back into port. We were waiting for him at the boathouse. Must've been about three in the morning. The boat came out of the fog like a phantom—hell, for a second it was like the old *General Kearny* had come back from the grave. Or maybe it was just Maggie's story that night gave me the heebee-jeebies.

"The tricky part came later. You can't just remake a yacht in a couple of hours, and we had to modify it enough to look convincing. Marcus was no help. He didn't know a head from a halyard. So Irene and me had to do it all, taking shifts so that it wouldn't look too suspicious. Which meant one of us had to be in the shop while the other worked in the boathouse. Pretty soon we realized we couldn't keep *Calliope* there. It was just too dangerous. We knew nobody would think to look there at first, not when everyone assumed he'd either gone under or to Cuba. But sooner or later somebody would come by, even you, David. That's when I remembered about Scilly Island, where old Cousin Sylvanus used to wreck his ships. It was perfect: a sheltered cove inside an island nobody knew about. We could anchor the *Calliope* there for as long as it took.

"Marcus didn't like it, not one bit. The idea of holing up in the middle of the bay spooked him, I guess. But I told him it was either that or take his chances on open sea, so he went along in the end. In the meantime, we had to keep stirring the pot. I knew they'd find out about Alicia sooner or later, but it did no harm to cook up a few other extravagant theories, just to distract everybody.

That's why I mentioned the Robie gold. Which, of course, is the goddamn-stupidest thing I've ever done in my life, since it made Mrs. Wally and the whole frigging town turn around and decide to go treasure-hunting. Oh, Irene was mad at me! You should've seen her. Neither of us had the heart to tell Marcus. He was already as nervous as a dog with ants up his ass, pacing back and forth in the *Calliope*. Whenever we came to work on her, he'd follow us around, peering over our shoulders. He was getting desperate. The good news was, we were almost finished. I took down the cabin and pilot house and was just about to rig up a spare jury mast, to make her look more like a sloop. It wouldn't be pretty, but nobody would know she was the *Calliope*. By now the town was out looking for her. Well, you know about that. I sent them off in all the wrong directions, and just did slow turns around Scilly Island until it was over.

"That should've been the end of it. But then that prince of all assholes, Wally Turner, takes out his scrubby little boat to investigate. You know his wife put him up to it. She must have told him we were hoarding the Robie gold or some shit, so he comes right up to the island and starts nosing around. Sure enough, he finds the entrance. We were on deck that day, working. It was almost sunset. I didn't see him come in at first; the sun was in my eyes. Irene had her back turned. But Marcus saw. He was right on the stern, drunk as a loon. Oh, yeah, I left that part out. He'd been hitting the bottle pretty heavily, partly out of boredom and partly from fear. He was on his fifth or sixth sundowner when he saw the *My-T-Fine*.

"Well, he just freaked out. There's no other word for it. Maybe if it had been anyone other than Wally, we might've talked our way out, but that dumb son of a bitch stands up right on his fantail and screams, "I knew it! I knew it! You've got the Robie gold, Constance!"

"'Wally,' I called back, 'I don't know what you think you're seeing right now, but there ain't no Robie gold, and you'd best be getting on back to port and sober up.'

"'Bullshit!' he piped. 'I'm gonna get Chief Dyer and the police and see what they have to say about it!' And then, if you please, he turns the *My-T-Fine* around and starts making for home with all sails set.

"Just then, I heard it, a whole series of pops like champagne corks going off. Marcus was standing, legs spread, holding the pistol with both hands. The first two shots went wide; there were plumes of water where they hit. The third just vanished, but I saw Wally slump over.

"For a long minute we did nothing, just stood there watching Wally drift out into open sea. Marcus hadn't moved; the gun was still in his hand. The Irene screamed. Or it might have been a sob, I can't be sure. Whatever it was, it woke Marcus out his daze. 'We've got to recover the body,' he said.

"I asked him just what in the hell he was talking about, and he turned round to look at me. I think he forgot I was there until then. 'We have to get the body,' he repeated slowly, as though to a prize idiot, 'and sink his boat so no one knows he came here.'

"Well ,this was just about enough. I'd listened to this man whine and carry on for a week, but this was the kicker. 'No,' I told him, 'the only thing we, me and Irene, have to do is go get Chief Dyer and tell him Wally's been murdered.'

"'But what story are you going to give?'

"'The truth,' I told him, 'always works pretty well, if no other options are available.'

"'You're going to turn me in?' he said, shocked. 'I could turn you in. We're all in this together.'

"That's where he was wrong. Irene and I might not be above taking a hush wrecking job, but this was murder. And the most incredible thing was that he naturally expected we would condone it, as though shooting poor Wally was just another unfortunate but necessary business decision. Well, that's not how I do business. And I told him so.

"For a long time we just stared at each other. Then I saw his hand come up, almost casually, like he meant to scratch his temple and just forgot he was still holding the pistol. And I remember thinking, *Well, Constance, old girl, you've cashed in your markers this time*. Can you imagine after a lifetime spent staring down whatever dirty business the sea throws at you, getting knocked off by some two-bit fairy mobster? Oh, sorry, David. No offense meant, I'm sure."

"None taken," I say, watching the expression in her eyes closely. I strongly suspect that was not an accident, that we are once again being led gently astray.

Yet Billy, like a bloodhound, keeps his nose to the scent. "But how on Earth did you disarm him?" he asks. "Did you throw the fire extinguisher at his head? How could you have closed the distance before he fired?"

She shrugs. "We were standing pretty close. I just clocked him before he could think twice."

Billy frowns a little. "But the wound was on the *back* of his head, just behind his right ear. How did you manage to..."

Constance turns anguished eyes to me. There is real pain there, and infinite sorrow.

"Oh, Billy," I say gently, "can't you see? It wasn't Constance that had the fire extinguisher. It was Irene."

None of us speaks. Constance stares down at her hands, folded on the aluminum desktop. Billy stares at me, open-mouthed. And I look over Constance's shoulder at the green ledgers, testament to sixty years of friendship. The Laughing Sarahs, loyal to the last.

"I'll deny that until my dying breath," Constance whispers.

"There's no cameras here, Aunt Constance, no microphones. Whatever you choose to tell the police later, you can tell us the truth now."

She thinks this over for a moment. "Irene didn't mean to hurt him as bad as she did," she says at last, her voice thick with emotion. "Just acted instinctively. She saw him raise the gun, knew I was a goner. I think she just wanted to knock him out. But, you know, she's stronger than she looks. In her day she was Ladies' Doubles Champion at the Newport Tennis Club three years' running, with the meanest backhand in the business. So she backhanded him with the extinguisher, and he just fell right over the side. We heard the splash, looked down. But with the *Calliope* riding so high, the water was fifteen feet below us. Even if we had a grappling hook I doubt we could have reached. Anyway, there wasn't time. After just a few seconds, Marcus Rhinegold disappeared. All we could do was hope we'd seen the last of him." She draws a deep, ragged breath, sits a little straighter in her chair. "And if either of you ever repeats a word of that, I'll throttle you myself. Irene Belcourt is the sweetest, kindest soul on this whole miserable Earth, and I'll be God-fucking-damned if I'm going to let her spend the remaining years she's got locked up in a cell." Constance turns from one of us to the other, nostrils flared.

"What about your remaining years?" I ask.

She shrugs indifferently. "I don't think I'll mind prison. Uncle Warren always said you meet a better class of people there. Maybe I'll get some reading done, finally. When you get down to it there's not much difference between prison and an old folks' home, except prison's less depressing. Gotta be one or the other, right?"

Her voice is casual, but there are dark pools in her eyes. I know she's thinking of Blue and Petie, her sons. And of the little pre-Revolutionary colonial on Westover Lane that she's spent forty years restoring, finally excising every trace of three ex-husbands. "Oh, come on, Billy," I cut in, "Surely there must be some alternative to prison? Home confinement, community service, or something?"

"That's for shoplifting or peddling a dime bag. This is murder."

The awful finality of the word makes even Constance cringe.

Billy sits back a bit and steeples his fingers, thinking hard. "When we saw the *Calliope*," he says slowly, "she looked like you'd been doing a lot more than modifying. She's about half-gone."

"Well, of course," Aunt Constance answers, surprised. "We couldn't just leave her there. You can't imagine what it was like that day, with Irene wailing and saying she was gonna turn herself in, and me trying to talk her down. We stayed out long past dark. In the end, I got her to see sense. Nobody was looking for Marcus Rhinegold anymore, not here anyway. People were moving on. And it was a helluva thing about Wally; I couldn't be sure if, by hiding Marcus, we weren't accomplices or accessories of something."

Billy shrugs. "Actually, I'm not sure either."

"So, there it was. Wally was gone. Marcus was gone. One corpse followed another out to sea. The only thing left was the *Calliope*."

"So you decided to scrap her," I offer.

"Sure. Not all the way down to the keel—you can't do that without cranes and heavy equipment. But I figured to take off all the valuable stuff, everything we could carry, then open up the seacocks and let nature do its work. Got a bit of dynamite to hurry things along. Those holes in the side are for when we sink her, so she goes down easy. Not that I'll get the chance now, of course." Aunt Constance flicks her eyes at Billy.

I look over at him too. "What do you think, Chief?"

He considers before replying. His face is still stern, coldly judicial. "I was just thinking how much fun I'd have telling the FBI that their golden snitch was knocked off by an eighty-year-old ex-Ladies Doubles Champion."

"No," Constance protests, half-rising out of her chair, "I told you, I don't want…"

"You know what this means, right? I'll have to bring them back in, and the Staties, too. It'll be a frigging holiday. Shit, with the *Calliope* still out there I'll prob'ly have to call in the Coast Guard. And all the camera crews. This'll light up the networks for weeks."

"You'll be famous," I say sardonically.

His mouth gets even thinner. "Yeah, cuz that's just what I want."

"You'll damn well tell them I did it," Constance insists, throwing herself into the cannon's mouth. "That's the deal. It was me with that fire extinguisher."

"And you that single-handedly scrapped the *Calliope*?"

"It wouldn't be hard to believe," I mutter. "Honestly, Billy, what would you even charge them with? Aiding a fugitive? He wasn't a fugitive from justice, just his wife and the Molinaris. Murder? That was acting in defense of another; no court in the world would convict."

Billy shrugs. "Seems kinda weird there could be two dead bodies and a half-sunk yacht, and nobody's responsible for anything."

"Sure they are," I answer back. "One man, anyway. The same man who brought all this trouble from the beginning: Marcus Rhinegold. It was him, Billy. Nothing ever happened in Little Compton, not until he showed up. Now look. He was the one that killed Wally, and I say he got the end that he deserved. Let the dead bury the dead."

He considers this for a long time. For the life of me, I don't know whether I'm talking to Billy or Chief of Police Dyer. "Come on," I press, "it's Christmas morning. I'll buy you a coffee and a Boston Crème donut and you can come crash at Grandma's place. We can decide whether to put my aunts in jail after breakfast."

"Oh, for shit's sake…" Against his will, he starts laughing. The tension breaks; even Constance settles a bit more easily in her chair. "Okay, okay," he says, throwing his hands in the air, "I'm too frigging tired, I don't want to write all this up, and I wouldn't know where to begin." He turns to Constance. "Can you have that boat gone by New Year's?"

"It'll be fish food before the week is out," she promises eagerly.

"Okay." He heaves himself up. "I guess that's it, then."

Not very dramatic, perhaps. Not how Hercule Poirot would have done it. '*Mesdames et messieurs, I have the honor to retire from this case…*' But this is Little Compton, not the Orient Express. It gets the job done.

"Thanks," Constance says dryly, but I can tell she means it.

We leave her still sitting at her desk, staring with a slight frown at the pictures of Irene, Maggie, Emma, and herself. She seems lost in thought, and very far away. I have a feeling she'll be there for some time.

Billy's truck is where we left it, blissfully unaware of the momentous happenings since we saw it last. I hug my knees in front of the heating vent, marveling that so much could have gone down in just a few hours. Sometimes the Earth moves slowly, other times fast, and once in a while it jolts right out from under your feet and lands you on your ass.

Billy is thinking the same. "This is not where I expected the day to go," he says quietly.

"It might end better than you think."

He gives me a look that is at the same time hopeful and a little nervous. "Really?"

"Wait and see. It's Christmas, after all."

We drive for a long time in silence. I'm trying to imagine the thoughts going through his head. Some of them probably involve Debbie, an empty house covered in her Christmas decorations. Most, though, will be back on the deck of the *Calliope*, endlessly replaying the scene where Marcus shoots, turns, raises his gun, and is swatted by Aunt Irene. Billy will be wondering if he just made the greatest mistake of his career, throwing away the chance to humiliate the FBI and make his reputation among his brother officers. There aren't many opportunities like this one—certainly not in Little Compton. He knows he has just consigned himself to a lifetime of writing parking tickets and carrying drunks back home from the Boy and Lobster. Maybe, too, he's wondering what it means to be attracted to me, and whether he can go where that question leads. Maybe he's already decided this is more than he can handle, and just doesn't know how to tell me yet. If so, I can't blame him. He's given me back my aunts; that's a fair trade.

While he's putting all this together, on the passenger side I'm readying my armor, my all-forgiving smile when he says this just isn't going to work, my sympathetic notes of understanding for the enormity of what he is being asked—told—to face. "Of course," I'll say, "this was never fair to you, Billy. I still want to be friends. Please believe that." I turn my face toward the window as if I'm staring at the Christmas lights. Never letting him see that losing him this time will be infinitely harder than the last.

Finally, it is Billy who breaks the silence, and the suddenness of his voice in the truck cabin almost makes me cringe. "Hey," he says, very seriously, "are you sure that Dunkin Donuts is open on Christmas?"

Chapter Sixteen

It won't be that easy, naturally. Three times that morning I nearly have to wrench the steering wheel out of Billy's hands to keep him from hot-footing to Tiverton and giving up the whole show. He's worried about his job, of going to prison, but mostly of what would happen if some "damn fool"—as he put it—comes upon the Aunts while they are administering last rites to the *Calliope*. I tell him he's absolutely right, and the only thing for it is to give them a police guard for the task. Billy doesn't like that at all. But he comes to Grandma's house anyway and helps me lay out the plates for Christmas breakfast.

What is the etiquette for a cop, a boat thief, and a murderess sitting down to flapjacks? We are in uncharted waters here. If this were a mystery novel of the old school, the problem would solve itself. I can see it now: Billy gathers us all into the parlor, Irene cries out "You can't prove a thing!" whereupon Billy produces a damning note that Irene claims never to have seen but which, incredibly, is *written in her own hand*. Irene collapses, police stream through the doors, curtain falls.

Reality, I discover, is less dramatic and more surreal. The Aunts show up at nine precisely with Grandma in tow, exactly as if we hadn't all met in the boathouse a few hours before. Irene has even put on her special evergreen jumper with light-up ornaments. Constance opts for somber dark blue trousers and a grey cardigan. "Merry Christmas!" they both cry, pecking me on the cheek. Billy gets a warm handshake from Constance and a hug from Irene. I should have known. Naturally, they'll pretend nothing happened; it's the New England way. Folks here go right on moving in their established grooves—knock them out and they may wobble for a bit, but they'll fall back in as soon as they can.

The only sign of anything untoward is that both women are elaborately polite. Constance helps me in the kitchen, while Irene and Billy take turns trying to engage Grandma in something resembling normal conversation. Finally Irene switches on *A Christmas Story* marathon. Grandma sits happily in front of the television and tunes the rest of us out. She'll watch the same movie loop again and again and be just as delighted each time. I feel a pang of guilt—*shouldn't let her watch so much TV, it'll rot her brain*—which on further consideration seems darkly funny.

Breakfast is a strange affair. While Grandma giggles in the front room, the rest of us pass around bundt cake and tell lame jokes, exchange stale gossip, and take turns going to "check on Maggie." Constance asks Billy an intelligent question about inshore smuggling, and seems genuinely interested by the answer. Irene fusses over me and tells me I'm getting too thin. But they both cast furtive glances Billy's way like small children afraid of being scolded. It's a relief when Mariana arrives from Central Falls in the afternoon, clad in a red sweater with a sack full of presents like some belated gender-confused Santa Nicolá. Grandma gets a stack of coloring books and a five-pound brick of Hershey's chocolate. "At that age, what's the harm?" Mariana asks unanswerably. I receive a toolkit, which I'm sure is a regift from one of Mariana's many cousins, but is much appreciated all the same. Both Aunts get a freshly baked Barbadian rum cake with enough moonshine to light itself. Billy helps me plow through the toolkit and explains each item. He is patient but not condescending. Constance's gift to me is an electric razor, complete with attachments. "Get used to that first, and later on you can use a blade," she says gruffly. She cuts off my thanks with a curt wave and suddenly becomes very interested in the portrait over the fireplace.

Irene pads over and presses something into my hand. "Meant to give this to you ages ago," she tells me. I look down into my palm, and gasp. It's a gold pocketwatch with a hinged lid and a long glittering chain. "Wow, Aunt Irene, it's beautiful."

"In good Rhode Island families," she says with dignity, "it was customary for fathers to present their sons with a watch like that when they reached maturity. Your daddy should've done it, by rights but…well, anyway, if Maggie was herself, she'd want it done, too. But I can't take credit. Look inside."

I pry open the lid. The watch is a Waterbury, at least a century old, but the inscription is freshly cut. *For David Hazard*, it reads, *from his loving Aunt Emma*.

"Oh." Traitorous tears well up in my eyes.

"She wanted you to have it," Irene insists. "Told me so, not long before she died. There was a house full of jewelry, but she knew you'd want this the most. It belonged to her daddy, and his daddy before that. I guess it was her way of saying she understood."

"One more thing we had to smuggle out of the house before those rotten relations of hers took over," Constance adds, smiling with satisfaction at the memory. "There's a pair of diamond earrings, too, but I reckon we'll just have to sell those. Unless you change your mind again." She smiles to let me know she's kidding.

"Thank you both," I say, looking into each of their faces in turn. "Thank you so much."

The Aunts have brought their usual contributions to the Christmas feast, which Mariana augments with a curious assortment of dishes in Tupperware containers from her own table. Conversation, already halting, sputters to a stop. Mariana doesn't seem to mind. She worked many years in hospice care, so she's used to making her own entertainment. *A Christmas Story* blares from the front room, while someone—likely Aunt Irene—has found the old Perry Como records in Grandpa's den. The house is a perfect simulacrum of Christmas cheer, absent any actual cheeriness.

While Mariana bustles from room to room, Irene drops in to the kitchen for a conspiratorial whisper. "Connie thinks we oughta do it tonight."

"Do…what?" I ask, momentarily nonplussed.

"The *Calliope*," she hisses, and instantly turns round to see if anyone—Mariana or Captain Barrow or the Hired Help, presumably—has overheard.

"On Christmas?" I ask, surprised. But Billy is nodding.

"Makes sense. No patrols today. Harbor's as empty as its ever gonna get. Not even the fleet will be out."

"Billy's offered to guard us while we sink her," I tell them.

The tension, which had been gathering in the house like an electrical cloud, dissipates at once. Billy shrugs, stares down at the linoleum counter, but doesn't correct me. Irene bestows on him a smile that is all but a promissory note for a lifetime of baked goods deposited on his doorstep every Sunday. But Constance, who materialized at the refrigerator in search of a Pepsi, looks at me. "*We?*" she asks, eyebrows raised.

"Sure," I reply. "You think I'm going to let you two have all the fun *again*?" I point to my new watch, which has already become my favorite possession. "Time's a-wasting!"

Constance turns to Irene. "I told you we should have just given him the earrings," she says.

• ● ⬤ ● •

So it is that we all find ourselves on a piercing midwinter evening out in the bay again, sou'westers tucked up to our chins, wool caps pulled over our ears, leaving only a small cavity of cloth through which to view the spectacle. The *Eula May* pitches and rocks in the swell, carried by a sharp breeze that searches through our coats like a pickpocket. Grandma is back at the house, sleeping peacefully in her easy chair with an afghan around her knees and Mariana watching nearby. I envy her.

"You set the charges, right?" Constance asks for the third time.

Billy simply nods. The *Eula May* has towed *Calliope* out to a deepish stretch of water off Dolphin Rock. The yacht is still riding high with her cabin and pilot house gone, seemingly suspended in space. *Her keel doesn't touch the water, just glides over it*, Grandma had said. The yacht rests on the glassy bay like a white-shrouded body on a funeral bier, waiting for the torches to set it alight.

"Reckon we better get started then," decides Constance. A small table has been set up on *Eula May*'s stern, covered in a tartan blanket. We gather round it, and Constance pulls back the cloth. On the table are a cluster of white and red candles of various lengths, a golden bowl with three oranges, a dragon-shaped incense holder, and two photographs. One is Marcus Rhinegold, cut from the *Providence Journal* around the time of his disappearance. The other is a Polaroid of the *Calliope* herself. Constance takes a Zippo from her pocket and solemnly lights the candles. She hands the Zippo to Irene, who puts the flame to four sticks of incense and gives one to each of us. Irene turns to the yacht, silent and ghostly a few yards away, and bows three times, slowly. Constance steps forward and does the same. Billy and I follow, bemused.

"Put the incense in the holder," Irene whispers. Even as we do so, Constance begins to chant in a low, deep, carrying voice:

"*Namo tassa bhagavato arahato samma sambuddhasa, Kusala dhamma, Akusala dhamma, Abyakata dhamma...*"

There's something deadly serious, almost ennobling, in Constance's chant for the dead. Where she learned the words I can't imagine. It goes on and on, droning, carried over the water to the dying ship.

"Connie saw them do this in Japan," Irene explains under her breath, "at the scrapyards in Osaka. They believe every ship has a soul. No Japanese scrapper will touch the hull until it's been declared officially dead—not respectful. Well, that made sense to Connie. Said she felt sorry for all the ships she tore apart without sending them off first; it was almost like she was gutting them alive. So now we go through this bit of business every time. I dunno. It's pretty, don't you think?"

I do. It's also a side of the Laughing Sarahs I've never seen before. I feel like we're initiates into some dark and secret ritual. We are seeing something rarer than the Awa or Yanomami tribes along the Amazon, and just as fragile. *Femina Novus Angliae Senes* in their dying habitat. Finally Constance finishes, and spreads her hands. At that exact moment there is a low rumbling from the *Calliope*. "Watch it!" Billy cries, flinching. A crash answers him, and a tall sheet of flame bursts through the deck. The percussion from the blast reaches us and makes the *Eula May* shiver in sympathy. Now the *Calliope* is groaning, a remarkably human sound, heeling over slowly and letting the seawater fill her shattered hull.

"Poor thing," Irene mutters.

"Told you we should've opened the seacocks first," Constance grumbles. "She's going down sloppy."

Calliope is almost on her beam ends. Loose boards and detritus shattered by the blast tumble into the frothing water. For a moment I imagine her as I first saw her: glittering with lights from stem to stern, paint and brightwork gleaming in the moonlight. I feel Marcus standing beside me now, watching. "I'm sorry," I whisper, though I don't know for what.

Anyone who has seen a ship go down always describes the last sound it makes as a weird kind of death-rattle. Nobody really knows what causes it: boilers bursting, decks collapsing, pipes exploding as the lower decks fill up with water. Perhaps all of these. But I hear it now: a long, rasping, keening screech. Impossible not to believe it must be made by a living thing. Impossible, too, to think this ship is not experiencing humiliation, even pain, as she surrenders herself to the sea. But her agonies are almost over. The bow disappears and *Calliope* turns almost vertical, plunging and thrashing her way down. A last, long sigh—which might just be air escaping from her vents—and the *Calliope* is gone. The sea boils for a moment, then goes still. Except for a few bits of floating wreckage she might never have existed at all. Such is the all-consuming, all-obscuring power of the Atlantic. Marcus Rhinegold and Captain Bilodeaux and Sylvanus Hazard and Wally the Postman—and countless others—all sought its favor, bargained with it, cursed it, blew themselves apart upon its surface and writhed their way down into its depths. Yet the sea remains absorbed in its own inscrutable affairs, pricking out the music of the tides.

"Well," says Constance gruffly, "that's that, then."

"Good-bye, Marcus," I say quietly. "I really hope you got wherever it is you wanted to go."

Constance restarts the engines on the *Eula May*, which toss up a glutinous bubble in lively defiance. Even the old minesweeper seems to want to put as much sea as possible between herself and what we just witnessed. I wait for a moment on deck, breathing in the frigid air, staring back at the blank piece of ocean where a man's dreams now lie submerged. It's then I remember the date: Christmas Day, the same day the *General Kearny* exploded. Perhaps some watchers on shore were finally gratified by a mysterious orange glow. *Calliope's* death has served a greater legend. How strange, I think to myself, the symmetry of things.

Inside, Irene has turned up the heat in the cabin till it's almost suffocating. But the warmth is a comfort, as is the hot chocolate she presses into my hand. Life, it seems to say, goes on. And truly, the further we get from the wreck, the more it seems as if all that passed before was just a weird and terrible dream. Marcus, Alicia, the Molinaris—none of them really belonged in Little Compton. Even the *Calliope* was, after a fashion, swallowed by the *General Kearny*. The Laughing Sarahs have performed last rites; life can go on as before. Billy is at my side and wraps a protective arm around my shoulders. Irene stares into her mug, lost in thought. Constance begins to sing. It's an old hymn, and I remember it. Grandpa used to call it the sailor's prayer, but Grandma said it was what the old drunks sang down at Oddfellow's Hall when they closed out their meeting.

"*Dark the night of sin has settled, Loud the angry billows roar!*

Eager eyes are watching, longing, for the lights along the shore..."

Then me and Irene and even Billy join in for the chorus. The words fill the stuffy little cabin like an incantation:

"*Let the lower lights be burning, send a gleam across the wave,*

Some poor fainting, struggling seaman you may rescue, you may save!"

Just then Constance points out the wheelhouse windows. The spotlights are on at Dowsy's Pier, and a string of colored bulbs stretches down from the Boy and Lobster. White glittering lights twinkle from a dozen mastheads. These are the lights along the shore, welcoming us in.

Chapter Seventeen

Every New England winter is the longest and worst ever. This is a rule. Nobody can remember one as bad as this; it is definitely worse than when they were a kid; and everyone swears—swears—that this is the year they're finally moving to Florida.

The worst part is that once Christmas and New Year's are over, winter is just settling into her stride. January is bitter, February cruel, March unbearable. Daybreak paints the world in a palate of gray, black, white and beige. You forget colors. Outside the air is like chalk dust to breathe, and you can't remember what it is to simply walk around in the sun. Faint stabs at cheeriness—stupid fake holidays like Valentine's and Presidents' Day—are ignored. Each day passes like the one before.

Nowhere is this truer than in Little Compton. The whole town is a charcoal smudge: gray skies, gray water, dirty gray snow, gray faces peering out from gray clothes. Every now and again the bay whips itself up into a storm, yet even these are only momentary distractions. I spend my mornings at the gym, afternoons applying for jobs I'll never get, and evenings watching television with Grandma.

She's getting worse. Dr. Renzi says not to think of it like

that. "The disease," he told me, "is running its progression. That's all." Well, okay, fine. But he doesn't have to listen to her rant for three hours because she thinks she's been kidnapped, or cry hysterically because she wanted banana ice cream and got chocolate instead, or wake me up at three in the morning because she's decided the house is floating away. Even Mariana is exhausted. She'll only come in the afternoons now, puts headphones on and races through the house, cleaning. I'm grateful for the help, but laundry and dishes are the least of my problems. Constance and Irene do what they can. Constance brings Domino's and sits with Grandma in front of the television; Irene comes by every now and then and takes her out for a long lunch, to give me a break. They remember things like doctor's appointments and random bills and dates at the hair salon. It's hard for them, too. Most of the time Grandma still recognizes old friends, but her conversation has gotten wilder. They know it's not her fault, but one day I watched helplessly as Grandma accused Aunt Constance of sleeping with Grandpa Mike. She called her a bitch and a whore and tried to spit in her face, but her mouth was dry from all the yelling. Constance just sat there, unmoving, unflinching, her lips a thin line. When it was over, she pulled a handkerchief from her pocket and wiped the spittle off Grandma's face. "Thank you," Grandma said, demure as a girl. But later I saw Constance lean over the draining board and wipe away tears. "You gotta get her into a facility," she told me quietly, on her way out.

I know I do, but it's not that easy. Mrs. Everard at the Methodist Home finally did go, but her place was taken by elderly organ player from the Woonsocket church, much beloved by all, and unfortunately healthy enough to last for years. "She still *drives*," Constance reports, disgusted,

"So what the hell does she need to be in a home for?" Irene calls around, but the Catholics, Episcopalians, Baptists, and even the Jews are full up. "No room at the inn," says Constance laconically. Everyone is dying, but nobody is dying fast enough.

February brings other, more welcome changes. One morning Irene calls, breathless as usual, and tells me to put on a jacket and tie. I've got an interview with the Chair of the URI History Department that afternoon at four. "How?" I ask, dumbfounded.

The answer is long and involved, and very Rhode Island. Irene's second cousin's husband works in the provost's office, and heard the department was about to post a search for someone that could teach history of gender and sexuality. "That's you, right?" Irene asks a bit worriedly.

"That's me."

So Irene, acting swiftly and stealthily, copied out my CV from an old Xavier web page and sent it along to URI, along with a glowing recommendation from a professor at Brown I've never heard of, but I suspect must be another of Irene's very old friends. Now she hands the whole story to me like a birthday present. Oddly enough, it's only a week away from my birthday.

The interview goes surprisingly well. Clearly Irene has briefed the Chair on the circumstances of my last dismissal. "This is a secular institution, Dr. Hazard," he tells me seriously. "We tolerate no discrimination of any kind."

That must be true, because a few weeks later, I find out I got the job. Billy takes me up to the Capital Grille. I won't start teaching till the fall, but at least I won't have to worry about starving once the food stamps run out. After dinner we celebrate by going to a tattoo parlor on Wickenden Street. The Artist sits by himself behind the counter, playing

Candy Crush on his phone. He is about six-four, bearded, and looks like he might have done professional wrestling. They say he's the best there is.

"Damn," Billy mutters, "you sure about this?"

"Yup."

I've been thinking about it for a while. The scars on my chest are smaller now, but they'll always be there, two flat tombstones over Rosalie's boobs. I'm sick of looking at them. So one afternoon I started doodling on a pad. Gradually the design took shape: a flush-decked schooner with all sails set, figurehead of Marylee Hazard cleaving through the waves with her arm extended and an arrow in her fist. The waves arc out like eagles' wings, lifting the bow of *Marylee's Revenge* upward and holding her aloft. For weeks I kept the drawing folded in my coat pocket, pulling it out now and again to add a line here, a detail there. Finally, I showed it to Billy. "What do you think?" I asked tentatively.

He studied it for a long time, fingering his chin. Oh God, I told myself, I've gone too butch even for him. "Needs a flag," he decided finally.

"What?"

"Every proper ship needs a proper flag. Else how's anybody gonna know who you are? Or what you stand for? You can put it just here"—he indicated the stern—"fluttering out behind."

I spent all night thinking about it. Then, at about four in the morning, I knew. I pushed Billy aside, as gently as I could, and padded into the kitchen where the markers are kept in a drawer. In a few minutes I had it: a rainbow flag with pink and blue horizontal stripes and, in the center, a skull and crossbones.

Now I pull it from my pocket and hand the drawing, with some trepidation, to the Artist. "What do you think?"

He holds it with both hands like a slice of bread and stares with a quizzical expression. "Two-fifty," he says at last. "And about three hours. Where d'ya want it?"

"On my ass-crack, where d'ya suppose?"

The Artist stares at me blankly. Then his face splits into a grin. "You trans dudes are always so tough. Okay, take off your shirt, and let's see the damage."

Billy stays with me, holding my hand. When I had the arm done, I was lying on my stomach with my face pressed into the leather headrest, but there's nowhere for me to go this time. I'm on my back, staring up at the fluorescent lights, listening to the angry buzz of the needle as it scrapes across my chest. It feels like surgery without anesthetic. But the Artist has surprisingly refined taste in music, and runs his pen back and forth to a Vivaldi concerto. "Do you know what it is?" he asks rhetorically.

"*Storm at Sea*," I answer automatically.

"It's…yeah. Yeah, it is. You like classical music?"

"Ouch," I tell him.

"You okay?" Billy asks, solicitous.

"Sure. But don't expect any action tonight."

He blushes a little and casts a glance at the Artist, who is bent close over my left nipple, filling in a wave. "You can lie on your back easy enough," the Artist mutters. Billy suddenly becomes engrossed by the pictures on the wall. This goes on through six more concertos, until finally the Artist says, "I'm just shading a bit now," and I look at myself in the mirror.

My skin is red and raw, swollen and sweating blood at the seams. But that hardly matters. The scene is exactly as I drew it, except a million times better. The colors are sharp and clear. *Marylee's Revenge* looks as though she's exploding from my chest, bows pointed defiantly at the world, flag proudly flying over my heart. "God," I whisper, "it's beautiful."

The Artist smiles. "Yeah, I liked that one. Bet it comes with a good story."

You have no idea, I think to myself.

Chapter Eighteen

The drive home from Providence is long, made even longer with every bump and pothole sending a shot of pain across my torso. Billy looks contrite at the wheel. After he apologizes a fifth time I snap back, "Just shut up and put on a podcast." We listen to Radiolab until the lights of the Mount Hope Bridge appear over the dashboard. He offers to take me back to his place, but I know Mariana's gone home by now and Grandma is all by herself.

Her house is never dark; she always leaves the hall light on to discourage burglars. But tonight it's switched off. Billy swings into the driveway and stares. The place looks gloomy and funereal. Inside, time has no meaning: in Maggie Hazard's cockeyed world it could be high noon or three a.m., yesterday or 1957. Walking through the front door is like coming upon a play mid-scene.

"Want me to stay with you?"

I do, but I'm crabby and in pain and not good company. Mostly all I want is some ibuprofen and a scotch. "It's okay, just drop me at the door."

The sound of the tires on gravel echoes against the house, but no light appears. Good, I think, she really is asleep. "You working tomorrow?"

"Six-thirty in the morning. They're sending us all up to some protest at Salve Regina."

"Come for dinner? I'm making meatballs."

"Sure. I'll bring the wine." He kisses me on the cheek, just like an ordinary couple. "Your tattoo looks great."

"Just wait till the bandages come off," I promise, and kiss him again, longer.

Nevertheless, I can't restrain a slight shudder of apprehension as his truck pulls away. The key sticks in the door, and it takes a few minutes of fumbling before it finally opens with a creak. The front hall is completely black. I trip over the hall rug and bark my shins against the table. Something overbalances and hits the floor. The lamp. Now I'm groping in the darkness, running my hands along the wall, trying to find the switch.

"Who's there?" a quavering voice calls. Grandma is at the top of the stairs, the light through the stained glass window turning her hair blue. "What do you want?"

"It's okay, Grandma!" I shout up.

But clearly it's not. Somehow she has managed to find Grandpa Mike's service pistol, and she's holding it with both hands. "Get out of my house," she growls.

"Oh, my God, put that away! You know me!"

The shot goes wide, taking out a beveled mirror. The sound of the explosion fills the room.

Now she's on the second landing, peering down with rheumy eyes. I finally find the switch for the chandelier and turn it on. Recognition and relief flood her face. She lowers the gun.

"*Teddy?*" my grandmother sputters, her eyes widening.

"Huh?"

"Teddy Johnson!" She sees the resemblance, and in some cold and mossy part of my soul, I see it too. Blond hair, blue eyes. Like my father. But Grandpa's hair was black, and his eyes were hazel. "Teddy, you can't stay here!" she cries. "Emma's on the warpath, she found your letter. Fucking postman sent it to the wrong house." Now she is grabbing my sleeve, pulling me toward the door.

I could end it now, but I don't. "What letter?" I ask. "Do you still have it?"

"Sure! Here." She pulls out a drawer in the hall table and extracts a frail piece of parchment, the same one Emma handed her all those years ago. It looks old enough to have the Ten Commandments written on it.

June 18, 1951

Dearest Babs,

All day long I've been trying to pack, putting in this pair of socks or that shirt, looking out at the windows as if I expected the view to change, doing all the dumb things one does before they say goodbye to the place they love most in the world. So I guess it's only right that I say goodbye to you, since you're what I love most about it. Do you regret how we met? Sometimes I do. But other times I think it had to be like this. In a way, the war's a blessing. Gives us a chance to sort things out. Once I'm at base I'll write to Em and tell her it's over. I won't tell her about you, not yet. But that way we can start making plans for my return. And I will return, darling, I promise. I'm not such a fool to go throwing my life away now that it finally means something.

Em's got a million things for me to do, so I don't know if I'll have the chance to see you before I go. She's yammering on about underwear and suspender-belts and I don't know what, and all I can think about is how your hair smells of lavender, the soft weight of your breast in my hand like a fluttering bird…

I can't read any more. Teddy Johnson knew something

that no one, not even Aunt Emma, did. Something that would not come out until I had to dig up Grandma's birth certificate for the application papers to the Methodist Home. Margaret is my grandmother's middle name. Her full name is Barbara Margaret Hazard.

Poor Emma. Poor Teddy. Poor Grandma. "But you're hurt," she says, touching the bandages on my chest.

"It's nothing, it's okay, don't worry…"

"*What did that bitch do to you?*" Grandma demands, eyes bugging out of her head. "She killed you, didn't she? Oh, my poor Teddy, she's killed you!"

"It's okay," I murmur to her. "Emma's gone, she's gone now."

A strange look comes into my grandmother's eyes. Sly. I don't who I am talking to, whether this is Maggie or Babs or Grandma or some other creature I have never seen before. Different ages, different personalities bubble up to the surface. "You bet she is," she says. "That's all fixed. Stupid cunt. Smashed her like an eggshell with her own frying pan. Bam, bam, bam. Ha!"

"What are you talking about?" But I know, of course I do. I can see it playing out before my eyes like a Kodochrome. It's early October, and Grandma wants some strawberries. She knows Emma has a deep freeze, so she puts on her carpet slippers and crosses the lawn. Emma sees her old friend bustling over and lets her in through the back door, the one that leads to the kitchen. There on the draining board is the lobster, waiting for the inevitable. Something snaps. It's June, 1951. Emma has just confessed to murdering Teddy Johnson. The lobsters lie next to the body. Grandma stands there, numb with rage, staring down at the man she loved. And she hears Emma's voice droning on about a misdelivered letter, a letter that was meant for her.

Emma comes toward her and asks her what's wrong, why does she look like that, does she still need the strawberries? Strawberries, or lobsters? Without even thinking Grandma grabs the frying pan from the stove and brings it down. Teddy Johnson is avenged.

She leaves Emma's house, stumbling back over the yard. It's cold for June, too cold. She needed something. Yes. The strawberries. Emma has a deep freeze. So Grandma turns around again and heads back to Emma's place. She taps on the door, on the glass. She peers through the window. She sees the body of her best friend spreadeagled on the floor, and in a panic she rushes back and starts telephoning.

Telephone. I tentatively reach into my back pocket and pull out my phone. "It's going to be okay, Maggie," I say as gently as I can. "Just let me make a call."

"Call? Call who? She's dead, I tell you. There's nothing for it now. What is that thing? Put it away." She slaps the phone out of my hands and it lands on the floor between us.

"Grandma," I say, willing my voice to remain calm, "listen to me. It's past midnight, and everyone is asleep. You need to go to bed now."

Her eyes slip out of focus. She is still holding the pistol. "But my bedtime's not until later," she insists. "Dad said I could stay up to watch the parade. I want to see the parade."

"You can see it from your bedroom window. Go on now."

She stands for a moment, irresolute. I can feel the house shifting and morphing around us, jolting back and forth through time. Captain Barrow is seated in his chair by the fireplace, studying us with an ironic smile. Sunlight streams through the windows, then disappears, then comes back. We are in the eye of the storm. The paper on the walls is faded green, bright red, soft blue with silver swans flying past. I can even feel my own face melting, realigning, taking the shape of Teddy Johnson and Grandpa Mike and Great-Grandpa Ezekiel and God-knows-who else. "Just give me the gun," I say, lowering my voice to an authoritative growl.

"The gun?"

"It's dangerous, Maggie. It's not a toy. You hand that over now, like a good girl."

Her hand outstretches. The gun dangles limply from her fingers. But then a shaft of light comes through the windows and throws my face into sharp relief.

"You're not Teddy…"

The pistol is pointed at my head now. "Who are you? What do you want? What have you done with Teddy?" She takes aim, and her arthritic fingers fumble with the trigger.

At that moment the front door bursts open and there, like sentinel guards, are the last surviving Laughing Sarahs.

"It's going to be all right, Maggie."

This is Aunt Constance, who steps forward bravely and takes the gun from her hand. "But…Teddy," Grandma protests, "she killed Teddy!"

"Yeah, honey, I know. Come on now." Constance takes her by the shoulders and propels her firmly, but not unkindly, toward the stairs. She never turns around.

Aunt Irene puts a soft hand on my arm. "Don't worry, love," she says. "We'll look after her. You go on to Billy's place and get some sleep. It'll be all right in the morning." She kisses me on the cheek.

"How did you know to come?"

"Your phone. You dialed Connie, didn't you know that? We heard the whole conversation. Course we were both racing over before you'd even finished. I'm just glad we got here in time."

"But Aunt Irene," I say, confused, "it's past midnight. What were you doing with Aunt Constance at this…? Oh."

Her face is completely closed. "You go on to Billy, now. We'll be fine."

I should have known. How arrogant I was to assume mine was the only transformation in Little Compton! It was theatrical, that's all. Theirs was quiet, unassuming, quintessentially New England. Two old ladies tending garden together. This is a fascinating revelation, but there's no time to consider it.

"Grandma's dangerous," I stammer. "I can hardly believe it, but I think she brained Emma. Now she's convinced it's 1951 and I'm Teddy and..." I can't go on.

Irene sighs. There is no surprise in her expression, only pity. "Damn. You shouldn't have heard all that. And you really, really shouldn't have to see her like this. It's not fair. But, honey, you can't mind anything she says or does. It's not her fault. We know, we've been through this before, the night poor Emma died. Why do you think we had that scumbag Marcus Rhinegold hanging on us? But it'll be okay."

I am standing dumb, shocked into silence at the compact precision of Yankee speech. But I can translate without difficulty. Grandma told me as much herself. She'd seen Marcus Rhinegold hanging around Emma's house that day. But why?

Here's how it must have happened. Grandma finds the body of her best friend and calls the Sarahs. They come at once. It doesn't take long for Irene and Constance to discover the truth: Emma's body on the kitchen floor, a bloodied skillet nearby, Grandma confused and agitated. Perhaps she slipped back into 1951 and told them the truth herself. So, once again, New England Wrecking and Salvage swings into action. Irene wipes off the skillet, pulls down a pile of pans onto the body, hiding the tree in the forest. Constance sits with Grandma Maggie, asking her pointed questions. But it's clear she doesn't remember a thing. So far, so good. But then, disaster. Maggie looks out the window and sees Marcus Rhinegold standing in Emma's yard. Constance confronts him. He came to see his grandmother. Instead, he found her best friends covering her with cookware. Constance tells him…something. But clearly it's not enough. Turns out Marcus has a plan of his own, and now he has two accomplices ready at hand. He offers them money, and his silence. Reluctantly, they accept. And so begins the dark chapter that ends with a sunken yacht in Narragansett Bay.

I can see them now, the Laughing Sarahs, leading my grandmother up to bed, tucking her in, coming down and straightening the pillows on the sofa. Three old ladies with four murders between them, and yet I can't find it in my heart to condemn them for any of it. Not so long ago, Billy said it was odd to find so many corpses and so little responsibility. Truth is, he literally didn't know the half of it.

Or is this all the product of my grandmother's dying brain, spinning out its last fantasies, groping about the all-enveloping mist for something real, something absolute, something she can cling to as the rest vanishes?

Finally, the Yankee conundrum. Does resilience come from calling a spade a spade, or transforming it into a diamond through sheer will?

There are no more answers. Irene smiles rather sadly, disappears into the shadows. The door closes in my face.

Chapter Nineteen

Two weeks later, Grandma is dead. It was not anything sinister: she had a stroke. Doctors say it could have come at any time. Sometimes I wonder if the excitement of that night tore something inside her brain, a tiny fissure that widened into a gulf, but they say no. The brain doesn't work like that. And it must be true, because the next morning after Grandma confessed I came over to the house from Billy's and found her in the kitchen, eerily normal, flipping pancakes. Aunt Irene was sitting at the breakfast table reading the paper aloud. It was clear that Grandma's mind had, in its last reaches of mercy, kicked over the traces once again. She knew who I was, asked me about my job, if I had anybody special in my life. I told her the truth, selectively edited. Maybe I'm becoming more of a local.

In the meantime, Aunt Constance and Aunt Irene went on exactly as before. Of course neither ever said a word to me about that night, then or later. By no gesture or sigh did they reveal any of their thoughts. Irene treated Grandma like a nurse with her favorite patient; Constance, in her gruff way, let it be known she was ready to take on any extra duties. As if their best friend didn't kill her fiancé; as if Grandma, the fiancé's lover, didn't kill Emma; as if Irene didn't brain

Marcus Rhinegold after Marcus shot Wally the Postman. But this is Little Compton, where nothing ever happens.

They say she was happy the night she died. I wasn't there; I had a conference at the college. But the Laughing Sarahs kept her company, made her a frozen pizza and put on old tapes of *The Honeymooners*. Grandma laughed so hard she choked. Then she choked a bit more, her eyes widened in surprise, and she slumped sideways in her chair. The seizure hit both sides of her brain like a lightning bolt. Constance says she was gone before she hit the ground.

Several times I've had to ask myself if I feel any real grief. I'm still not sure of the answer. There's regret, of course, and a stately kind of sadness that comes with reflecting on the impermanence of all things. But real, raw, actual grief...I don't know. I feel like I've been saying good-bye a while now. Hers was a ship that left port long ago and only just passed over the horizon.

The day of the funeral is April 25th, a Tuesday. The fog is back, a damp chill that settles over everything. It could just as well be that day in late October when we put Emma in the ground. Strange, I think, that one fall and one spring day should be so like one another, as if there were no real passage of time. Just fog, and shapes that move through the fog.

Aunt Irene and Aunt Constance lay wreaths on the grave. Irene shivers in her black skirt. Her legs are bare. "I hope I die in summer," she murmurs. "It's too darn cold to make everyone stand outside."

"I hope I die in January," Aunt Constance answers with a grim smile. "Let the fuckers freeze."

"Maybe they won't come at all!"

"You will, Irene. And David, too. You'll bury both of us, David."

In that moment I realize it's true. The Laughing Sarahs are down to two, with three replaced knees, arthritis, cataracts, and a pacemaker between them. How long before I'm here again? But they are with me now, standing on either side, their warmth giving me strength.

Constance asks, seemingly apropos of nothing, "So you'll be home as usual on Saturday?"

Still thinking about mortality, I answer, "Sure, why?"

"Why do you think?" she replies with a hint of her usual tartness. "With you and Billy that makes four for bridge. Haven't had a decent game since we lost Emma. You *do* play, don't you?"

My mouth opens and closes. "Grandma tried to teach me the basics, but it never really stuck. And I have no idea if Billy..."

"Oh, we can teach you both!" Irene says brightly. "Your Grandma had to learn, and she ended up the best player of us all."

"Except for overbidding her hand," avers Constance. "Maggie always thought she was on a winner. Sign of an optimistic nature, I guess. So we'll see you then?"

They're both looking at me closely. I know what they're asking. The Laughing Sarahs, the most exclusive society in the world, are about to induct two new members. There'll be no black hoods, no swearing of oaths. They will simply go on doing what they have always done, our mutual acquiescence binding as any blood oath. In truth, the induction already happened—on the deck of the *Eula May* as we watched *Calliope* go down. The bonds that keep this club together have nothing to do with bridge. "Sure," I tell them. "I'll see you then."

"Lovely!" Irene cries. "Can I give you a lift back to the house?" Her new pickup, cherry red with a crew cab and fog lights mounted above the grill, glitters nearby. I have a shrewd suspicion it came from the Save Marcus Rhinegold $500,000 Fund, just like her slate roof and the landscapers that chopped down poor old Melvin the Oak. But there is no tactful way to ask.

The crowd of mourners is thinning out. Billy stands dutifully by, but he is scraping his toe in the dirt. "No," I tell them. "Take Billy home. I'd like to be here myself a little while."

"Of course." Irene and Constance go have a word with Billy and I see them depart, arm in arm.

Now it's just me and Grandma. No, that's not entirely true. At her left is Grandpa Mike, a small flag marking him as a veteran. Just as well, since that's the best that could be said of him. I'm standing amongst the long rows of Dyers, Thurbers, Butlers, Tinkhams, Browns and Hazards, all jumbled together by marriage and issue, with names like Frances Tinkham Butler and William Butler Brown. Here is Harold Hazard Dyer, 1929-1961, who had an enormous collection of Dresden figurines and a wife named Luley that nobody could stand. Grandma called her "Physic Face" for the look of intestinal discomfort she habitually wore. The marriage was childless, and Harold took to spending more and more of his summers with his artistic friends on Fire Island. Luley's discontent deepened. But it was Harold who put a bullet through his mouth, April 14, 1961, the same day the CIA invaded Cuba.

Stories pulled out of the cupboard, dusted off, and presented at the table with the same loving care as Limoges china or Great-Grandma Hattie's silver set. But it's not my family—or, at least, only half as much as I supposed.

I've been thinking about blood a lot recently. Not the kind that goes drip, drip, drip down the walls in some gothic horror. The other kind, passing its thin blue identity chip from one generation to the next. A couple days ago I sat down with a pad and pencil and wrote it all out. Pretty soon the whole thing started to look like one of those Old Testament catalogues. Emma Godfrey and Teddy Johnson begat Annabelle, who begat Marcus Rhinegold. But Teddy, randy bugger, also begat Walter Hazard (my dad's name is Walter, can't think why that never came up before) with Grandma Maggie, which means Marcus and I are actually related—all thanks to our mutual Grandpa Teddy's wandering pipe.

I'm not a Hazard at all. I don't know whether to be relieved or sad.

• • ● • •

It's still only early afternoon when I get back, but the fog makes it seem like evening. I was expecting the house to be dark but the porch light is on, lamps lit in the front hall and kitchen. There are two covered dishes on the draining board and a note: "*Just something to tide you over till Saturday. Love, I & C.*" I pull back the foil and find fresh-baked lasagna in one and blueberry crumble in the other. These were my favorite dishes as a kid. I dip a fork into the still-warm lasagna, and sigh. The comfort comes not from the food itself, but from knowing there is still someone that remembers.

The house is not as depressing as I thought. In fact, without the turmoil of Grandma's uncertain memories, it seems to have settled into something resembling normality. The ceramic owl still gazes beadily down from the banister. The Rockwell plates line the kitchen. In the front parlor, Grandma's knitted afghan rests neatly folded on the arm of the old leather sofa, her rocking chair drawn up to its usual spot near the fireplace. Someone—Constance probably—has even drawn up a fire. It throws warm shadows on the room.

My room, I remind myself. My house. Which means things will have to change. It's not a prospect I relish. Academic life required that the sum total of my possessions fit within the back of a pickup truck. I've never had anything larger than a bedroom to decorate; suddenly it feels as if I've been given Versailles.

Sure, I could leave the house just as it is. Pack up her old clothes, clean out the closets and attic, but otherwise leave well enough alone. And yet, without even acknowledging it, I'm already moving from room to room, deciding the fate of all things: what to give to the Aunts, donate to charity, consign to the curb. It's a strange and terrible power, enshrining some memories and discarding others, becoming the final custodian of someone else's life. Keep all the family heirlooms, of course. The upstairs bathroom, too, will remain untouched as long as I'm alive. And Grandma's bedroom set is actually quite pretty: late Deco, with lots of little mirrors and inlaid mother-of-pearl. My own, on the other hand, is heavy, blond, and hideous. I slept on that bed for thirty years, but I can't wait to see it gone, along with all the other frilly horrors. Finally, I promise myself to make a bonfire of all Grandpa Mike's marine registers, his stacked and sorted copies of *The New American* and *The Federalist*, even the wooden models of the Herreschoff yachts on the mantle. The first thing to burn will be that little leather ottoman he used to bend me over to deliver what he called "discipline."

I pass by the dining room and there, sitting all by itself, is the tape recorder. There's a cassette inside. I don't remember leaving it, but in the confusion of the last few days I could have walked around the house with two live lobsters and a pair of fire tongs and not known. The recorder is four-square on the table, looking up at me, practically begging to be played. I press the button and Grandma's voice fills the room:

"*...a bit of Sylvanus in all the Hazards. Good and evil, rage and comfort, wrecking and salvage. We became wreckers to have the power of gods on Earth: choose what to save, and what to destroy...*"

To see more Poisoned Pen Press titles:

Visit our website: poisonedpenpress.com
Request a digital catalog:
info@poisonedpenpress.com